Protection

Molly McCloskey is the author of two acclaimed collections of short stories, *Solomon's Seal* and *The Beautiful Changes*. Born in Philadelphia, she has lived in Ireland since 1989. *Protection* is her first novel.

WITHDRAWN FROM STOCK

Protection

MOLLY McCLOSKEY

PENGUIN
IRELAND

PENGUIN IRELAND

Published by the Penguin Group
Penguin Ireland, 25 St Stephen's Green, Dublin 2, Ireland
(a division of Penguin Books Ltd)
Penguin Books Ltd, 80 Strand, London WC2R ORL, England
Penguin Group (USA) Inc., 375 Hudson Street, New York, New York 10014, USA
Penguin Group (Australia), 250 Camberwell Road,
Camberwell, Victoria 3124, Australia (a division of Pearson Australia Group Pty Ltd)
Penguin Group (Canada), 10 Alcorn Avenue, Toronto, Ontario, Canada M4V 3B2
(a division of Pearson Penguin Canada Inc.)
Penguin Books India Pvt Ltd, 11 Community Centre,
Panchsheel Park, New Delhi – 110 017, India
Penguin Group (NZ), cnr Airborne and Rosedale Roads, Albany,
Auckland 1310, New Zealand (a division of Pearson New Zealand Ltd)
Penguin Books (South Africa) (Pty) Ltd, 24 Sturdee Avenue,
Rosebank 2196, South Africa

Penguin Books Ltd, Registered Offices: 80 Strand, London WC2R ORL, England

www.penguin.com

First published 2005
1

Set in 12/14.75 pt Monotype Dante
Typeset by Rowland Phototypesetting Ltd, Bury St Edmunds, Suffolk
Printed in Great Britain by Clays Ltd, St Ives plc

A CIP catalogue record for this book is available from the British Library

ISBN 1–844–88071–0

Protection

One

Through the tall bay window, Gillian could see the guests arriving, pulling into the small car park down the slope, then shouldering their bags and trudging through the drizzle up the path to the front door, where Elspeth would greet them and direct them to their rooms. She could also see, through the open swing doors that led into the dining room, two posters mounted behind glass and hanging side by side. Elspeth had chosen them. The first one said, in bold black letters:

> It was not by making yourself heard but by staying sane that you carried on the human heritage.
>
> – George Orwell, *1984*

Beside the Orwell was an image of a meditating monk in a saffron robe sitting placidly under a tree. The caption read:

Silent retreat, Mihintale, Sri Lanka

The monk poster irritated Gillian. If he was a real monk, what was he doing meditating for the camera? On the other hand, if he was a monk minding his own business and the photographer had sneaked up on him, then the whole image was an offence against personal space, against silence and stillness and a lot of other things they stood for here, or were meant to stand for. She did, however, admire the juxtaposition of saffron robe and periwinkle sky and had so far managed to tolerate the poster on the basis of that.

It was Sunday. She had just driven down to the Farm from Dublin, where she'd spent the morning in Seapoint with an estate agent, going through her aunt's house. Gillian had no desire to sell it; she'd grown up there with her aunt and uncle, but now Martin was dead and Grace had come to live with them in Howth and there was little point in hanging on to the old place out of sentiment. Already, only a month after Grace had moved out, the Seapoint house was showing signs of neglect. Grace and Martin had bought it decades ago in the expectation of having a family. But it hadn't happened for them. Gillian had been their family, and they'd been hers.

A guest walked past, close to the window, startling her. A heavily built man in hooded raincoat. She caught a glimpse of his face. English, she thought. Late fifties. Retired upper management of some sort. Self-made, definitely. Probably widowed. Cheerful, but lonely.

She put her fingers to her forehead and rubbed it hard. God. She'd been here an hour and already it felt old. It was her, she was tired. She was spending five days a week at home with Grace now and only two in Meath, a reversal of the schedule she'd kept since she started the Farm three years ago. She'd have thought that Grace's company – the repetitive questions and the vacant stares, the sad periodic silences – would make her hungry for stimulation by Sunday, but all she wanted to do when she got to the Farm was sleep.

She checked her watch. There was time for a lie-down before six, when the new arrivals would gather in the common room. For the first year or so, Gillian had allowed arrivals and departures every day of the week. Guests got acquainted naturally, in their own time, in chance moments of connection she'd enjoyed witnessing. She saw the group as a living organism that was perpetually reinventing itself, and had resisted the idea of formalizing the process of getting acquainted or of streamlining arrivals and departures. But this lack of structure had produced headaches of its own. People were forever ringing up to move their arrivals forward or back by a day, or wanting to extend their stay. She and Elspeth were spending far too much time wrestling with the room plan.

Finally, Gillian had been forced to concede that the constant trickle of new arrivals was actually replicating the feeling of transience and unending novelty the Farm was aiming to combat. After much agonizing, she had decided to designate Saturday as the day for departures and Sunday the day for new arrivals, and to offer packages of precisely one, two or three weeks. Now, as she sat staring blankly out at the dozen cars huddled in the drizzle, she could hardly believe she'd ever felt passionately about the subject.

Gillian had initially conceived of it as a decompression chamber – a slow-down zone dedicated to doing things at their natural speed, to recapturing the joy of performing one task at a time, a place in which no activity would ever be preceded by the word 'power' used as an adjective. The idea had come to her one sunny April afternoon when she'd gone to town to buy a new cordless phone. The old one at home was going from bad to worse. Friends said she sounded as though she were speaking from inside a tunnel. *Are you on the cordless?* they'd ask, the tone oddly accusatory. Gillian had begun to detest the thing; it was one of those pieces of technology that seemed to have plateaued in its evolution, the aggravation it caused threatening to overshadow whatever advantages it conferred. She wasn't entirely sure that a newer model would be much better, but she couldn't do without a cordless. Like everyone she knew, Gillian believed that doing a range of other things while talking was both necessary and natural; without quite realizing it, she had come to regard the notion of undivided attention as an indication of poor time-management skills.

She'd been working at the time as an information consultant, conducting on-line research on behalf of those who were too busy or not savvy enough to navigate the morass themselves. Most of her days had been spent googling, skimming, cutting and pasting, all at high speed, boiling hundreds of pages of documents down to a few so that her clients read only what they needed to read. All day long she'd conducted eye-blink assessments, and this ruthlessness had started spilling over into her non-working life. When having a conversation, she'd sort what she heard into 'relevant' and 'irrelevant' categories. Or she'd find herself sifting clinically through Heather's mix of evasions, economical answers, white lies and verbal doodling, as though her daughter's idle adolescent chatter were a stream of statistical contradictions she could synthesize into the truth.

And she'd been having trouble sleeping. At bedtime, her head whirred with the possibility that there was some informational stone she had left unturned. She would close her eyes and see her computer screen, darkened and silent and taunting her, and know that with every passing minute gigabytes of data were filtering on to the Web from around the world and that, even if she never slept again, she would not make the merest dent in this infinity.

The day she went shopping for a new cordless, she was exhausted. She'd had a particularly bad night's sleep and was feeling mildly disoriented as she stood on the corner of Nassau and Dawson streets, in the midst of a throng of pedestrians watching the seconds tick down on the display unit attached to the traffic light on the opposite corner. The units had been put in place in an effort to encourage patience and cut down on jaywalking. The pedestrians were looking quickly from the red numbers to the oncoming cars, back and forth, back and forth, like nervy oversized birds. Some, with the precision timing of children skipping rope, threaded themselves through the moving vehicles.

Boo-boo-boo-boo-boo . . .

The light had changed. The crowd pressed forward out into the street, meshing halfway with the crowd crossing from the opposite corner. Gillian weaved her way through and continued in the direction of the phone shop.

The first thing she saw when she stepped inside was a large poster depicting a man, hands to the side of his head, staring miserably at his answering machine, over which hovered a speech bubble, containing a jumble of tightly packed words. Underneath the picture, it said:

You love your friends, but don't you sometimes wish they'd get to the point? Ask us today about our manual speed-control message minder.

Gillian browsed around the shop while waiting for guidance, because that's what another sign told her to do, to wait for guidance from one of the telecommunications consultants.

'Tell me about your manual speed-control message minder,' she said, when one of the sales assistants floated towards her, having soundlessly detached herself from two young men ruminating over a mobile.

Gillian felt suddenly dispirited by the scene. She was old

enough to recall the days when phone shops were of the humble and clunky semi-state variety, before they'd reinvented themselves as state-of-the-art retail. Minimalist and sleek, with their polished wooden floors and tiny technology, their floating consultants with the long glossy hair who looked so two-dimensional you wondered if they got folded up and put away at closing time.

'Oh!' the sales assistant said silkily, as if caressed by unseen hands, and proceeded to explain to Gillian that the speed-control unit was a time-saving device aimed at friends who tended to go on a bit. 'It is *such* a wonderful system. The technology compresses the pauses between words and phrases, and makes the actual words your friend uses take up less seconds. But,' she hastened to add, 'it doesn't make them sound funny.'

Gillian nodded and looked absently in the direction of the door.

The woman shrugged. 'Don't ask me how,' she said, and rolled her eyes and smiled dazzlingly at Gillian.

Gillian managed to smile back. 'It's not something I need.'

Now the sales assistant nodded. She was mildly irritated, less by Gillian's lack of interest in the message-minder system than by her general lack of enthusiasm. 'Do you know about voice dial?' she asked. Her tone was oddly challenging.

Gillian knew about voice dial. It was when you told your phone what to do. She felt saddened, not for the first time, by the fact that she would never again actually dial a phone, never feel the slight *clickety* resistance as she push-pulled the dial round to its stopping point, never hear the reassuring *zznnnzzznnnt* as it slipped back into place. What patience dialling had required! She wondered what was the sum total of time saved since the introduction of push-button phones. She had no doubt an estimate had been arrived at.

She cast her eyes woefully about the shop. Choosing a cordless phone suddenly seemed a huge and unappealing task. The sales assistant, sensing she was losing her, suggested to Gillian that she might like to spend a few moments with 'the literature', an invitation Gillian politely declined before heading for the door.

As she made her way down Nassau Street and back towards the car, she felt sluggish and headachy. People were whizzing by her, jostling her, but instead of picking up her own pace Gillian imagined all these people slowing down, falling into step with *her*. At the dentist's recently she'd been reading in *National Geographic* about one of those also-ran species of the genus *Homo*, and as she trudged along tried to amuse herself by imagining that she was one of them, heavy of limb and simple of mind, making her unhurried way across the steppe or the savannah, haunted by some dim inkling of her own impending obsolescence.

If I were king of the world, she thought idly, I would outlaw learning-while-you-sleep.

When Damien came home that evening and asked about the cordless phone, she said, 'They wanted to put all of our friends on amphetamines.'

'The conspiracy continues,' he said.

She looked at him, but didn't bother explaining.

Her timing had been good. Slow was the new fast. Even more than the attentions of certain salespeople – Gillian had been pitched everything from motorized scalp massagers to Planet Earth DVDs ('soar over the seven seas to the accompaniment of calming flute music . . .') to packages for managing her on-hold advertising space – the enthusiasm of her bank manager encouraged her to believe she was on to something. He had her seeing Deceleration centres dotting the landscape, ubiquitous as petrol pumps but looking more like the log cabins of the American frontier. She felt a distinct buzz coursing through her that had very little to do with space or silence or healing.

To lessen this inappropriate excitement, she had visualized her bank manager as a future client of the Farm. He was exactly the kind of person who needed to slow down. And yet, Gillian worried, he seemed quite happy at his near-fever pitch, with his materially saturated and spiritually vacuous life, happier than she was, in fact. Maybe he would crack up, such people often did, but she didn't want people to have to crack up before coming to her. Anyway, if they did crack up they would need something more than she could provide; they would need professional help. No, she would have to convince them of the benefits of Deceleration while they were still functioning at fever pitch. If she was going to do other than preach to the converted, she would have to offer something more than self-congratulatory organic farming and the absence of muzak. She ordered a slew of books by people who, down the ages, had imagined a better world. Reading Comte and Marx and Thomas More, she began to believe that if she could just affect the way a few people interfaced with time, there might be a trickle-down effect (though the trickle would be horizontal, more like a ripple, because Deceleration wasn't about hierarchies), and that if enough people slowed down at once, we might actually alter the rate of change in the world.

Elspeth was her first employee. They had met through an old professor of Gillian's at Trinity, who was then supervising Elspeth's postgraduate work. She was completing a dissertation called *Bonding Alone: How the Desemanticization of Place and the New Extraterritoriality of the Globetrotting Elite Will Affect Attachment-forming in the Twenty-First Century.* When it was finished, she wanted to see the ideas she'd been researching explored in a real-life setting. Gillian told her about her plans for Moilligh Farm (she'd scoured foreign dictionaries, Buddhist meditation manuals and the *Encyclopaedia of Utopias* for a name and settled on the Irish for 'slow down'), and Elspeth applied on the spot for the job of her assistant.

'I used to sit there wishing for the perfect controlled experiment,' she'd said. 'But the only possibilities that seemed even remotely suitable were like those preferred flyers' lounges in airports, and that's such a limited glimpse of the developments I'm interested in. Not to mention,' she laughed, 'a depressing environment. Talk about a lack of fresh air, my God. But the Farm, the Farm is perfect. I *already* believe in it.'

Elspeth said the whole nature of 'relationship' was changing for the worse, that we were undergoing a phase of 'radical loneliness'. But this was only temporary: things had to fall apart before a whole new way of being could come about. 'Virtual relations have in a few brief years become the standard. I mean, okay, their time had come, we'd been preparing for them since the sixties, all we were waiting for was the personal computer. Now our real relationships are apeing our virtual ones. They have to be flexible, right? Disposable, undemanding, constantly fun or we're out of there, etc, etc. But the real will come back. And that'll be the interesting part, to see how we manage that.'

'*Will* we manage that?' Gillian asked.

'I think so. Because we aren't actually designed for this infinite procession of identities and places. It's like eating tapas every day of your life. Who wants that? Rootedness will become a radical position, so will monogamy. That's already starting, in fact. So the next step is they get subsumed into the mainstream and then they're back as the standard, but with a difference. They're not reactionary, they're not conservative, they're not even retro – you know, lifestyle options masquerading as ethics. They're intelligent choices, because the alternatives have proved too painful.'

Gillian loved her. She was also a little bit in awe. Although she was forty-one and Elspeth only twenty-eight, she felt at times as though she were the younger of them, the more innocently eager. Elspeth was ironic and supremely confident. She had a little hook to her nose and high cheekbones and almond-shaped eyes. Her black hair was bobbed with a heightened and deliberate severity that managed to suggest self-parody. In comparison, Gillian felt harried and uncertain, but she also felt Elspeth's faith working on her. Listening to Elspeth ratcheted up her missionary zeal, her confidence, her sense of responsibility towards those who would entrust themselves to her. Gillian wanted Moilligh Farm to play a part in healing the 'radically lonely'. And Elspeth seemed sure that it could. The two of them took drives down to the old house in Meath, where renovations were already under way. They talked late into the night at Elspeth's apartment on Ormond Quay, standing out on the balcony, drinking wine and looking down at the Liffey, high enough up that the figures of addicts on the boardwalk blurred into a benign tableau. They met designers and visual artists, and poked around kitchen shops and galleries. They hired staff: Peter, who was taking a year off from social work in Dublin and would be at the Farm part-time; three local women who would share the kitchen duties; Helen, who would look after the garden.

The first couple of years had been bliss. Watching the

Farm's guests unwind over the course of their stay, Gillian thought of tight fists opening to the world. Watching them depart, slowly, down the long drive, she felt like both a successful hostess and a proud parent.

Back then, she had participated in almost every aspect of the Farm. She planted and meditated alongside the guests. She was with them when they cooked a meal from scratch. When they compiled 'not to do' lists of habitual neurotic activities, Gillian compiled her own. In the evenings, she gave brief talks on things like how paper is made – from the felling of the tree to the shop shelf – in order to remind the guests of how many resources and processes, how much effort, went into some of the things we used and tossed thoughtlessly aside.

She was busier than she'd ever been, and the paradox of that wasn't lost on her. But it felt like a healthy kind of busy because she loved her work. She was energized rather than exhausted, and she hadn't felt such a sense of community since university. And, aside from when Heather was a toddler, she'd never felt so trusted. Sometimes the guests would look at her, and the look in their eyes told her that she had the answer and was simply waiting, patiently, for the right question to be asked.

By six o'clock, the new arrivals had assembled in the common room. Gillian greeted them and explained in her customary Sunday-evening welcome voice – a tone both eager and conspiratorial, although she was feeling neither – that it was time to get acquainted.

'What I want you to do,' she said, 'is pair up. We're going to help one another get dressed.'

Raised eyebrows all around. For once nobody made the can't-we-help-each-other-get-*un*dressed? joke.

'On the table over there are a number of coveralls and several pairs of shoes. I want everyone to take one suit. Leave the shoes for now.'

The coveralls were standard-issue, dull grey, Great Leap Forward-wear. The shoes were a haphazard collection: large silver slippers, Wellingtons, flowered Doc Martens, snorkler's rubber flippers. Everybody took a suit and returned to their places in the circle, full of childlike curiosity.

The idea, Elspeth explained, taking over from Gillian, was to find the coveralls with your partner's name in the pocket. 'Then you must dress each other, because all the buttons and snaps and hooks are in the back of the suit. When that's done, you have to choose a suitable pair of shoes for your partner . . . based on what you think your partner would look best in.'

A grumble made its way around the room. The two repeaters in the group, who knew the drill from their last visit, sought collusive eye contact with Elspeth and Gillian. Gillian had developed a dislike for repeaters but Elspeth indulged them with a wink.

They gave the signal for the game to begin. As usual, great merriment ensued as the guests set about locating the right coveralls amid the mayhem, displaying an exaggerated pride when presenting them to their partners, as though the coveralls were actually of value and their procurement the result of an arduous and profound journey. They took great care when dressing one another, the men, particularly, their thick fingers awkward on the unfamiliar hooks and eyes. Finally, they all stood in a circle – identically clad but for the inane footwear – pointing at one another's feet and laughing.

When the hilarity died down, Gillian explained where the idea of mutual dressing had originated. 'This was practised in a community based on Comte's principles, as a way of developing a sense of responsibility for others. It's a symbolic act. Fostering interdependence. Helping to break down the hierarchies that so quickly take shape in a group.'

Among the guests there were nods of understanding. Gillian knew what they were thinking: that here at Moilligh Farm, behind even the most seemingly silly activities lay challenging, revolutionary ideas.

After dinner, as on every Sunday night now, they had Ice-Cream Koans – Elspeth's idea. She'd first proposed it over dinner one night with Damien and Gillian, during a phase some months ago in which she had been reading a lot of Zen Buddhism. Damien, who had stopped in Meath on his way home from a meeting in Belfast, had nodded and offered a distracted murmur of approval. Gillian had thought she was joking. By that time she'd unhappily accepted the fact that Elspeth viewed the Farm primarily as a laboratory, but increasingly she'd felt Elspeth applying the same sort of academic scrutiny to her, as though she might be writing a book, an insider's view of self-help, in which she would deconstruct Gillian's gullible, distracted and hypocritical manner of playing the guru.

Gillian had looked at Damien and said in a stage whisper, 'She's testing me. She's seeing if I'll take the idea seriously. If I do, she'll know I've really lost it.'

Elspeth affected indignation, and Damien said, 'She's only having a bit of fun. You should too. You take the place very seriously.'

'Of course I do,' Gillian said. 'It's my responsibility to.' She didn't like discussing the Farm with him; his regard was always tinged with irony.

'I'm not against serious,' Elspeth argued. 'But if we package serious things humorously, then people don't feel intimidated.'

'Why does everything have to be funny?' Gillian asked. 'And why must we always be "packaging" things?'

Elspeth put her chin in the air, one hand caressing her neck. 'Okay. Supposing we say to our guests: tonight we're going to present you with some Zen koans. Koans offer contradictions of the known. They are paradoxes meant to reveal the inadequacy of logical reasoning and provoke in you, we hope, sudden enlightenment. You know what would happen? Everybody would freeze up.'

Gillian chewed her lip. It was one of those increasingly frequent moments when she felt she'd lost her bearings, the inner compass that told her which things were a joke and which not and how seriously she should be taking her life.

By the following evening, Elspeth had gathered a sufficient number of koans and typed them on thin strips of paper, which she then had laminated so that they could be put through the dishwasher.

When your mind is not dwelling on the dualism of good and evil, what is your original face before you were born?

Now, every Sunday night, a single koan was tucked inside each cone, which was then topped by a large scoop of homemade ice cream.

Tonight, it was caramel, and the guests mingled happily as they licked. As Gillian watched them chatting – warmly, excitedly, the occasional wet dollop lodging on an upper lip – she couldn't help it; she wished them all the best.

Two

Instead of skirting city-centre traffic via the East Link, Damien was heading right into the thick of it, and all because of Glorianna. He had to be at the office by ten, and there was just enough time to call into the Boots on Grafton Street.

Chemists seemed to Damien benign versions of hospitals – the crisp white coats but none of the actual trauma, the griefs that were small and primarily of vanity. He liked the way they were organized according to the needs of the various body parts: eyes, teeth, hair, nails, feet, skin. He particularly enjoyed the sight of someone popping an emergency paracetamol right there at the counter, and was proud to be part of a species that had figured out how to relieve the common headache quickly, publicly and cheaply. Sometimes, having fallen prey to some new and minor affliction he'd either never heard of or been too young to bother about (what were corns, for instance? he still didn't know, though they must be big because there were corn cushions, corn caps, corn relief pads and a corn knife), he'd gone to the chemist and found the treatment there waiting for him. It was reassuring, knowing that there was nothing he could come down with or break out in that others hadn't suffered before him and for which someone, somewhere, hadn't already devised an antidote.

And then there was Glorianna, the girl with the gold-tinted face. They had a little thing going, not an actual thing, just a flirt-thing. Glorianna had densely curling shoulder-length hair, the kind you couldn't tame or straighten, and with her gold face and her kinky red-blonde mane she was like some feral thing, raised in the jungle by her adoptive lion parents until rescued by civilization and taught life skills. First a knife and fork, then language, then a job at Boots. Even her name – Glorianna – sounded to him like a gentle roar.

He saw the billboard just as he reached the old railway bridge on the North Strand Road. It had been there for weeks, it should have become wallpaper by now, but it never failed to catch his eye: a man and a woman leaning towards each other over a kitchen worktop, smiling smiles that were conspiratorial, marital and clearly post-coital. The kitchen was a cool blue. They were wearing silk dressing gowns. Steam from their two cups rose between them like a just-loosed genie. It could have been an ad for coffee but it was actually for the cock clinic in Sandymount. Above their heads were the words:

SIGHS MATTER. DO IT FOR BOTH OF YOU.

He crossed the river at the Custom House and headed up the quays and into the clogged-up centre, towards the underground car park nearest Boots. Once he'd found a space, he got as quickly as he could back out into the open air. As he was making his way up Grafton Street, he saw her, standing in the doorway, her feet on the premises but her upper body and head thrust out to catch the breeze, as though she were a sprinter crossing the finish line. He wondered if there was some kind of Boots regulation, insurance-related, about keeping your feet on the property during your shift.

'Hi,' Glorianna said. 'How're you?' She recognized him, but she didn't know his name.

Damien had the sudden urge to growl, but then remembered that he had never let Glorianna in on his little jungle joke. Anyway, she probably wouldn't blink an eye. Glorianna was imperturbable. She'd probably just say something like, 'I'm not from the jungle, I'm from Ballymote.'

She was from Ballymote. She'd told him that the first day he'd ever seen her, when she was helping him to locate contact lens solution. He'd heard the country accent and asked her, then they'd swapped reminiscences of the west, of charming small-town chemists, the bell going *ding-a-ling* over the door and everybody knowing each other's name. Glorianna said they'd had the tiniest little chemist, like a closet filled with magic potions. Back then she'd wanted to be an actress when she grew up. *But*, she'd shrugged cheerfully, *here I am*.

'I'm very well, thank you, Glorianna.' He glanced at her name tag as he said it, as though he weren't quite sure. 'And you?'

'Grand,' she said, following him inside. 'What can we get for you?'

Damien was in the latter half of his forties. It occurred to him that young women had begun to humour him, to regard him as harmless. On the other hand, perhaps he was not yet old enough to be harmless and they found him middle-aged and lecherous. The best-case scenario was that he was not yet considered old enough to be either lecherous or harmless and was still a plausible sexual object for women between the ages of twenty-one and forty-five. Perhaps, if he tried very hard – if he got his timing just right and honed his self-awareness and promised to fall prey to no illusion – he could somehow pass from the stage of plausible sexual object to cute doddery harmlessness, leapfrogging lechery altogether. Perhaps there was a remedy right here in Boots which would enable him to do just that. He was tempted to ask Glorianna, to see if it would get a laugh, but the joke was a bit too close to the bone and if she failed to roll her eyes and glance sideways at him in a way that said *You? Old? No way!* and instead just smiled stiffly, he would be mortified.

'Something for heartburn,' he said.

She looked at his heart and gave him a little smile of sympathy. 'Follow me.'

And follow her he did (though he knew where the heartburn section was and was pretty sure she knew he knew), enjoying as he went the sight of her hips in her white dress as they ticktocked smartly from side to side, sailing past the skin food and foot butter and body milk, the wax for men's chests and women's everywhere, beyond the Verruca Accessory Pack and the wonderfully medieval Toenail Pliers and the supports for fallen arches, which conjured up visions of Romans in the sunset of their glory. There was a bit of a bottleneck in the Hair Care aisle, and Damien tore his gaze from Glorianna's behind to scan the options (Big Hair, Cool Hair, Dream Hair, Bounce Control) and the range of colours (Florida, Virginia, Kenya, Havana, Oslo, Helsinki). All lined up in a row, they sounded like a menu for an escort service.

They passed into the make-up section, which also disturbed him, though for entirely different reasons. There was something militaristic about this display of mass production on such a tiny scale. Rows and rows of angled lipstick and mascara, like mini-missiles eager to be launched. Squat, square-shouldered bottles of nail polish – brown, cream, flesh-toned, black – a multi-ethnic army standing at attention. And the samplers! How many women's lips had touched the oddly planed tips of those little missiles? How many fingertips, all having dipped into the same well, had rouged how many cheeks? The off-handed intimacy of women! He thought of a writhing heap of them, fleshy and powdered, like in a scene from the *Antony and Cleopatra* production he and Gillian had seen years ago in London.

They were moving again, Glorianna's hips in front of him, side-to-side in time with the click-clack of her shoes on the tiled floor. Her hair was pinioned to the back of her head with two things that looked like crossed chopsticks. How did that work? Escaped wisps of it trailed kinkily down her neck, which was smooth and delicate and curved gently where it joined her shoulder. He thought of a carriage in the snow and the sound of horses' hooves. Hedgerows, newly white. A rustling in the seat beside him. Bustles and hooks and pre-Wonder Bra cleavage, the slightest sheen of damp on the skin above, the rise and fall of her breasts, her body beside him heavy with desire. He didn't know if the fantasy was a sign of chivalry or of sexism, or if he'd just watched too many TV serializations of nineteenth-century novels.

Glorianna had stopped and he nearly collided with her. She was turning over a box of Gaviscon, squinting at the fine print. He crooked his neck to get a better look at her, a look of rapture and timidity, as though he'd just dropped in from another planet where they didn't have gold females.

'I love the gold,' he said.

'It's something-something jaundiced.'

There were words in the middle he hadn't caught. Did she just say she had jaundice? He felt the heat in his own face. Surely it was skin dye. Wasn't it? As he struggled to think of something sensitive to say, she spoke again.

'Don't you think?' she said. 'Or maybe I just used too much.'

He smiled with relief. 'No, I don't think you look jaundiced. Not at all. You look like . . . an Egyptian statue. You know those gold statues. Oh, what are they called?'

'You think I look like one of those gold statues?' She weighed this up, her gaze trailing off somewhere. 'That's okay,' she said, nodding. 'I like that.' Then she handed him the Gaviscon. 'Go for these.'

'Okay. If you say so.'

She nodded again. They stood for a moment.

'Thanks, Glorianna.' He smiled, like a man with heartburn. Like a man passing through the lecherous stage.

She smiled back. 'Mind the heart,' she said.

'I will, of course,' he said.

She gave him a little finger-fluttering wave and disappeared into the slow-moving stream of bodies, which were bumping their way around each other up the too-skinny aisles.

What did she mean by 'mind the heart'? Was she referring to the increased risk of heart attack in men his age? Was she referring to the stirrings she knew his heart was undergoing as they spoke, in which case she meant, *You haven't got a snowball's chance in hell so don't upset yourself trying*? Or did she simply mean, *Watch what you eat and don't make the heartburn any worse*?

He headed towards the till, past the pregnancy tests and condoms that were displayed next to one another, locked in their eternal co-dependent tussle. Glorianna was at the till, her gold face matte under the ceiling lights. Had she seen him looking at the reproductive items? The things to do with fucking? She was holding his gaze as he came closer and, just like that, he knew. He'd seen it in her eyes: he was plausible.

By the time he'd taken the last few steps to the till, a fine mist had released itself under his arms. He was not so brazen as to look her in the eye as he handed her his money and said, 'Thank you, but I don't need a bag.' Ten years ago, even five, he would have looked straight at her in confirmation, but now humility was called for. Odd how everything reversed and what an enormous thing gratitude could be.

He touched her hand, neither too little nor too much, as she handed him his change. Just before turning towards the door, he permitted himself a look; he took the risk of seeing nothing in her eyes and realizing he'd been mistaken. But no, she was waiting for him to look at her and her lips were slightly parted and she had that little stunned, or fake-stunned, look women have at such moments, when fucking you has just occurred to them for the first time and they realize you've been thinking about it for a long time and their own loss of innocence on the subject is serving only to heighten their arousal. They'd had a moment. He was not so out of it, so washed up, that he didn't know a moment when he had one, or that he imagined a moment where there'd been none. As he donned his favourite sunglasses and made his way back down Grafton Street towards the car, his step was lighter and his legs felt stronger and his body sang a little song of thanks.

By the time he'd exited the car park, the Glorianna glow had faded and he was thinking about money. He wanted a pay rise. Heather would be going to university in a couple of years. Eventually, Grace would have to go into a nursing home. The sale of the Seapoint house would help pay for that, and though Gillian didn't want to let it go, when the time came, she would. Gillian's income had recently surpassed his own. Damien was glad for her – he liked having a wife who made good money; it was sexy – but he'd prefer the imbalance didn't grow any larger. He had been with Experience Ireland for more than twenty years; his pay had risen steadily. If Kill was a success, he would almost certainly be in line for another increase. Twenty-five million was the village's estimated potential

market in Europe alone. Out of that number, how many could he actually convince to visit Kill? EI's latest Worldwide Visitor Survey revealed that what tourists still expected to find in Ireland was a native population that was: friendly, honest, charming, convivial, witty, blessed with an ethnically specific verbal dexterity, superstitious, fun but untrustworthy, roguish and mystical. Damien had studied a number of EI visitor surveys, and the results could be summed up in a single line from one of them: 'Even the people who don't read seem really literate.'

Damien knew, however, that once tourists scratched below the surface of such people, they discovered minds awash in Manchester United, American television and the latest *Hello!*-sponsored nuptials. As for friendly, the Irish were tired of being friendly. How many letters had Damien read attesting to the increasing belligerence of the native population? *When we have visited your country in 1970 the people had been so nice . . . I am apologizing it to report that I can not say as well now.*

Prosperity was to blame. The country was losing its Unique Selling Point as a First World destination that retained pockets of the pre-modern. But Kill was going to be a pocket, a pocket of the 1950s. It was going to help reverse the trend of visitor dissatisfaction. By standardizing the tourist experience, delivering a reliable supply of convivial wit and verbal dexterity, it would alleviate the frustration that resulted from the irksome unreliability of people: the frustration that arose from your having followed the same Limerick–Kerry–Cork itinerary (even alighting in the same pubs) that your next-door neighbours from Chicago or Dusseldorf or Sheffield had followed only the week before, but having had a radically different experience. While your neighbours, through sheer undeserved luck, had stumbled upon that delightful ad hoc fiddle-and-

Guinness session, you had got stuck all night next to drunken bores you'd convinced yourselves were verbally dexterous though they were hardly capable of speech.

Damien understood this frustration. He knew that there was often the thinnest line between a great holiday and an anticlimax, and what made the difference was the very thing you couldn't control. It was the sheep factor. The sheep factor wasn't just the good luck, while motoring in rural areas, of getting stuck in the midst of a flock of sheep being herded up the road by a red-faced man in a cap who hailed you amiably as you sat enchanted in your car watching the bumpity-bump of sheep rumps recede. No, the sheep factor was shorthand for so much more, for the *je ne sais quoi*, the thing-in-itself that a visitor couldn't quite name but knew to see: life as a graciously enacted burlesque in which the laughter was sweet and the sorrow worn lightly, and in which everyone outside of Dublin looked like they were stranded in the seventies.

Damien had high expectations. Kill wasn't going to be like any other heritage attraction in the country. For one thing, it wasn't going to be about facts. Gillian was right: people were tired of information. They were tired of timelines and voice-overs and videos on a continuous loop and of squinting at labels telling them how significant some little hunks of iron were. They were tired of the number dead, the number wounded, the number enslaved or emigrated, even, Damien had noted on his visits to countries where such statistics applied, the number of concubines. Between the boredom and the drowsiness and the guilty inability to feel much of anything for the 40,000 dead, visitors tended to leave such places feeling not much better about themselves than when they'd arrived.

Kill, on the other hand, was going to make people feel good inside, the way castles and dolmens and display cases couldn't.

All anybody wanted was refuge, even for an afternoon. And what better place to take refuge than right here? Because Ireland was a place of spiritual homecoming, and people somehow knew that, without exactly knowing they knew it, and that was why they came. Nostalgia was a kind of modern epidemic, and the thing that opened Kill up to a potentially infinite market was that people were no longer required to actually remember the time or the place for which they were feeling nostalgic, or have even the most tenuous connection to it.

Some in the trade thought theme parks had already peaked. Jimmy, one of EI's other Heritage Strategists, worried that people were getting too sophisticated. Jimmy and Damien had worked together since the mid nineties, after Europe had started pumping money into cultural tourism and Damien moved to heritage from marketing, where he'd produced such EI classics as *Tackling Seasonality: All-Weather Tourism in Non-Sun Destinations* and *Roots Tourism and the North American Visitor*. Damien liked Jimmy. He was cynical but only on the surface. He was reliable and loyal, and looked like a clown: bald on top with a ring of brown hair in a horseshoe shape around his head. Jimmy was married to a woman nearly as funny-looking as he was and the two of them were happy, in what seemed to Damien an old-fashioned way, meaning they knew what they had and didn't engage in neurotic speculation about what other lives they might be leading.

'I thought people were getting dumber,' Damien had said.

'Yeah,' Jimmy had said, 'they are. But somehow . . . even as they're getting dumber, they're requiring more sophisticated products.'

They'd been in the middle of one of their informal brainstorming sessions that usually began with an exchange of guesses as to how the latest international atrocity or air disaster would affect the industry and graduated to bemoaning the increasing banality of the country's Unique Selling Points. Although visitor numbers to Ireland were growing, the curve wasn't as steep as it was in places like Cambodia and Libya. People wanted countries that had a whiff of danger about them: a languid and semi-redundant military presence; power cuts, even if the result of mismanaged public funds and an overstretched grid; a market economy in its primitive form (the recognizable gleam in the eye of a half-naked coconut salesman). Post-conflict destinations were increasingly popular. There was something romantic in the residue of war. And ethnic minorities were always a draw. Mongolia, Guihou in China, the hill tribes of Vietnam and Laos. Dirt roads and bumpy mountain passes. *Living conditions unchanged for centuries*. Bhutan was up-and-coming. Apparently, the Bhutanese still wore traditional costumes by order of the king. What had Ireland got? Travellers in Hiace vans by the rubbish-strewn side of the road. Beehive huts on Slea Head and Inishmurray. Admittedly, the huts were beautiful, but nobody was living in them. What if they could get people to live in them? Actual monks, maybe. Just for the summer months.

'I wish we were Mexico,' Jimmy had said. 'Except less fucked up.'

Black-spot tourism was getting bigger; the grassy knoll in Dallas had got that going. Adventure sports, too. And multi-purpose packages were gaining in popularity – the scalpel safari, for instance, cosmetic surgery plus safari and recuperation time at a five-star hotel. They gave you lip-swelling agents or resurfaced your face with a laser or sucked cellulite out of your ass, then loaded you, all sutured and bruised and bandaged like you were just back from the front, into canopied buses to gawk at wild animals. It was the kind of development that made Damien feel old-fashioned, like he wasn't weird enough to keep up any more.

The EI office was in Donnybrook, not far out of town, across from the TV studios. But twenty minutes after exiting the car park, Damien still hadn't reached the dual carriageway. Traffic leaving town had come to a near-halt. They were digging up the road in the outbound lane. He tapped the back of his head against the headrest and glanced at the clock. He seldom gave himself enough time. He refused to accept that he had to allow three-quarters of an hour to go a few miles. It now took longer to get across the city than it did to fly to London. If you were in a taxi, it cost more, too.

He was meeting with Judith later to make some final decisions regarding Kill. Judith was going to be the live-in director at the village. He and Gareth, his dull but competent boss, had hired her. She was smart and efficient and knew how to put people at ease, but she was only twenty-eight and had lived in the city all her life, and Damien wasn't entirely sure she'd be happy stationed in the middle of nowhere; on a good day, Kill was a two-and-a-half hour drive from Dublin.

She and Damien had selected the cast. They'd held two rounds of auditions and had come up with a mix of amateur actors (which was what they called the locals they'd hired) and professionals. They had the Irish-speakers, the soon-to-be-emigrating, the couples-at-home, the bachelor farmers, a priest and a nun, two publicans, the singing, step-dancing teenagers, the background cast of OAPs, and the poet-philosopher. He was the gem. Sean O'Gara was sixty-three and had never married. He'd attended the Sorbonne forty years ago but a breakdown suffered in Paris had landed him back home in Boyle, where he'd spent his life since, working at the library, reading Irish history and the classics and speaking Latin, Greek, Irish and French to locals and tourists alike. The townspeople doted on him. He was a rare combination of erudition and modesty. In the summers he led tours of Boyle Abbey. He could recite Yeats and chunks of Beckett, passages from *Ulysses* and the *Táin*, and he knew the 1916 Proclamation by heart. And it was Sean who introduced them to Irish bingo, a game he'd played with package-tour groups who came to Boyle. Instead of numbers, the cards had several words in Irish printed on them. Damien saw bingo as the solution to Kill's Irish-language problem.

The only slot they hadn't filled was the woman-at-her-loom-dispensing-wisdom. Two women had auditioned but both had been too young. Judith had suggested last week that they rethink it, forget the wisdom and do a girl-on-the-cusp-of-womanhood-at-her-loom. A stunner. Judith was in favour of sexing up Kill.

'There was always a stunner in every village,' she'd argued. 'Two stunners – one guy, one girl – and you've got a storyline. They want to marry but they can't because her parents want to send her to England, or his parents want to send him to Australia, and what are they going to do?'

Damien had liked her idea about the stunners. But he wasn't in favour of replacing the wise-woman-at-her-loom with the girl-on-the-cusp-of-womanhood. Better a female counterpart to Sean. People liked the elderly. They found them comforting. Someone appropriate would surface. There was no shortage, it seemed, of old folks eager to participate. The EI scheme was the first sign of life they'd seen here in some time and they welcomed it; it meant they hadn't been forgotten after all. In recent years, Kill had become one of those West of Ireland towns that seemed to have no reason for continuing to exist other than to offer itself as a case study when academics needed to highlight the corrosive effects of emigration on rural life or emphasize the dangers of over-reliance on foreign direct investment. The post office had closed, as had the butcher's and the draper's, their shopfronts faded into photogenic dereliction. Of the dozen or so businesses that had once lined the village's three streets, only a small shop-cum-pub still functioned. And in the scattering of cottages and bungalows in the townlands surrounding Kill, the only people left staring out at the scutch grass and bog were the ever-diminishing clutch of OAPs. Soon, even they would have gone, carted off to nursing homes by sons and daughters who couldn't be blamed for believing that the place was depressing them. Now, encouraged by those same sons and daughters, they would be part of Kill's revival.

They'd been given only the barest outline of a script – just prompts, really – then asked to reminisce about life in the fifties. Even those who'd appeared reticent at first soon became animated; a number of them could sing. Most of the OAPs would be planted at strategic locations around the village, in one of the two pubs or sitting on the low wall that ran along the main street or pushing their bicycles through town, available if visitors wanted to stop and chat with them, but not under the kind of pressure that would come with being one of the main attractions.

The teenagers had been trickier. Reared on reality TV, they already regarded performances at Kill for a potential audience of a few dozen at a time as a squandering of their potential. A boy named Bryan had wanted to know if any talent scouts would come to Kill. Alexa, Bryan's female counterpart, had been beside him at the time, nodding in agreement. Her hands were in the back pockets of her jeans and she was twisting her torso rather severely, the way that members of girl and boy bands did, making it difficult for Damien to ignore the exposed, ever-so-slightly flabby (but not the less attractive for that) strip of sunbed-tanned flesh at her midriff. Was Alexa auditioning for him? He had half-expected her to right herself dramatically, look him in the eye and burst into a chart hit. Instead, she had tucked her chin down and peered up at him for a moment before lapsing back into a more unstudied pose.

She and Bryan had continued to eye Damien expectantly, waiting for him to confirm that Kill was, indeed, a springboard to fame. He couldn't blame them. Many seemingly unpromising situations *were* brilliant opportunities. And who'd want to be singing 'The Fields of Athenry' in Kill when you could be doing Barry Manilow covers for a major label?

'Let me have a think about it,' he'd said. 'There's no reason you shouldn't make the most of this. What's good for you, after all, is good for us.'

Had he really said that?

By the time Damien inched past the massive hole being dug in the road it was coming up to ten. He switched on the radio to catch the news headlines. The tail end of an appeal from Concern, a high-speed verbal assault insisting he shop at Power City, then a voice he recognized.

Immerse yourself in the familiar. Establish personal stability zones. Resist pointless reorganization. Manage the rate at which acceleration enters your life. Gradualize. Monogamize. Recognize.

She was fading to a murmur.

Gradualize . . . Monogamize . . . Recognize . . .

Gillian had started doing her own ads again. It was an attempt to reassert some control, now that she was at home with Grace for the better part of each week. Damien didn't think it was a good idea. The tone was all wrong. There was the slightest trace of insistence in her voice. It was the sound of accumulated stress.

He wouldn't go so far as to say he was sorry she'd ever started the Farm, but it had changed her, in ways directly opposed to the changes she aimed to bring about in her clients. There had been a honeymoon period – a time of nervous elation towards the end of that first year, when it was clear the place wasn't going to go under, that they weren't going to lose the savings they'd put into it or have to re-mortgage the house – when Gillian had started appearing on television chat shows and in the papers and was sometimes recognized around Dublin. When she'd become an author.

She had rung him one day almost breathless with excitement. A UK publisher of self-help literature had asked her to put the principles of Moilligh Farm in print. Books on the quietly growing Slow Movement were already beginning to appear and the publisher reckoned Gillian was perfectly placed to capitalize on the appetite for such literature.

'I'll be an *author*,' she'd said, with a mixture of pride and self-mockery. There was a tiny part of her, he knew, that could hardly believe she was being listened to.

The book was short and to the point, encapsulations of the workshops she'd developed. But he could hear her voice in it. In her author photograph, she sported an earnest and upbeat we-can-beat-this-thing-together kind of smile. In the beginning, she'd smiled a lot.

Now she said things like, 'I hate playing the swami. I'd just as soon write the software and let them at it.'

Where were they that day? Damien could still see her, sitting across a table from him, looking off to the left as she spoke. Invariably, he pictured her in a turban, because of the swami reference, though of course she wasn't wearing a turban. There was nothing behind or beside her. It was like in one of those plays where you had a single actor seated on a stage against a white backdrop, talking about her life with a kind of inadvertent insight.

Three

On the Dystopia Channel, a woman (or was it a man?) was talking about the utopian/dystopian cause–effect thing. Heather knew the DTV ad by heart at this stage: nice ideas that produced nasty results, nasty ideas that produced nasty results, nice ideas that produced nice results, and just dreadful things that happened without having been anybody's idea. Heather wondered if nasty ideas had ever produced nice results, accidentally. It didn't seem so.

As the woman (or man) spoke, phrases in different colours appeared and disappeared on the screen. They were some of the subjects that would be featured on DTV programmes that week: the mental life of lottery winners, the city of Atlantis, Hesiod's *Works and Days*, heaven, Hawaii, Huxley, Philip K. Dick, *Gulliver's Travels*, space travel, the noble savage, *Candide*, the rainforests, the Manhattan Project, the nuclear winter, genocide, lotus-eating, the history of the *ménage à trois*, Ecstasy, Icarus, Lincoln, Marx, Margaret Atwood, fundamentalism, socialism, *A Vision*, *Walden*, phrenology, Leibniz, William Gibson, the Romantics and childhood, mass production, the Prozac revolution.

Heather didn't have a clue who or what half of the people and things were, but they all sounded interesting. She was a DTV addict. Her friend Emile had got her into it. In the programme that had just finished, experts had predicted that due to an ever-mushrooming population, the one-child family would eventually be enforced by law in countries throughout the world, resulting in the gradual disappearance of such concepts as 'brother' and 'sister'. Heather was an only child, and though she was aware that there were perks to her position, she also envied her friends and the obvious – if sometimes begrudging – loyalty they shared with their brothers and sisters, and suspected that a little part of her wouldn't be altogether sorry to see such concepts disappear. However, the enshrining in law of the single-child family was apparently a few years down the road, by which time the more pressing issue for her would be offspring.

The condoms were still upstairs, the box unopened, its plastic wrap intact. Her mother had presented them to her almost three months ago. She'd said that even if Heather had no need for them just yet, she wanted her to be comfortable with birth control and to get used to the idea of taking responsibility. She also said that if Heather were to get involved with a boy with whom she wished to be sexually active, she might want to consider a hormonal method as well, as condoms were not entirely reliable.

'But,' her mother had added, 'you know this doesn't mean that you *have* to become sexually active. Remember, you can just say no. You own your body, and you are entitled to say no without having to explain.'

'I *know*, I *know*,' Heather had said, rolling her eyes at the wall, careful to avoid the kitchen table, where her mother had placed the box. On the front of the box was the word 'lubricated', a word whose existence Heather did not wish to acknowledge while in the company of her mother.

Though she was deeply embarrassed by the little speech (more, she told herself, by its combination of New Agey blah-blah and just-say-no anti-drugology than by the subject of sex itself), and though she had scant faith in her mother's ability to imagine the temptations she might be subject to, Heather knew that the official presentation of birth control was not an insignificant event. It was the formal recognition of a certain inevitability, and while outwardly she affected disinterest, secretly she felt she'd been issued a pass to somewhere thrilling. The feeling reminded her of how she'd felt when she was small and her father would take her to the funfair and hand her a fistful of tickets he'd just bought, and there'd be so many tickets she'd know she would never be able to use them all, which could only mean that the rest of her life would be spent at the funfair, which was all right by her. But the tickets got eaten up at an alarming rate because some things required three or four tickets, and Heather could see her funfair infinity shrinking down to a day, then an afternoon, then an hour. And before she knew it, it was time to go home.

The day she'd placed the condoms carefully in her dresser drawer she'd had that fistful-of-tickets feeling again (which caused her to wonder if perhaps only a certain number of feelings were issued to each person and you had to kind of recycle them as you got older). Unfortunately, the belief that a lifetime of fun was about to commence was turning out to be even more groundless than it had been at the funfair. Heather had imagined that once she was the authorized owner of birth control, she might send out a pulse of some sort, a signal that she was ready to receive, like a satellite dish inviting radio waves or a flower a bee. But three months later, she was still a virgin. Of course she could remedy that if she really wanted to, but she hated those stories you heard about kids setting out to lose their virginity. Something about that depressed her.

Now DTV was running a trailer: *Just as families with one*

child are on the increase, children with more than one family are on the rise. Next week: the disappearance of the single-family child.

This was confusing. One week the family was disappearing, the next week it was proliferating. Which was it? Oh, well. That's life, Heather thought, shaking her head and smiling. *C'est la vie.* A few weeks ago she'd seen a teacher at school do that, a substitute French teacher who was actually French. First the woman had said it in English, to another teacher, then repeated it in French. Then they'd both laughed, the way women sometimes laughed together. When Heather had got home from school that day, she'd stood in front of the mirror over her dresser and shrugged, world-weary. *C'est la vie*, she'd said. A French film star after a million affairs and as many would-be lovers squashed underfoot. Men gone *splat* on the footpath as they dive-bombed into love with her. *C'est la vie*, she would say, turning on her heel, grinding a few more hapless admirers to dust.

She made a mental note to watch that programme next week. Sometimes she wanted her parents to do something exciting and tragic, something that would place her at the centre of a drama. Like get a divorce. Heather knew they'd almost done that a few years ago, though they didn't know she knew. She'd heard them talking about it once, late at night, sitting stock-still in her bed, unable to imagine how such an upheaval would affect her life. For a while after that, she had watched them obsessively. She had gone round the house in a state of anxiety, awaiting the announcement, afraid to ask, lest her asking might somehow force an outcome that was otherwise not inevitable. But though she took every opportunity to eavesdrop, she never caught them speaking of it again, and had finally concluded that divorce was one of the many things parents considered doing and seldom actually did.

No, now that she thought about it, a divorce would be a bit much. Maybe they could just separate for a while. Like for a week. And by the time *The Heather Show* came back on next Friday, everything would be patched up again. Emile's family was always having a drama. The latest one involved his sister Nathalie, who was twenty and a drug addict. Or not exactly a drug addict any more, because she no longer took drugs, but she kept calling herself a drug addict. It was part of her therapy. Heather hadn't known Emile when Nathalie was a coke fiend, but apparently it had been *quite* dramatic. When Emile had first told her, Heather had said, 'Cool,' because she hadn't wanted Emile to think she was the kind of girl who'd get all freaked out about someone doing drugs, but Emile had rolled his eyes and said, 'It was not cool.'

According to Emile, Nathalie had lost two stone and at the end was living with her appalling boyfriend who was a dealer. Nathalie was beautiful, just like Emile, and she'd been dating this hot rich guy and he was the one she'd started doing coke with, but then she'd ended up shagging the rich guy's dealer, who was by then her dealer, too. The whole thing ended when Nathalie went to Benidorm with the dealer and had some kind of a breakdown towards the end of a week-long party. Emile said Nathalie was more embarrassed afterwards about the fact that she'd actually gone to Benidorm than she was about the fact that she'd rung them crying in the middle of the night, asking their father to come get her, like she was only down at the shops or something. Now Nathalie was back at home again, working as a secretary somewhere and going to NA meetings every night, living what looked to Heather like a very dull life in comparison.

NY25 was starting. This was DTV's most popular drama series. It was on every Monday night, and they repeated it

Wednesday afternoons and Friday nights. It was about a group of surgeons in New York in 2025 who specialized in inserting small CCTV-like computers in people's heads. These implants, which were manufactured by the massive Mnemon Corporation, were expensive and thus not available to all. But those who had them were able to record everything they saw and heard, thereby relieving them of the burden of having to remember things. The implant people ruled the world. Then there were the grubby people – the steaming underclass, as Heather's mother called them, because it was always raining and warm in New York in 2025, and steam rose off the grubby people like they were wet dogs. The grubby people, who couldn't afford implants, could hardly remember their own names but worked in jobs so menial that it didn't matter. One of the surgeons, Dr Swinford, was always trying to get the government to have implants subsidized and made available to the grubbies for practically nothing.

Heather felt sorry for the grubby people, trudging to work in the morning and having to pass by the shotza bars where the future captains of industry hung out, rich kids popping penny-sized disks in and out of their skull pads. Four or five at a table, eyes closed and smiling to themselves, sipping various shades of nutrient cocktail. If she were grubby, she'd be pissed off, too. But she also sensed that if Dr Swinford got his way and there were implants on the medical card, or whatever they called it in the States, a certain tear-jerking element of the story would be lost. She wasn't sure she'd watch it any more if the grubby people disappeared.

Aside from the implant people and the grubbies, there were the Refuseniks. The Refuseniks thought the implants were evil, though some of them possessed implants, having got them when they were young, before they knew any better.

Now they wanted to have them removed, but there were very few doctors who could, or would, perform the operation; no one had ever had an implant removed except as a consequence of a separate trauma, like a brain tumour, so the effect on healthy people couldn't really be predicted. But whatever became of their own implants, the Refuseniks wanted to stop the industry from growing. They were trying to save human nature. They lurked in the shadows plotting terrorist actions against the implant clinics. So far, all their plots had been foiled by the implant-enhanced police.

Right now, the Refuseniks were having a meeting. The head Refusenik was totally hot. His name was Mymar. He was Slovakian. The problem with the Refuseniks was that they were always arguing. About whether to bomb or to hack; about what exactly was wrong with having a camcorder in your head; about whether they should work for an implant ban or educate the grubby and let them make their own decisions; and about whether they should go undercover or be completely 'out'. Because even though, technically, it wasn't illegal to refuse an implant, if you weren't grubby and you didn't have an implant you were regarded with suspicion. What was wrong with you that you didn't want your life on mini-disk? Were you a terrorist? As a result, some of the implant-free Refuseniks went round in grubby drag, arguing that it was better to be thought stupid and poor than to be thought a terrorist. Others argued that such an approach only contributed to the shame the grubby felt. They said that part of their mission was to stand with the grubby by making clear that they themselves had chosen to be implant-free. The problem with that argument was that the only thing the grubby seemed to want were the implants.

This was Mymar's dilemma. He had come from the steaming underclass but had bettered his lot in America and been the first in his family to get an implant. Now he was ready to throw this privilege away. He felt torn. His parents had been so proud of him the day he'd showed them his first disk. Just gazing at the disk in Mymar's palm, knowing it contained the memories of their first-born son, had been one of the high points of their sad, steaming lives.

Mymar was talking to Dr Harding, who was a colleague of Dr Swinford's, and who, it was revealed last week, had been in contact with the Refuseniks. Heather wasn't entirely surprised. Dr Harding had always been a bit iffy, asking his girlfriend Mitya to put her implant in *pause*, mode when they were having sex, that sort of thing. Mitya was really thick. She spent her days lounging around on curvy furniture in a leopard-skin jumpsuit and she was always on for it and couldn't understand why anyone would question any kind of technological advance. When Dr Harding asked her to *pause*, Mitya would purr at him and say, 'But darling, what ever will I do while you're at work all day and night?'

'Well, you could just . . . think about me instead,' Dr Harding would say. 'Or, I don't know, you could . . . *do* something.'

Then Mitya would pout and say, 'Mmm, no, I want to watch you,' and rub her leopardy breasts against his chest.

It was clear that even though Dr Harding was sexually enslaved to Mitya, the two of them weren't going to last, especially now that he was getting mixed up with the Refuseniks. And there was a beautiful and kind Refusenik named Claire who was obviously next in line for the doctor's affections.

Dr Harding was telling the meeting about his 'keep-fit' exercises.

'Every day I dwell on something old and real,' he said. 'I

press *pause* and sit in the dark and don't slip in a disk and don't sleep. I just see blackness and know that I'll never see that particular blackness again. It's important to retain the notion of unrepeatability, because unrepeatability is exactly what we're in danger of losing.'

'Aren't you afraid you'll miss something, Doctor?' That was Mymar. Poor Mymar. His humble roots were not his only problem. Dr Harding was also a problem. He needed Dr Harding, and he respected him, but Mymar was in love with Claire, and he could see the way she looked at the doctor. He knew he was losing her. Heather wished she could give Mymar a big hug. He was a good man; he just wasn't as rich or as slick or as powerful as Dr Harding.

'Of course,' Dr Harding said. 'The temptation to re-enter the *record* mode is great. The Zapruder Syndrome. It's half the problem. Mnemon recommends spending at least one hour a day in *pause*, but people won't do it. Because who knows when something's going to happen? Something you don't ever want to forget.'

Those around the big table shifted and grumbled.

Heather bit her lip. They were always on about Zapruder. At first she thought it was something from an earlier episode she'd missed, but then she gathered it was something or someone from the real world. She'd ask her father. She wouldn't ask her mother, her mother was busy stressing about Aunt Grace, who had Alzheimer's. Apparently, Aunt Grace was going to go slowly crazy until she was eating stuff that wasn't food and sneaking out at night with no clothes on. That was what it said in one of the pamphlets Heather's mother had given her to read. It sounded awful but also kind of interesting. Maybe it was the family drama she'd been waiting for.

'And what about those who don't keep fit?' Mymar was asking.

'Well, we can't be absolutely certain, but we suspect the neural connections are just atrophying. Your memory's like a muscle: use it or lose it. However' – Dr Harding leaned forward, elbows on the table – 'I believe it can be rehabilitated. That's one of the things you'll have to confront if you're ever going to convince people to let go of the implants, the fear they have of finding their post-implant minds a total blank. It's terrifying to contemplate, and no amount of rhapsodizing about the sanctity of human nature is going to overcome that fear.'

'Doctor . . .' It was Claire.

'Yes, Claire?' He turned to look at her. Claire was everything Mitya wasn't. The viewers saw it. Dr Harding saw it. He was dying to have unrecorded sex with her.

'What do you think our chances are? Honestly.'

Dr Harding sighed. The double meaning of Claire's question was apparent, but he didn't let on. Dr Harding was so cool.

'I think you've got to look to younger people,' he said. 'Younger people and the economic underclass. As for those who've had the implants for twenty years, there's no way they're even going to consider letting them go. I'm an exception,' he added.

The camera panned around the table as all the Refuseniks took in the irrefutable fact of Dr Harding's exceptionalness.

The camera cut to a new scene: Dr Harding walking home through the rain. He had the collar of his raincoat turned up and he was thinking about Claire, you could tell by the sad, preoccupied look on his face. When he got home he made himself a glass of purple shotza. Then he sat in his kitchen and chewed on his knuckle, like he was trying to make some kind of decision. He walked to the living room, lay down on the sofa, and started fiddling with the remote for his implant. He closed his eyes. Next thing, you saw what he saw. It was the recording from the meeting. There was Claire's face, asking him, *What do you think our chances are?*

And again, *What do you think our chances are?*

What do you think our chances are?

What do you think our chances are?

Heather wondered whether, in such a world, she'd be a Refusenik. After all, it would be cool to be able to do what Dr Harding was doing. She would love to look at a recording of Emile like that, to be able to carry him around with her wherever she went. And the implanted people were always dining out in posh restaurants and driving around in Lamborghinis, and whenever they had sex they looked really clean and fit, like people on the covers of health magazines. The Refuseniks, on the other hand, had more dangerous and thus more exciting lives, but they were always angry or paranoid, pounding on the table and creeping around in the dark, and they really did seem to be on the losing team. Nevertheless, she hoped that if it came to it, she would cast her lot with the Refuseniks. Some gut instinct told her it was the right thing to do. And besides, Emile said he would definitely be a Refusenik, and she wanted to be on Emile's team.

Emile's father was half-Egyptian, half-French, and his mother was Irish, which Heather reckoned made Emile one-third of all those things. Mostly, Heather thought, he looked Egyptian, from what she knew of Egyptians. He had curly black hair and dark eyebrows and beautiful smooth light brown skin. There were little black moles at the corner of his left eye and on his neck. He lived on the south side and went to a different school, where he was a year ahead of her.

Heather had met him in a café next to the place where they both went for grinds. That first evening, they'd started talking about *NY25*, arguing over whether Dr Harding was a double agent. That was a theory of Emile's, which he abandoned not long after.

Emile didn't have a girlfriend, though of his friends who were girls Heather was definitely number one. He had invited her over this weekend to watch DTV. There was a programme on about people who lived in trailer parks in America and won the lotto and how it totally fucked them up. Emile loved watching programmes about dysfunctional people. Heather was thinking that maybe that night, if Emile didn't make a move on her, she would make one on him. It didn't always have to be the guy, she knew that from films, but she didn't know exactly how she should go about it. She'd been thinking of asking her friend Miriam. Miriam had a boyfriend, and though she and Heather had never explicitly discussed the extent of Miriam's sexual experience, Heather knew it was far greater than her own. You could tell by the way Miriam handled guys, like they'd all been put on earth for the purpose of doing favours for her.

Heather didn't want to ask Miriam. Miriam didn't even know she fancied Emile. Heather hadn't told anyone; Emile himself didn't know. If only she weren't a single-family child, she might have a step-sister she could talk to. What about Elspeth? Even though Elspeth didn't have a boyfriend, she apparently had a constant supply of admirers; Heather had heard her mother say to her father, 'There's always one or two sniffing around.'

A dumb programme about hunter–gatherers was coming on. Heather switched off the set and switched on some music. Her current favourite was a German band of four guys called the Milkmaids. One of them wore a kilt and another wore a long black evening dress. It was said that the kilt and the evening dress were lovers, but Heather wasn't sure. Months ago she'd found a picture in a bus kiosk of two men doing it and she'd been fascinated. Really manly men having it off with each other under a waterfall. One of them was lying on his back, while the other one was standing – or was he kneeling? she couldn't remember – and they were facing each other, doing it just like a man and woman would, which had surprised Heather because she'd thought men could only do it from behind. She'd put the picture in her bag and stashed it in her room. Sometimes she took it out and looked at it, turning it this way and that. She thought she might like to watch two guys having it off, just sit there and watch, the way you'd watch the TV.

She was still half-lying on the sofa, flicking at her navel ring and toying with the idea of writing to the Milkmaids and asking if perhaps, the next time they played a gig in Dublin, they might arrange a little private viewing for afterwards, as she had a very healthy curiosity and was in no way homophobic and would in fact be delighted to spread the word, act as a kind of ambassador for homosexuality, when she heard her mother's car pull in the drive. She didn't get up, though she did go to the trouble of sitting up. She lowered the volume on the Milkmaids till all that could be heard was a high-pitched clatter that sounded, even to Heather's loving ears, like dishes being done behind the scenes in the school cafeteria.

Her mother peeked in the door, and Grace appeared beside her. 'There's Heather,' her mother said to Grace. Her mother was smiling that fake smile, the one she'd developed after Grace came to live with them.

'Hi, Grace.' Heather smiled back. Her smile felt fake too.

She loved Grace, but sometimes she just wasn't in the mood. Grace was so needy, even when she wasn't actually asking for anything. It was just the way she looked at you, like you were neglecting her even when you weren't. It made Heather feel guilty of something.

Grace came in and sat down in the armchair. She was wearing one of the new outfits Heather's mother had bought for her. The outfits were all bright colours – yellow and red and orange – with matching trousers and tops, the kind of clothes Grace would not have been caught dead in when she was normal. But her mother said that it was good to dress Alzheimer people like that. Heather had said, 'Why? It's not like Grace is going blind,' and her mother had said, 'It just is . . . it's good.' Like she couldn't remember why. Her mother was such a spacer. In fact, Heather found it difficult to square the person who stood in the sitting room looking stressed out and confused with the famous person who appeared in magazines. Heather had read articles where people who'd been to the Farm claimed that it had changed their lives. They talked about her mother like she was Mother Teresa. Heather didn't know what to think and so, for the time being, tried not to think about it at all. She figured maybe her mother's value in the real world was one of those things she wouldn't be able to properly assess until she was older.

Sometimes Heather wished that her mother was famous for something else, like being a radical environmentalist movie star or inventing a vaccine for that virus that made your organs melt and blood spurt out your pores. But she guessed it was better to be famous for having a slow farm than not to be famous at all. Also, if her mother were a movie star or genius doctor, then she – Heather – might not be here because, under the circumstances, her mother probably would never have met her father. Or she might only be half here, the half of her that was her mother's half, and what would it feel like, being only half of herself? And who would the other half be? Or, if her mother had had her with someone else, she mightn't even be *half* herself, the mix might have resulted in someone else entirely. This particular thought made Heather's head spin, and caused her to conclude that if things really were different, as she often wished them to be, she probably wouldn't be around to enjoy them.

'Tea?' her mother was saying. 'Would you like a cup of tea?'

Grace nodded. She looked like someone who was deaf or didn't speak English.

Her mother went to make tea. Barney appeared out of nowhere and slithered along Heather's ankles, then leapt up on Grace's lap.

Grace was so startled she let out a little cry and her sunglasses fell off the top of her head and hit Barney on his head. Barney registered the impact, blinked heavily, then began to knead Grace's thigh, which was very skinny.

Heather looked sideways at the stereo. The Milkmaids were still crashing away, but Grace hadn't seemed to notice.

'Ni-ice,' Grace said, scratching Barney's back. 'Aren't you the lovely puss.'

Heather leaned over and tickled Barney under the chin.

'He's a very good puss-puss,' Grace said, then looked at Heather. 'Is he yours?'

Heather swallowed. 'Mmm . . .' she said, and looked away. Barney was Grace's cat and had lived with her in Seapoint for years. Maybe Grace would remember later. Grace was like that. Sometimes she remembered things she'd forgotten.

Heather retrieved the sunglasses from where they'd slid

down to the side of Grace's other skinny yellow thigh and held them up to show Grace in case she wanted to put them somewhere. But Grace didn't look interested. Heather put the glasses on Barney instead and held them in place. For a moment Barney was stunned and didn't move.

'Look,' Heather said, 'Barney's on his holidays.'

Grace opened her mouth wide in delight like it was the best trick ever. Then Barney wriggled free and jumped down, in a huff at having been made sport of, knocking the glasses to the floor as he went. Grace looked down at the glasses, puzzled, as though they'd just dropped out of the sky.

Then she turned to Heather and smiled and said, 'Barney's got a flight to catch.'

Heather laughed. She was pretty sure it was a joke.

Four

Before Grace had moved in with them, she'd lived for forty years on Trafalgar Lane, near the DART track and the bathing places at Seapoint. For the last six of those years, since Martin's death, she'd been alone. Gillian had tried not to worry about her – Grace didn't invite it – and it wasn't until the day she discovered the print-outs in the study that she'd had any idea Grace herself was worried.

They had just finished Sunday brunch and were sitting in Grace's kitchen. Between them on the big table were coffee cups, fruit rinds, slices of brown bread, three kinds of cheese on the cutting board, and the array of computer print-outs. The computer had been a gift from Damien the year Martin died. Gillian and Heather had come over one afternoon and got Grace connected and taught her how to search for things on-line and send e-mails and find out whether the book she wanted was in the library and, if it wasn't, how to get it delivered from Amazon. Grace had sat back in her chair and clasped her hands together, gazing at the screen, wonderstruck.

'Isn't this *mar*vellous!' she'd said.

They'd found the website for the school in Dun Laoghaire where Grace had been a teacher for nearly thirty years. Heather clicked on the slide show and, as the images stuttered into being, Gillian saw tears gathering in Grace's eyes. After that, Grace had found a gardening chat room. Within days, she'd made a number of new on-line friends in various parts of the world, whom she talked about with the same warmth and familiarity with which she talked about her neighbours of many years.

The print-outs on the table that day concerned dementia prevention. Some of the stuff was futuristic: pumps implanted in the brain to feed it nerve growth factor, plaque-dissolving antibodies, immunization against beta-amyloid build-up, shunts to drain spinal fluid. Other sheets had information on micro-nutrients, folate, B12, Vitamin E. *Tests are currently under way to investigate the possibility that fish, nuts and oily dressings containing polyunsaturated fatty acids may help protect our brains from the ravages of Alzheimer's.* There were articles on Motrin, Aleve, Exelon, Aricept, Reminyl and Memantine, and an order form for Ginkgo biloba.

Ginkgo biloba enhances blood circulation and has antioxidant properties. It is possible that these properties may lower your risk of memory impairment associated with ageing. This statement has not been evaluated by the Food & Drug Administration.

Finally, there were several sheets Grace had stapled together, headed *The Memory Protection Plan*. Gillian turned the page. There was a neat little acrostic to help you remember the tools you would need to help you remember.

R each out to others
E xercise your brain
M ake an effort
E motional associations
M ake notes
B e organized
E at right
R est

Gillian looked closely at her aunt, who was calmly buttering a piece of bread while Gillian skimmed the print-outs. She looked at Grace's hair – whiter than white – and at her liver spots and glassy eyes and swollen knuckles, at the near-transparency of her fair skin. Grace had remained at a certain plateau of ageing for an unusually long time. Even at seventy, Grace had still appeared post-middle age rather than elderly. Now, she was old. Perhaps it was Grace's self-containment that had allowed her to slip over the divide unnoticed. Or maybe it was the fact that in so many ways she was very much alive. She read and cooked and shopped and gardened. She made things – yoghurt and jumpers – and dug fresh beds in the garden. People still enjoyed her company. Students from years ago occasionally called by to see her, and Grace would serve them tea and cake, then they'd walk down to the sea and watch the year-round swimmers brave the icy water. Grace, all bundled up, would wave a gloved hand at them as they emerged, their shocked flesh gone pale in the cold. But Grace was old now, and life was speeding up, getting away from her. When Gillian was younger, she used to think that life moved slowly for old people – all she could see were what looked like long stretches of monotony, lives in which the element of surprise had been reduced to the emergence of pain in some part of the body one would not have thought capable of producing its own distinctive ache – but now she knew the opposite to be true: time moved faster with each passing year.

The world worked against you. Grace had grown up in a time when the-way-things-are was a feeling, a texture, an assumption, a collection of facts reordered only by major events like a birth or a death, or the coming of electricity. Otherwise, the days ticked by, bracketed and reassuring. But now the world was like a single draft under continuous revision, a cityscape of quick successions, the imploding and flowering of structures on every side, as though in time-lapse, and you didn't have a say in any of it. You just trusted some unseen force to keep resculpting your world. Meanwhile, if you were Grace, your own inner workings were getting slower all the time. You shuffled, you chewed carefully, you peered, you cupped your ear to hear better and took twice as long to learn anything, you repeated yourself and asked others to do the same, you erected tiny bulwarks against the changes that surrounded you, building for yourself a little fortress of stasis. And then you sat there in your chair and watched the world pull away, like some monstrous train you kept just missing.

'If you're concerned about your memory,' Gillian said finally, 'we should see a specialist.'

'I've been,' Grace said.

'You have?'

'I've informed myself. As I informed myself about the menopause.' That was true; when the change came, Grace had been armed for battle.

Gillian pushed the print-outs aside. 'When did you see the specialist?' she said.

'June.'

'*June?* That's five months ago.' Gillian stared at her aunt, and shook her head. 'Why didn't you tell me?'

Grace, still unperturbed (though refusing to look Gillian in the eye), sliced off a bit of blue. 'It's not as though there's anything for you to do,' she said. She paused, then added, 'I don't want to be watched, I don't want to be monitored.'

'What kind of doctor was he? Or she. What did he say?'

'He's a neurologist. Ray Shipsey recommended him.' Ray was Grace's GP. 'He gave me all sorts of tests and at the end he said I have Mild Cognitive Impairment.' She pronounced it with ironic care.

Gillian wasn't sure if this was bad news or relatively good news.

'Which means . . . ?'

'I can't remember sometimes, but I'm not losing my mind. Half the people my age have it –'

'Oh. Well.' Gillian's palms opened to the heavens.

'It might get worse and it might not.'

'Get worse how?'

'Then you get Alzheimer's,' Grace said.

'He told you that?'

'He told me not to worry. He said stay active.'

'I don't think you're getting Alzheimer's,' Gillian said. 'If you can worry about having Alzheimer's, you haven't got it. Isn't that what they say?'

'I didn't say I *had* Alzheimer's. I'm saying there's a much higher chance I will get it now that I have this other thing.'

Gillian was silent. Grace sounded almost eager for the worst, but that was Grace, overcompensating for her fear with this willingness to meet the worst halfway.

'I'm only telling you,' Grace said.

Gillian looked closely at her. 'So did he put you on anything?'

'No,' she said. 'They only put you on something if you've got Alzheimer's.'

'Well, look,' Gillian said, tapping the stack of print-outs, 'don't take anything without talking to us first. Or to the doctor.'

The following Sunday, Grace had come to their house for lunch. (Gillian met her nearly every Sunday, before heading off to Meath for the week.) She'd been in fine form and had spent half the lunch talking about the GM foods debate, explaining the difference between the current crops of GM foods and the old-fashioned hybrids we were so used to we didn't even know they were hybrids. She'd been reading about it on-line and discussing it with some members of an organic gardening chat room she'd found and had even signed up to receive the English-language version of an electronic newsletter from a GM watchdog group in Germany.

After she'd gone, Damien had said, 'If this is cognitive impairment, give me some,' and Gillian had shaken her head and smiled and said, 'I know. She's fine.'

A few weeks later, Gillian had gone out to Seapoint to take Grace for a swim. It was one of those beautiful autumn afternoons that seem to come out of nowhere and feel like a reward for something you've forgotten you did. She was due to drive to the Farm afterwards, though she'd half thought of skipping tonight's getting-acquainted session, inventing an excuse and spending the evening in the garden with Grace, opening a bottle of wine, having a good long chat. It was a far more appealing prospect than listening to the predictable anxieties of twenty neurotics, anxieties she was finding it increasingly difficult to care about.

She didn't bother knocking when she got to the house, but let herself in through the side gate and went round to the back garden – a walled jungle of light and shade and trailing vine that opened on to a brighter square beyond which Grace had her vegetable plots and a small greenhouse full of seed trays and geraniums and tomato plants. Gillian peered hard into the landscape of shadows, as though at one of those puzzles full of hidden figures, until she heard a rustle of movement. Grace was deadheading buddleia. Her spine was crooked with scoliosis and her posture had been deteriorating, and instead of troubling to straighten up as she inched forward or back she remained stooped, lending her work an air of stealth.

'Hi,' Gillian called. 'It's me.'

Grace lifted her head in response to the sound. She looked like someone who'd heard a bird's song or a twig snapping ominously in a forest. Her gaze made the rounds of the garden before zeroing in on Gillian.

'Oh, it's you!' she said.

'I didn't mean to startle you.'

Grace shuffled towards her, listing with the scoliosis, peeling off her gloves as she came. Gillian kissed her on the cheek and rubbed her back, her fingers passing over the pronounced bumps of vertebrae.

'Come in, come in,' Grace said. 'Isn't this a lovely surprise.'

It wasn't a surprise. They'd discussed it on the phone yesterday.

'I came for a swim . . .' Gillian said, eyeing her aunt.

Grace looked at her, considering it. 'Grand,' she said, with a single decisive nod. 'But we'll have a cup of tea first.'

In the kitchen, the usual array of projects covered every available surface: yoghurt-in-progress, a stockpot simmering, apples drying on newspaper, a string of onions waiting to be hung. Gillian sat at the big table, watching Grace fill the kettle. She was wearing an old olive-green blouse and loose cotton slacks that had elastic at the waist and ankles, though her ankles were so thin the elastic hung redundantly. She had a headband the same colour as her blouse. Her hair was pure white and a bit wild from her having been out working all afternoon. From behind, stooped, Grace looked oddly like Einstein.

'Have you lost weight?' Gillian asked.

Grace looked over her shoulder and pursed her lips thoughtfully. 'I don't think so,' she said.

She put the cups and saucers on the table, and some slices of Madeira cake she'd baked. A sugar bowl and a carton of milk.

'I'll get the milk jug,' Gillian said. Although they were having tea at a table on which a small soil-encrusted gardening trowel was lying and on to which Grace's cat Barney occasionally leapt, Grace would never have served milk straight from the carton.

Gillian looked in the cupboards and the dishwasher and on the tea tray that had been left in the sitting room. 'Where is the milk jug?' she asked.

Grace shook her head. 'I don't know,' she said. 'I can't find it.'

'Oh well. Not to worry. This is fine.'

When they'd finished their tea, they put their swimming costumes on. They were careful crossing Seapoint Avenue (Grace couldn't dash across like she used to), and their footsteps down the hill and the ramp were small and tentative. Grace had been swimming here for years, and several people greeted her by name. It was nearly high tide and they had only to descend the first steps from the curved promenade before they were waist-deep in water. Grace pushed off and Gillian watched her move smoothly, slowly out, her pink-capped head bobbing as she went. Gillian followed, turning on her back to see the tower and the sun still high above it, the families grouped on the promenade (the children shivering, the fathers and mothers handing out sandwiches), the wizened but fit old men, two of whom were playing chess on the terrace above the promenade. It all looked lifted from some bygone era, as though this small half-moon of space, sheltered by the high wall on one side and bounded by the sea on the other, was a pocket of the city that had eluded change.

They'd gone back to Grace's after swimming and Grace had insisted on slicing some Madeira cake for Gillian to take to the Farm with her.

'You'd like something to nibble after they've all gone to bed,' she'd said.

But in the few seconds between having sliced it and going to get something to wrap it in, Grace had forgotten what she was doing. She'd stood with her hand on her hip, looking intently at the tiles on the kitchen floor.

'Grace?'

Grace didn't answer.

'Shall I get some kitchen foil?' Gillian asked.

'Kitchen foil?' Grace said, lifting her head.

Gillian got the foil from the drawer and wrapped the cake while Grace watched with curiosity, as though she'd never seen it done before.

Gillian found the missing milk jug a week later. It was in one of the spare bedrooms – what used to be her room and where Grace now kept some of the linens – in the wardrobe with the towels. There was milk still in it, long since curdled. The smell when she'd opened the door had made Gillian think of Heather vomiting in the back of the car as a child. On the shelf below the milk was a plate of biscuits.

'Phew!' Grace said, when Gillian handed her the milk.

'I found it in the spare bedroom. In the wardrobe, with the towels . . .'

Grace wrinkled her nose and looked slightly disapproving, as if to say, Now who'd have put it *there*?

Gillian didn't mention the biscuits.

*

Driving home from Grace's that afternoon, Gillian had wondered whether, if it came to it – Grace incontinent and wandering the streets – she would place her in a home. Even allowing herself to think it felt like a terrible betrayal. Grace, after all, had not placed *her* in a home. She and Martin had raised Gillian after the accident and there had never been the slightest intimation that they had considered doing otherwise.

The accident had happened when Gillian was five. Her father – a civil servant, but also an amateur photographer and naturalist – had taken her mother to the Pyrenees on what was their first proper trip away from Gillian. On a mountain road, while attempting to avoid a stream of rocks that was tumbling down a hillside, her father had swerved and taken the car, with the two of them in it, over a cliff and into a ravine.

Four days after Aunt Grace and Uncle Martin had sat her down and explained to her very carefully and quietly that she would never see her mother and father again, and almost a week before the bodies were returned to Dublin for the memorial service, Gillian received a postcard from her mother. It came through the letterbox to rest on the floor of the entryway, its script slightly rain-smeared but instantly recognizable. As Gillian, through a combination of denial and genuine confusion, had not yet accepted the finality of her parents' departure from the world, her receipt of the postcard made instantly clear to her that her aunt and uncle had made a mistake. Or *she* had: she'd misunderstood them.

She turned down the corridor towards the kitchen to show the card to Grace, to let her in on the good news, the now-funny enormity of the misunderstanding.

But instead of laughing or reading the card aloud – which was what Grace did with post she thought might entertain

Gillian – her aunt looked at her and said, *Oh, child*, and began crying yet again, pressing Gillian to her breast and holding her so tightly and for so long that Gillian began to feel a crick in her neck as a result of its being bent at an unnatural angle. Gillian began to cry then too, tears cresting the bridge of her nose and running out of the corner of her other eye and into her hairline, which was now tickling with the dampness. She could feel the wet of Grace's cheek against her own and she didn't like it, the intimate clamminess of someone else's sorrow. When Grace finally let go, she called Uncle Martin to the kitchen and handed him the postcard. He read it – his eyes flicking from the card to Aunt Grace and back again – then the three of them sat at the kitchen table and the whole thing had to be gone through again, this time accompanied by a brief explanation of how the postal system operated, and how it was possible that a message could arrive from someone who was no longer there to write it.

No longer in Spain?

No longer . . . anywhere.

But how could someone not be anywhere, Gillian had wanted to know. Everybody has to be somewhere.

She was precocious enough to formulate profound and age-old questions, but not wise enough to grasp the bare-faced simplicity of their answers. And now she was being asked to comprehend too many abstractions at once: time, distance, death, nowhere. Even *never*, which she'd heard on countless occasions, didn't correlate to anything she could hold in her hand or verify. So she sat there, wide-eyed, bewildered and suspicious, her skinny legs swinging underneath the table, trying both to believe and not to believe that her parents were nowhere at all any more and never would be anywhere again.

*

Years later, as a philosophy student, Gillian had reflected on that day, the day of the postcard's arrival. She liked to imagine that it had, in some small way, disrupted her limited view of time as a linear entity. She even thought that perhaps it was the day that had pointed her in the direction of philosophy.

It wasn't a theory she shared with anyone, until she met Damien. He was from the country, and had been three years ahead of her at Trinity, studying history. He was someone she'd been vaguely aware of, so that when she met him at a party almost a year to the day after her graduation she remembered his face and knew where she knew it from, but she could not remember whether they'd ever spoken. What she did know, the moment she was introduced to him, was that he wanted to sleep with her, and she spent much of the rest of that evening weighing up the pros and cons of that eventuality.

Over the course of the party they had several moments of collusion, smiling at one another over the idiocy of other people, most of whom were quite drunk or just naturally stupid, but as the novelty of that form of flirtation wore off, her interest in him began to wane, until the moment she drew close to him to whisper something in his ear, something irrelevant and silly and probably slightly insulting to one of those other people, and felt her body brushing against his. She put her lips to his ear and felt the heat of her own breath, felt the tips of her breasts grazing his chest and upper arm (a pale muslin shirt she still remembered), his hipbone bisecting her abdomen; she noticed her hand slipping around the slight heft of his middle so as to anchor herself while whispering in his ear (though in fact she hadn't whispered anything yet and was merely breathing); she allowed her forehead to rest gently against the side of his head, just feeling what it was to be close to him, and by then she'd forgotten whatever it was she'd intended to say.

She drew her head back a little from his and looked at him; he was already looking at her out of the corner of his eye and she knew that he knew what had just happened. She took one small step away from him, using his hipbone to push herself gently off. She stood beside him then, but with her head turned slightly away, looking at something across the room, biting her lip, knowing he was watching her and enjoying that. Then one of those other people intervened and clapped Damien on the back and drunkenly inserted himself (sweat on his upper lip and a moon of it under his arm) into their little space, and though Damien continued to look at her over the shoulder of the guy, who didn't even notice he wasn't being listened to, and though Gillian looked straight back at him, and though the connection was anything but broken, the interruption allowed her to gather herself, and she made her decision. She was definitely going to see him again and she was definitely going to fuck him when she did.

They went out for dinner. Following her half of the life-stories exchange, which she'd capped off with the parents-dying chapter and a vague reference to the disruption of the temporal, Damien had asked, quite earnestly, leaning far enough forward over the table on which the dregs of their meal remained that she worried for his shirtfront, 'How do you mean? You mean you feel like your notion of cause and effect is actually different to other people's?'

What *did* she mean, exactly? She wasn't sure. In the face of his question, she felt unmasked. And yet his tone also left her feeling oddly protected. It was okay for her to admit that, in fact, she had no idea what she meant, because his willingness to take her comment seriously suggested that there was something in it after all. It made her suspect, maybe for the first time, that there might be more to her than the flat reflective surface she felt herself to be. She looked at him looking at her, waiting for an answer she suddenly suspected she possessed, and knew instinctively that this was what it felt like when someone loved you.

Finally, she said, 'You know, people used to say to me, *Aren't you the lucky girl!* All the time. Whenever I got a new dress or when my aunt and uncle took me somewhere nice, or whatever. *Aren't you the lucky girl!* And I could tell from the way they said it that it had to do with my parents because they always looked sad when they said it.' She shook her head. 'It was confusing. Apparently, I was the luckiest girl in the world. Nobody was as lucky as I was. And yet, my luck was apparently a source of great sadness. Every time someone said that to me as a child, I felt undeserving of my good fortune. At the same time, I couldn't figure out what my good fortune was.'

'That *is* confusing,' Damien said.

'And now I'm sitting here with you, and you're so nice, and I can hear this voice in the back of my head saying: *Look at you! Aren't you the lucky girl!* As though because of who I am, isn't it remarkable – literally – that anything good happens to me at all.'

A woman came and took their plates and left two dessert menus, which neither of them looked at. A small circle of sauce had made its way onto Damien's shirtfront, resembling, Gillian thought, a bullet wound.

'I'm rambling.' She rolled her eyes.

'It's okay.'

'I wonder would I have felt better if adults had kept saying to me, *You poor thing. You poor pet.*'

'You'd have felt different.'

She looked at his bullet wound. 'How?'

'How do you think?' he asked, tipping his head to one side.

'Well, I guess I'd have felt it was okay to be sad. I might've felt justified. Instead of confused. Or muffled.'

'Muffled,' he said. 'I can imagine. If your parents die, and everybody keeps telling you how lucky you are . . .'

'It gives you a strange idea of what parents must be like.'

He laughed, then grew serious again. 'So do you remember them?'

She fiddled with the tassel on the spine of her menu. It splayed limply on the tablecloth.

She could remember the rooms in the house in Rathgar and being in them (she could place herself there mentally any time she wanted); she could remember how the back garden looked in summer and a large crack that ran across the concrete of the drive and the trellis of roses trying to climb the gable wall and how frightened she'd been of their tenacity and what a marvellous word *trellis* had seemed. She could see it all still. But it was a place where nothing ever happened. There were no other inhabitants and there was no noise. Her parents never appeared, not even in cameo. It was as though she'd chosen to assemble her album of mental snapshots on a day her home was inexplicably deserted.

'I don't know if I remember them,' she said. 'There are some photos – my father liked taking photographs – and my aunt and uncle have told me lots of stories about them, and I think that's what I remember, the pictures and the stories. But the real stuff . . .' She shook her head. 'No.'

Damien folded his hands atop the table and nodded. When the woman came back they ordered coffee. All the hard-edged desire Gillian had felt coming to meet him tonight had melted into something softer. She half-tried to think her way back to that place, into the mind-set of conquest and dismissal, but there was no point. She liked him too much.

'Let's talk about something else,' she said.

He agreed, but the conversation drifted back to her parents, and by the end of that night she had resolved to travel to the Pyrenees, to the scene of the accident. It wasn't that she'd never thought about it before. From the age she'd first realized that the tragedy had occurred in a particular physical place that one could go to – that the place hadn't disappeared along with the people – she had thought regularly about making the trip. But she'd lacked courage. The cliff she'd seen in her mind a million times both obsessed and repulsed her, drawing her to it, as heights draw people, but with the added complication of inspiring an emotional vertigo as well. When Damien asked her that night why she hadn't done it yet, she said to him what she always said to herself.

'The time just hasn't seemed right.'

He smiled, a small sad smile. The coffee came. It had a slightly greenish hue from having sat stewing for hours in a glass pot on the hob.

'Well . . .' he said, sipping his green coffee, 'I could go with you.'

And with that she started to cry, as much from the generosity of his offer as from the prospect of finally seeing her parents' death place; from the whole welter of kindness and awfulness, of how people who were somewhere one day could the next day be nowhere at all and of how people you hardly knew existed could the very next day be your life.

Five

A large German behind jutted in the direction of Damien. Its owner was pumping a butter churn while its owner's colleagues whooped encouragement and Damien stared, absently, managing an occasional ironic cheer. It was late May. Kill was opening the following week, and he and Judith were conducting an introductory tour of the village for a group of twenty-two tour operators and travel agents from abroad, several of whom were having a go at the churn. The churn was in Bartie and Oona's house, one of four 'Real Homes' in the village.

'Visitors,' Judith was explaining, 'can wander into these open houses and chat with those who live here as they engage in their daily round of domestic chores.'

Damien wasn't sure there were enough domestic chores to keep Bartie and Oona going all day long; they were looking a bit redundant (though maybe it was stage fright) as they stood beside their dresser full of delph, in front of their lace-curtained windows, under the photos of what he supposed were their children or grandchildren and one luridly coloured image of Jesus, open-armed and with a molten-red heart.

The German abandoned the churn, sighing dramatically and wiping his brow. An American woman stepped forward, pounding her chest with mock machismo and provoking more cheers from the group, a few of whom were glancing intermittently at Damien and Judith, as though seeking approval. Damien forced a smile. Though he was always relieved to see a project come to fruition, he abhorred this sort of moronic horseplay. He was a strategist, an ideas man, and such exercises as these were beneath him.

Damien had done history at Trinity. His plan had been to continue into postgraduate work, then to look for a lecturing job. But the summer before his final year as an undergraduate, he'd taken a three-month internship at EI's New York office, more for the chance of living in New York than because of any particular fascination with tourism.

Day after day, in an eloquent patter peppered with witty asides and accompanied by periodic jerks of his head to realign the lock of black hair that tended to drop fetchingly over his forehead, he had charmed his listeners with images of persecution and valour, of dignity in penury, of revelry and sublime silence, and of green fields undulating towards cliff edges: his beloved, beleaguered land waiting only to receive them. And while his listeners marvelled at this erudite young salesman, what Damien marvelled at was how easily he placed his erudition at the service of the sale.

His knack for spin hadn't gone unnoticed. Back in Dublin, the EI office kept in touch with him during his final year and, just before graduation, offered him a full-time position in marketing, which he accepted. Once he had a wage, the thought of giving it up to undertake another round of studies came to seem less and less attractive.

The path not chosen didn't play much on Damien's mind these days. But scenes like the one he was now witnessing tended to encourage rumination. The butter-churner had just thrown a look over her shoulder and was jiggling her behind like a chorus girl.

'Olé!' someone cried, incongruously.

'No,' someone else said, 'oleo!'

*

Damien's mother had lace curtains, as well as a dresser full of delph and framed pictures of a red-hearted Jesus. She lived in Mayo, less than an hour west of Kill. After the tour had finished today, Damien had driven to her house instead of heading straight back to Dublin, as he would have preferred to do: a result of the latest in a string of resolutions to be a kinder, more attentive son, brought on this time by Grace, by her illness and impending disappearance. This was ironic, because Grace was a sore point between his mother and him. Though his mother had never accused him explicitly, she suspected him of being fonder of Grace than he was of her. Except for that lumpen blood-love that no one could ever usurp, she was right. Grace was – or had been – spirited, progressive, engaged and nonjudgemental, all the things his mother wasn't. And now, in order to show his gratitude to his wife for her having spent the better part of four years away from home running a self-help clinic (always 'self-help' accompanied with a shake of his mother's head and a wave of her hand), he had agreed to take in her demented aunt.

Some weeks ago – in what must have been a lame attempt at bonding – Damien had complained to his mother about Grace's latest aggravating habit: she'd begun to follow him around the house. 'Like a bored child,' he'd said. 'At first I thought I was imagining it, but no, she actually follows me.' Even as he was saying it, he felt it was a cheap betrayal, an odd sort of boast.

'You must be a saint,' his mother had said. Saint, in this instance, meaning *a bit of an eejit*. For although his mother believed in the sanctity of the family, she resented the fact that Grace was living with them, or rather resented the fact that she'd never been asked to do the same, though she wouldn't have dreamed of moving to Dublin.

'I suppose she can't be on her own,' she'd said, as though to highlight the fact that she herself still could be.

'No,' he'd said. 'She really can't.'

With his mother, Damien operated on two levels: the one that was engaging her in conversation, and the one that was calculating the minimum amount of time that needed to pass – and it varied depending on the reason for the visit – before he could leave without seeming callous, self-centred, uncaring or any of the other words he imagined were going through her head. Damien's theory regarding their relationship was this: that as a result of his having got into far less trouble growing up than either his brother or his sister, his mother hadn't had to pay as much attention to him. They'd left each other alone to get on with their business, a strategy that had led gradually to estrangement. In recent years they had both made half-hearted efforts at greater closeness, but the efforts seemed never to coincide.

His brother Francis could make her laugh. Unfortunately, Francis lived in Seattle. He came home once a year and, when he was around, their mother was a different person. Francis had a way of teasing her that made her coquettish. It was bizarre to witness. Damien attempted it with her on rare occasions – usually at some family gathering after too much drink – but it always caused them both embarrassment and he reverted quickly to his customary reserve. His sister Julia, who was in Australia and married to a guy who'd made money in fencing, pretended not to notice their mother's moods, on the rare occasions she was home. She was cheerful in a determined sort of way, hoping that her adamant good humour gave their mother a lift; Julia didn't know, any more than he did, how to engage with her.

His mother was in the kitchen now, slicing the loaf of

brown bread he'd brought from those Bartie and Oona had cooked in the pot oven at the cottage. She was insisting he have some, even though he'd assured her that he had already eaten several slices. He was in the sitting room, surrounded by framed photos of his father, eight years dead, and himself and Francis and Julia. His mother appeared in only two; being photographed brought out in her a shyness so intense it seemed a form of attention-seeking. He couldn't actually see most of the photos from where he was sitting, they were just smears of glare in the grey afternoon light. His mother didn't know about non-reflective glass.

A grandfather clock ticked against the far wall, in the strip of lemon-yellow between the doors into the kitchen and the hall. The effect was heightened in the silence, it drew attention to itself, like laboured breathing from the next room. It made him anxious. Damien didn't like this house. The quietness was of the oppressive sort, the newness sterile. The wall-to-wall carpeting had a muffling effect. The air felt heavy, thicker than normal, and yet there seemed a constant chill to the place.

He hadn't wanted his parents to move from the old two-storey house on the outskirts of the village, with its large front windows instead of these awful things divided into bitty rectangular panes. Where the stairs creaked and you had to hitch up the press to close it. There were accidental wonders everywhere, an organic aliveness – the gate that sagged out the back, droop-shouldered, like it was sad, and the briars that crept over the stone wall like they were coming to get you. Damien still saw himself running round the yard or through the halls of the house, Francis on his heels, not a memory of any particular day, exactly, but a composite of those early years.

Now that his mother was alone, he was sure she'd have

been happier in the old place. His father had had the heart attack a year after they'd moved into the new bungalow. They'd all known about the heart trouble, but had mistakenly believed that catastrophe had been headed off. His father had had a stent – an inflatable cage – inserted in his artery to keep up the blood flow. Damien used to imagine a tiny monkey inside the cage, inside his father's heart. It was a comforting image, it added a certain whimsy to an otherwise grisly business.

They'd waked him in this very room and Damien still remembered the strangeness of it – not of the dead body of his father but of the way the sitting room seemed perfectly suited to the occasion. For a while afterwards, he had thought that maybe if his mother wasn't alone in the house it mightn't seem so funereal. He'd hoped she might find some male companionship eventually, but he knew that if he even so much as hinted at the idea he would offend her. Many things offended her. She was a pious woman, an attender of mass and a sayer of the rosary, a woman who still, without irony, used the term 'living in sin'.

'You okay in there?' he called.

He heard clattering, then she emerged with a tray of sliced bread and butter and marmalade. Marmalade made him gag and his mother knew this but she served it to him every time he came, not out of nastiness but out of an unwillingness to adjust her behaviour to available information.

He stood up. 'I'll get the tea.'

He came back with the second tray and set it down on the table beside the bread and they stared for a moment at their picnic before beginning.

'There's a change in the weather,' she said, and poured the tea.

Damien looked out through the many-paned window. It had been dry earlier, and the sky, though not blue, had been a bright white rather than grey. Now a mist had come. It had got cool. Beyond the empty sloping lawn and the low wall, the sky met the ground.

He nodded and buttered his bread, his elbows resting on his thighs. 'It was forecast.'

His mother tugged the hem of her dress over her knees. The flesh around her knees, he noticed, was pocked slightly with fat. His father had got fat, too.

'So you'll have to come over to the village some time,' he said, a few crumbs escaping on to his lap. 'It's not far.'

She did something with her mouth, a chin shrug, bordering on concessionary, and said, 'What would I do there?'

'Well, you'd do what everyone does.' He picked the crumbs one by one off his lap and placed them carefully on the tray. 'Walk around, chat to people, look at things . . .'

'Sounds like what I do here,' she said, and he felt reproached, then realized it was an attempt at humour.

He smiled but didn't look at her and took another slice of bread and buttered it.

'They're going to serve bacon and cabbage, and buttermilk and spuds, and colcannon. Boxty, too.'

'And they come all the way from America to eat colcannon?'

'They'll come from all over,' he said.

She shook her head, mystified by the world's frivolity. They chewed in silence.

'Tcth,' she said. Or maybe she didn't. He looked at the grandfather clock.

'Oh,' he said, 'I almost forgot. I brought you something.' He put down his third slice of bread (he always ate quickly and too much when he was here), opened his briefcase and found the DVD, the one that would play on a continuous loop in Kill's interpretive centre. He'd bought his mother a DVD player last year and showed her how to work it, though he didn't think she'd ever used it and she probably wouldn't use it now. But none of the other souvenirs of Kill – Rubik's cubes and jigsaw puzzles, postcards and address books and mouse pads, all with black-and-white images of the old folks on them – had seemed appropriate. He'd got a Rubik's cube for Heather. He thought she might get a kick out of it, not out of solving it but out of mismatching the figures, a man's head on a woman's torso on another man's legs.

'It explains about the village.' He snapped open the DVD case and handed it to her. 'There's a little booklet inside, too,' he said, leaning over and tugging it out of its tight sleeve.

'Ah,' she said, 'so there is.' She held the booklet by its corners but didn't open it.

'I think it's really going to go,' he said. 'Next time I'm down, come for a tour.'

She opened the booklet and peered at the caption under the photo of the interpretive centre. 'The print is very small, isn't it?'

Damien leaned closer again. 'Too small?'

His mother, having registered her dissatisfaction, shrugged and turned the page.

'Is Jimmy there?' She loved Jimmy. She had only met him once but she'd remembered him. He'd handled her like Francis did, like Damien couldn't, refusing to take her seriousness seriously, managing to release in her some buried store of levity.

'No,' he said. 'Jimmy's in Dublin. In the office. I'll tell him you were asking for him.'

She was looking now at a photo of a flock of sheep, who

were being shepherded down the village's main street, as they would be a handful of times each day, by a rotating cast of three middle-aged 'farmers' dressed in quaintly ill-fitting suits and Wellingtons. The visitors today had loved it: the sheep factor! The only thing that had been a bigger hit was the American wake. Though the drinks at lunch and the Irish coffees after and the two rounds in the pub had likely contributed to a mawkish mood, the tour operators had been genuinely moved, the women particularly, a few actually getting teary-eyed in O'Dwyer's as they listened to a small group of young men singing 'Paddy's Green Shamrock Shore' while their female counterparts, in full flowered skirts and white blouses, wept softly, looking mildly surprised to find themselves being wept along with.

His mother turned the pages. There was a photo of the wake. She frowned.

'What's wrong?' he asked.

'Lassies crying. It's like someone died.'

'That's the American wake,' he said. 'Nobody died.'

She nodded. She looked almost disappointed. Like many people from the country, she was deeply interested in death. The most sacred, the most eagerly anticipated day of the year for her was the anniversary of his father's dying. In his meaner moments Damien allowed himself to think that the day was no longer about remembering his father but about remembering his mother. It was her day, the day she got to remind others of her suffering. There were times he found her fidelity to his father impressive, intimidating even, a form of loyalty that would pass out of existence when her generation did, but more often it seemed a fidelity to widowhood, and it struck him as arid and self-absorbed.

He cleared his throat and pushed the thought aside.

She had reached the end of the booklet. She pursed her lips and examined the back cover. Her thick ankles were crossed. She was wearing navy-blue shoes with short square heels and silver buckles on the toes. He felt ashamed of something. Of his wish that she were different or of the petulance he couldn't quite dislodge or maybe just of his own shoes, which were probably six times the price of hers.

Surreptitiously, without moving his head or his wrist, he checked the time.

Sensing his restlessness, she said, 'Will you have a bit of dinner before you go?'

'Oh,' he put a hand to his belly. 'I've been eating all day. Anyway, I can't.' Gillian wouldn't be home from Meath till tomorrow, but he didn't say that. 'I've got work to do tonight.'

His mother was staring, unseeing, at the picture of Kill's main street on the back of the booklet. The look on her face was soft and a little regretful, and if he didn't know better he'd think the tension between them had been all in his imagination, a years-long misunderstanding that he had created and could as easily dissolve.

After checking his watch again (this time openly), and communicating in some subtle but unmistakable way what a costly concession he was making, and loathing himself momentarily for the pettiness of that, he managed to amend his response.

'Maybe a quick bite,' he said.

Six

Articles about the Farm had appeared in the lifestyle sections of the *Sunday Times* and *Der Spiegel*; Gillian had been featured in dozens of women's magazines, in *Entrepreneur*, in *Men's Health*, *Psychology Today*, *Exclusive Getaways* and *Connoisseur*; her book – *Don't Just Do Something, Sit There!: How To Do Less and Get More out of Life* – had done well enough in its niche market; she'd been asked to plug a line of natural health-care products being developed in Edinburgh; and she'd received letters from schoolgirls wanting to be just like her. But until today, she'd never been asked to speak at a university.

Noreen from Queen's was on the phone. She had just invited Gillian to deliver a lecture next year at a conference on Gender and the Self-Help Industry.

'Sounds interesting,' Gillian said.

'Oh, it's an incredibly fertile area,' Noreen began. 'The exploitative potential of the self-help industry is old hat. We'd be more interested in some of the psychosexual, sociopolitical issues, the paradoxes inherent in the whole notion of "personal development".'

The inverted commas were audible.

'For instance, on the one hand, "personal development" is viewed as a source of empowerment, but is it just clothes and make-up in a new guise? The desire to gain access to some primordial wisdom has become a fetishistic pursuit. Do you know what I'm saying?'

Gillian looked up at Heather, who had just got home from

school. She was holding a long multi-coloured frozen thing, sucking it to a tapering point.

'Yeah . . .' she said to Noreen, 'I suppose.'

'And,' Noreen continued, 'what particular pressures does such a development place on women? And in an Irish context? Are we in Ireland reneging on our own birthright in order to sup from some generic global stew of pseudo-wellbeing? And then there's the question of the uncomfortable blend of capitalism and spiritual wellness. You've been quite successful, and that's a question you must've faced yourself: how to reconcile these two apparently antagonistic pursuits, money-making and a wellbeing based on the very rejection of the kind of frenzied lifestyle and superficial values that money-making generally entails . . .'

When Gillian had hung up, Heather said, 'Who was that?'

'A woman asking me to give a lecture at a gender studies conference.'

Heather took an elongated pull on the frozen thing, then turned it this way and that, gazing at it with a druggy absorption. 'Cool,' she said.

'Maybe.' Gillian checked the time. She was taking Grace to Reminiscence Therapy, her twice-weekly support group for early-stage sufferers. They should have been on the road by now. 'How was school?'

'Fine. We had career talks.'

'Yeah? Who talked to you?'

'People from the computer industry. They told us how to have a career in computers.'

Gillian frowned. 'Do they headhunt you straight out of secondary school?' she asked. 'Don't they want you to go to university any more?'

'Dunno,' Heather shrugged. 'Why do they call it headhunting anyway? Wasn't that like when cannibals captured people to eat?'

'I don't think so. I think it was when one side won a war they would decapitate their enemies and keep the heads as trophies.'

'No Geneva Convention back then,' Heather said.

'No.' Gillian looked at her watch again.

Heather's eyes were wide above the psychedelic freezie thing, which she was now sliding in and out of her mouth, piston-like.

'Do you eat those in public?' Gillian asked.

'Hunh?'

'You shouldn't eat in a suggestive manner in front of men.'

Heather's shoulders slumped and her eyes slid heavenward. She could just about indulge her mother's absurdity without dissolving from the strain. 'What?' she said. 'Like it's going to make them go totally out of control or something if they see a woman eating a Swirl.'

Gillian crossed her arms. 'It's tacky. And some men will use it as a chance to make vulgar remarks. Believe it or not, they will actually view it as a come-on. Tests have shown men consistently overestimate women's sexual interest in them. And they do not understand ironic forms of flirtation.'

'Well, I'm not going to eat in some certain way so that some Neanderthal doesn't think . . . whatever. Anyway,' Heather held the Swirl a little away from her face, 'how are you *supposed* to eat this?'

She had a point. How many ways could one eat a frozen phallus? 'Don't eat them,' Gillian said. 'Eat something round.'

'You're paranoid,' Heather said, and rolled her eyes again.

She bit the top off the Swirl. Through her half-open mouth, she gargled, 'That'll shut them up.'

Gillian laughed, relieved. She wasn't sure where she could take this conversation.

She called out the kitchen door to Grace, just as Grace appeared on the stairs.

'Ready to go?'

'Mm-mm,' Grace said.

'You look lovely,' Heather gargled, moving the bit of Swirl around her mouth.

Grace smiled. 'We're going . . .' – she looked at Gillian – 'somewhere.'

'We're going to the day centre,' Gillian said, once they were on the road. The centre was in the hospital, but Gillian had stopped referring to their destination as *the hospital*. It had recently upset Grace. 'You remember, you have therapy there today with Maggie and Leonora and Joe . . .'

Grace nodded placidly and gazed out the window, as though Gillian's explanation had nothing to do with her but she was willing to pretend a polite interest for conversation's sake. A tiny enigmatic smile, or what appeared to be a smile, played at the corners of her lips. It looked like an indication of tolerance, but it was impossible to tell whether Grace was indulging Gillian, indulging life itself or simply had no idea what the two of them were doing there but was willing to roll with it till the next adventure. It was an expression Gillian knew well by now and it meant that within minutes Grace would, with no fear whatsoever of irritating her, ask innocently, 'Where are we going?'

Gillian knew she should count her blessings, because there

would come a day when Grace wouldn't give a fuck where they were going, and after that would come the day when she wouldn't be able to go anywhere because she'd be bed-ridden, and the repetitive question-and-answer sessions would seem in retrospect a beautiful togetherness. But instead she found herself fighting the temptation to cast Grace as her confessor, to confide in her the things she'd never confided to anyone, knowing they'd all be forgotten; it was an unhappy sort of freedom that dangled before her, like the freedom to do something outrageous in front of a blind person.

'Where's Martin?'

Gillian glanced over at Grace. She was wearing her over-sized sunglasses. A year ago, they'd looked stylish. Now they just made her head look small. Grace was losing weight again; her whole form appeared to be shrinking, at a rate Gillian found alarming. With the glasses on, she was like one of those insects whose heads, under magnification, look top-heavy from the weight of impossibly massive eyes. She appeared to be recoiling slightly in her seat, as though bracing herself for a blow.

'Sorry?' Gillian said.

'Martin. Where is Martin?'

'Martin.' If they'd been at the hospital, Gillian could have distracted Grace, or asked one of the nurses what she should say.

'Martin,' Gillian said, 'is away.'

'Martin doesn't go away without telling me.'

Gillian hesitated. If she could wait it out, it might pass. Grace was capable of losing interest in a subject that moments ago had occupied her obsessively.

'Where did Martin go?' Grace said, more insistently this time.

'Martin . . . will be back tonight.'

'I think so,' Grace said sagely, and settled in her seat again.

As they pulled into the drive of the hospital, Grace smiled politely and said, 'This looks nice. What is it?'

'It's the day centre,' Gillian said. 'It's where therapy is. You like it.'

Grace had been in Rem Therapy for nearly three months and indeed seemed to love it, even when, according to the nurses, she made very little contribution. She smiled a lot and smiling was never a bad sign. Her group met in a small white room in which several chairs were arranged in a circle. On the wall was a timeline that listed significant events in Ireland and in the world from 1920 onwards, as well as memorable films and songs, and included some coloured illustrations. The nurses brought in old photos and recordings, pieces of clothing, foods, sods of turf, smoothing irons, whatever artefacts might set off long-term memories not yet obliterated. Then the group would talk about whatever memories arose. The early group was for people still in the 'awareness stage', people who remembered that they were forgetting.

Gillian left Grace with the nurse and went to the cafeteria. She got some tea, found a table in the corner and took out her notebook. She thought she'd make some notes for the gender studies lecture. In the car, she'd imagined it: the auditorium full of experts; the rapt gazes trained on her; her skilful deconstruction of neo-empowerment ('personal development' was not a term she favoured); the spirited debate that would follow. Now, however, as she tried to think how she might elucidate the guiding philosophical principles of the Farm, they struck her, and not for the first time, as an increasingly thin veneer. Last week Peter had called her attention to singlessearch.com, a website that listed the Farm among its 'Top Ten Hot Spots in Ireland for Discerning Mate-Seekers'.

> Tired of sweaty clubs, speed-dating and treadmill flirtation? Wise up, slow down and slip into something comfortable at this marvellous Meath sanctuary for multi-taskers in distress.

Besides making the Farm sound like a place whose *raison d'être* was romance (either they were going on very slim anecdotal evidence or there was a lot more happening after dinner than Gillian realized), the website's description of the clientele annoyed Gillian. 'Multi-taskers in distress' was, she supposed, not technically incorrect, but it sounded frivolous. She had to admit, though, there were days she'd be hard-pressed to come up with anything more accurate. Yesterday, for instance. She'd been leading the weekly discussion group in which all the guests explained what it was that had got them there. There was an odd competitiveness to these sessions, as though people were eager to appear more dysfunctional than their neighbours, and yesterday a rather attractive forty-something named Leslie had topped the charts.

'I was standing at the sink doing the wash-up,' she'd begun. 'At the same time, I was waxing my bikini line, printing out a long document, downloading a security patch, talking on the mobile, scanning the headlines that were crawling across the bottom of Sky News, and sort of kicking my legs out behind me in this arse-firming exercise.'

She'd looked at Gillian for approval, or disapproval.

Gillian had heard it all a thousand times before. Now and then she rallied, let her arms flop to her sides, went exaggeratedly limp in her chair and said, '*That* must be the record.' But yesterday she'd just shaken her head and made a lame attempt to look flabbergasted.

One of the men had said, 'So, sorry, Leslie, can we just go back? You were in the kitchen . . . waxing . . . so you're saying you had no . . . no . . .'

'No trousers on? That's right. Starkers from the waist down.'

'How *funny*,' a woman had said.

Gillian had offered the thinnest of smiles and said, 'Am I a human doing or a human being?'

Her mind had become a series of desk-calendar aphorisms.

The hour and a half had passed and, having compiled a shopping list and sheet full of doodles, Gillian headed upstairs to meet Grace.

The others from Grace's group were coming down the corridor, but Grace wasn't with them. Gillian kept going as far as the therapy room and poked her head in. Grace was sitting silently with one of the nurses. The other nurse, whose name was Anne, stepped out into the corridor and motioned for Gillian to walk with her. When they'd gone ten paces or so, Anne stopped.

'What is it?' Gillian said.

Anne gave Gillian that smile which is really more of a frown and said, 'Grace may no longer be suited to early-stage group.'

For a fleeting moment, an utterly implausible thought flashed through Gillian's mind: Grace is getting better!

'We think she might be ready for middle group.' Anne was wearing a bright blue trouser suit. All the nurses wore unpatterned clothes of primary colours, similar to the kind they advised carers to dress their loved ones in.

'Is she making too many mistakes?'

Anne shook her head, in a way that managed to look reassuring, just as her smile had managed to look unhappy. 'We don't like to think in terms of mistakes . . .'

Gillian nodded, as if she understood, though the statement shed little light on anything. 'Did you say it to her?'

'Oh, we talked about it in group,' Anne said. 'That's what group is for. It isn't about pretending that things won't change. It's about preparing for change.' Seeing the look on Gillian's face, she added, 'Believe me, it's easier with peers.'

Poor Grace. Poor defenceless Grace. 'So, what did she say?'

'Well, first she said she was fine, that she wasn't going anywhere. She became a bit . . . combative.'

Gillian smiled. Maybe Grace wasn't so defenceless after all. 'Do the others have a say? Do they think she should go?'

'They tend to go into a kind of collective denial when it comes to someone in the group moving on. Because, well, it's a glimpse of what awaits them all. Though you always have one or two diehard realists who insist on clear-sightedness over wishful thinking. They kind of brought the others round.'

Gillian winced. 'It sounds like everyone ganged up on her.'

'No,' Anne said, shaking her head. 'There's no ganging up. They're quite supportive. But they also rely on each other to tell the truth.'

Gillian knew Anne was right. She wasn't even surprised. The fact was that Grace had forgotten – if only temporarily – that her own husband was dead. But Gillian would never have ratted on Grace to the nurses.

'What should I do?' she asked.

Anne put her hands in her big blue pockets. 'Nothing for now,' she said. 'When Grace comes back next week, I'll talk to her again. Moving on is often a gradual process.'

'Moving on is a misnomer.'

Anne looked at the floor.

When they got into the car, Grace announced that she wanted to go to Seapoint, which was in the opposite direction of home.

'You mean to the sea?' Gillian asked. It was a warm spring day. It might be nice to get some air, though it would mean getting caught in rush-hour traffic on the dual carriageway heading back into town. 'Why don't we go somewhere nearer home? We could go to Dollymount Strand, or the pier at Howth.'

Grace shook her head. 'No,' she said. 'I want to go to my house.'

'You want to go to the house?'

'Yes.'

The house in Seapoint had begun to figure in Grace's occasional bouts of paranoia. She had recently accused Gillian of having tricked her into moving out of the house so that she could sell it and hide the proceeds in her 'private business'. In fact, the opposite was true. Selling it was going to break Gillian's heart. As for the proceeds, they would go into the pockets of nurses and consultants.

'Any particular reason you want to go to the house?' Gillian asked.

'It's my house. I want to go there.'

Gillian fingered the keys, which were hanging in the ignition. 'Okay,' she said, and started the car.

When she pulled into the drive and switched off the engine, Grace stared straight ahead. She showed no sign of getting out. She didn't even look as if she knew the car had come to a stop.

'We're here,' Gillian said gently.

For a moment, Grace said nothing. Then she shrugged and said, 'I don't know why.'

Gillian rubbed her chin and sighed. She felt a rising irritation, brought on as much by Grace's tone as by her insistence on a time-consuming and probably pointless detour; an imperiousness had lately crept into it, as though Grace found her somewhat stupid for being unable to follow the train of her thoughts. Worse, it was a tone she seemed to use only with Gillian.

'There must have been a reason you wanted to come here,' Gillian said. It was worth persisting. Grace could change her mind quite easily, and blame Gillian for the change. They could leave now and they'd be halfway into town and Grace would say, *I wanted to go in, I don't know why you insisted on leaving just as we got there.*

When Grace didn't answer, Gillian said, 'You did say you wanted to come to the house.'

'I didn't.'

'You didn't say it or you didn't want to come?' That wasn't fair, baiting the witness, who couldn't think straight anyway. But it was hard to draw the line sometimes between clarifying and bullying. 'Why don't we walk down to the sea? Look, it's a lovely day.'

Grace turned and gazed out the side window. She couldn't see much through the line of trees that edged the drive. 'No,' she said sharply.

'Okay,' Gillian said.

'I want to go now.'

'Okay, okay,' Gillian said again. 'We're going.' She started the car and turned it around in the oblong space at the top of the drive. As they pulled out, Grace twisted in her seat to get a look out the rear window, her expression anxious, as though the house was something bearing down on her instead of something she'd already lost.

'"When the parietal lobes are affected, tactile agnosia can occur."'

Gillian leaned over Damien's shoulder. They were in the kitchen, and he was reading from the booklet the Rem Therapy nurse had given her this afternoon. On the left-hand page were sketches of neurons and synapses in the hippocampus. The neurons looked like many-legged creatures that had gone *splat* on the road. Their dendrites hung on other axons, as though the axons were clotheslines, and all over these healthy dendrites synapses crawled, like bees over honey. But when you aged, the synapses started to drop off, fewer and fewer, your lights going gradually out. And then you got Alzheimer's, and what you were left with, finally, were just the tiny shrunken splats, stripped of their bumble-bee synapses, holding on for dear life to the axon clothesline with their two remaining dendrites. It was a distressing little cartoon.

'What's "tactile agnosia"?' she said. 'I don't remember hearing of that before.'

'It means . . . "unable to understand the meaning or source of touch".'

Gillian frowned. 'So if you touched her, she wouldn't know what it was?'

Damien shook his head. 'Or if she touched you, she wouldn't know what she was touching?'

They mulled this over. It was difficult to comprehend.

She put her head on Damien's shoulder and slipped her arm around his waist, thinking about tactile agnosia and how his lower back felt under her fingertips and wondering what would be happening right now if she had left him five years ago as she'd been close to doing, run off to London to be with someone else. Everything would have been different, including the frequency with which she saw Grace. She'd never have started the Farm if she'd gone to London. She would not have filled her mind with those thoughts or her time with those people. Trying to imagine an alternative life was not so difficult. What was difficult was attempting to think yourself out of the life you'd chosen.

Seven

Heather wanted clams.

'Clams?' Damien said. 'What kind of clams?'

'I don't know. We had clams at Emile's last night. His mother made them. They were really good.'

'Find out how she made the clams and we'll make them another night. How about Chinese?' He was on the mobile, on his way home from work.

'Sausages and chips?' Heather suggested.

'If we get Chinese, you can get chips.'

'Chicken curry and chips, then.'

He crossed the river and swung round behind the Custom House and on to Amiens Street. On the North Strand Road he saw the billboard had changed. Against a plain white background, large black letters now read:

JUST WHEN YOU DIDN'T THINK IT WAS POSSIBLE,
THE IRISH MALE GOT EVEN THICKER.
VISIT OUR SANDYMOUNT CLINIC OR OUR
NEW BRANCH IN SWORDS.

He felt vaguely offended. When had they put this one up? He hadn't noticed. He knew the old one had still been there last Tuesday because he and Gillian had discussed it on their way into town for dinner, and he remembered the date because it was the last time (and the first time in a while) they'd made love. She had pointed at the billboard and said she'd heard from someone who knew someone who'd once been a nurse there that the majority of customers came from the country. They had marvelled at the shift this suggested in the attitudes of rural men towards female sexual satisfaction. Gillian had recalled some old joke on the subject and they'd laughed, because they had just made love and were happy, or tentatively happy, which was as happy as they got these days.

The moment had surprised them both. Gillian had driven back from the Farm that afternoon and was just coming out of the shower when he got home from work. It had all happened without a word, almost solemnly (though that had as much to do with Grace being down the hall as it did with any erotics of silence). He'd sat on the edge of the bed, taking his shoes off, loosening his tie, untucking his shirttails, watching her while she applied her moisturizer. First the legs, then belly, then behind. Then the arms and breasts and neck. He leaned back on his hands and watched. He could tell she was getting aroused, by the fact he was watching her and by the feel of her own hands on her skin.

When she turned around to face him, he half expected himself to look away or to say something goofily suggestive – he was awkward these days – but he did neither and just let his gaze move over her. First her face, then her neck, down one side of her body and up the other. She took the few steps towards him and straddled his thigh, placed her hands on his shoulders to steady herself. The fabric of his trousers was rough between her legs, and she pushed herself slowly back and forth, arching her back a bit. He still wasn't touching her, just watching her – her breasts, her mouth, the motion of her hips. He fucked her with half his clothes on. She liked that and he knew it, she said it made her feel at his mercy.

Then they heard Grace stirring in the bedroom down the

hall, opening the wardrobe, searching for something (hangers clanging emptily on the rod), then calling Gillian's name. Gillian grabbed her dressing gown and kissed him on the tip of the nose and went to help Grace. He flopped back on the bed, thinking: *did that just happen?*

He picked up the takeaway and stopped at the Spar nearest home for soy sauce and milk. There was a Latvian man working there now. He was friendly, but Damien missed the Chinese girls who'd left a few weeks ago. He'd seen them regularly for maybe six months, though he had never learned their names. During the brief period that Gillian had got him meditating, he'd devoted the 'neutrals' segment of his loving kindness meditation to the Chinese girls in the Spar. He'd managed a half-lotus and wished the girls well. He hoped they would be free from suffering. He hoped they would make spiritual progress. The next time he saw them, he felt self-conscious and shady, as though he'd cast them in a fantasy or had an erotic dream about them.

One day he'd walked into the Spar and seen them standing face to face and saying to each other 'tree, tree, tree . . .' and giggling. They'd asked him what the difference was between 'tree' and 'three'.

'Well,' Damien said, 'a tree grows out of the ground and has leaves, and a three is a number.' He held up three fingers. 'But it's confusing, I know, because here some people say *tree* when actually they mean *three*.'

They stared at him, awaiting their initiation into this local secret. They were standing at a 45-degree angle to each other, as though posing on the cover of a top-shelf magazine. Somebody's Asian twins fantasy.

'Why this because?' the smaller one asked. 'Why say tree?'

'Why say tree?' Damien repeated. 'Why say tree?' It sounded like a name he might take were he to reinvent himself as a Native American tribe member. 'Well, it's not my area of expertise, but it's to do with the fact that there's no *th* sound in Irish, which is what we used to speak here before we started speaking English.'

'What your area?'

He looked at them and smiled, then tapped his head with his index finger. What he meant was: Guess, guess my area of expertise.

The two girls looked at each other.

'Headaches?' They giggled.

'No.'

'Thinkings?'

'Thinkings. Okay.' He wanted to see where it would lead.

'Ooh,' they said in unison, nodding. Then they looked at each other again and one of them added, 'Aah.' He wondered were they having him on.

'You are the doctor.'

'A doctor? No.'

'No? You look like doctor.' They laughed again.

The next day, when he was queuing at the till with a paper, the smaller one had looked straight at him and, while ringing up someone else's purchases, said to him in a tone that sounded wise and definitive, even mildly prophetic, 'You are the doctor of thinkings.'

Not long after that, they'd disappeared. To his slight shame, he wasn't sure how long they'd been gone by the time he noticed their absence. Eventually he asked the new girl, who was also Chinese but looked like much less fun.

'The two girls . . .' he said, and waggled his index finger at the tills.

'They go,' said the new girl.

'Oh.' For a second, he felt hurt. They might have mentioned they were leaving. On the other hand, he might have asked their names. If he'd asked their names, they might have told him they were leaving. Suddenly he wanted to know their names, to talk to them, to apologize for not having talked to them more. To tell them that he had once attempted to cultivate loving kindness towards them, and though it hadn't worked – for reasons he wouldn't go into – he'd felt much uncultivated kindness for them all along. To admit to them that although he'd once wanted to be a doctor, he really wasn't one.

'For good? They're not coming back?'

'They go away for job. They go to Galway,' the girl said.

Galway? He wanted to rescue them from Galway, from the dreadful mistake of having moved to Galway. As he left the shop that evening, disproportionately downhearted (what other abandonments had they caused him to re-experience?), he pictured himself driving on a whim to Galway, rolling slow as a kerb-crawler through the skinny streets until he spotted them loitering under an archway like teenage runaways. He'd roll down his window, 'Girls, girls . . .'

There would be much whispering in the shadows as they consulted, until one of them hissed, 'Who are you?'

'You know me,' he would say. 'You have nothing to fear. I am Why Say Tree. I am the doctor of thinkings.'

And out of the gloom they would bound, exclaiming, 'Why Say Tree! It is you!' And he would whisk them back to Dublin, make them sisters to Heather, and pay for every bit of education they ever wanted.

As he set the soy sauce and milk on the passenger seat and started the car, he wondered if the girls had forgotten him already and, if not, how long they'd remember. They might, for a time, actually recall his face. But then his face would start refusing to take shape. And then he'd be some man, somewhere, who was linked in their minds to the word 'tree', or was it 'three'? – their impromptu English lessons having by then grown legion – but who was he? Was he a dream one of them had had and told the other? Had he been a boss? A landlord from their days in damp, overpriced bed-sits? And had they really once used the phrase *doctor of thinkings*?

As soon as Damien opened the front door, he could hear the telltale sounds of a game being played: a high-pitched semi-automatic weapon punctuated by *whnngs* and *chungs* and *brnnngs*. Heather had spent most of her summer holiday so far playing video games, though Gillian had managed to get her out swimming at Seapoint recently. He put the takeaway bags on the kitchen table and poked his head into the sitting room. Heather was on her own. Gillian had taken Grace to Activity Night at the Alzheimer's Centre, where Grace was building a bird feeder.

'Chicken curry and chips,' he said.

'Hi,' Heather said, without looking at him.

'Hi. Are you hungry?'

'Un-hunh.' She didn't take her eyes off the screen. 'It's almost over,' she said.

As he was opening the steaming white boxes of duck and chicken, Heather materialized in the kitchen doorway. Lately, she seemed not to enter a room so much as ooze into it, around the sides of door frames, as though she were vaporous.

'Did you win?' he asked.

'More or less,' she said.

'What's the game?'

'*Spermicidal Maniac.*'

'*Spermicidal Maniac*?' He didn't look at her. 'What is that?'

'He's this guy who's always lurking around making a nuisance of himself and you have to try to kill him. Or you can just maim him, like, or cripple him, or make him get lost in the forest, all different stuff, and you get different points for each thing you do to him. It's really hard to kill him. If you do, you get bumped up to a higher level of the game, so it never gets easier.'

'Hunh. And what if . . . does the . . . is it possible the maniac . . . wins?'

Heather had taken some mayonnaise out of the refrigerator and was dipping chips straight into the jar, consuming them with a mechanical rhythm.

'How do you mean?' she asked.

He spooned chicken curry on to her plate, still taking care to avoid her eyes. 'Well, I mean, say, if he keeps eluding you, or you can't injure him.'

She stared blank-eyed at her plate, thinking. 'Then you just keep chasing him. Win, like you mean . . . what?'

'Well, kill you, I guess. Isn't that what win usually means in these games?'

'Yeah.'

He swallowed. 'Yeah what?'

'What?'

'And what happens?'

'If the maniac gets you? Well, the minute he touches you, you burst into all these tiny crystals and the game is over and you get points taken off your overall total.'

'I see,' he said.

'What did you get?'

'Sorry?'

She pointed at his plate.

'I got duck. Would you like some?'

She nodded, and looked encouragingly at him.

'You dyed your face again.' It was blue. Not like blue make-up. More diffuse than that, as though something iridescent were radiating from the core of her, a blue molten thing pulsing light, like a priceless jewel in a cartoon. The first time she'd done it, he'd panicked.

'It's nothing,' she'd said. 'It's like fake tan, except in different colours.'

She'd shown him a box labelled *Ariel Self-Colouring Capsules*. On the front were four grinning teenage faces – three girls and a boy – in red, yellow, blue and green. Heather's shade was called Blueberry. On the back, it said *Manufactured in Sussex*. Damien had expected somewhere more sinister, somewhere oozing with carcinogens. The Yucca Flats, the Bikini Atoll, Bhopal. Sussex sounded safe enough, though he was still pretty sure that turning yourself a different colour couldn't be healthy.

Now Heather's face was Blueberry again. Her eyes were brown. The effect was bizarre, but he was almost used to it now. Glorianna was gold. His daughter was blue.

'What colour would suit me?' he asked.

'You?' Heather looked at him, picking up a slice of duck with her fingers. 'Brown.'

'Brown?'

'Yeah. You'd make a good brown guy.'

'You mean like someone from India? Or the Middle East?'

'More . . . Tibetan.'

'Tibetan?' He thought about it. 'Tibetan's okay.'

'Tibetans are cool,' she said.

He followed her into the sitting room. She'd stilled the spermicidal maniac. Damien thought maybe it'd be better if the maniac wreaked some real virtual havoc, so that Heather would not develop the dangerous notion that if attacked by an actual maniac, she would magically energize into a thousand points of light and vanish into safety.

Oh my God.

It suddenly occurred to him that this eruption upon being touched might be a metaphor for orgasm. And what about the game's initials, *S* and *M*? On the other hand, spermicide killed sperm, didn't it? Maybe the joke was on the maniac, on men generally.

'Who made up that game?' He jabbed his chopsticks at the screen.

'Someone in Japan.'

Japan. He thought of a gaggle of perverts in a Tokyo skyscraper. It had to be men. Game design was a man's world.

'Does your mother know you play this game?'

'Hunh?' She minimized the maniac until he occupied a tiny square in the corner of the screen, which was now tuned to DTV.

'Your mother. Does she know you play the maniac game?'

'I dunno.'

'She didn't buy it for you.'

Heather shook her head. 'I got it myself.'

Damien asked the obvious question. 'Why?'

She shrugged and said, 'It's fun,' and stared at the chicken on her plate, pushing it around with a single chopstick as though she were playing hockey. 'I read this thing today,' she said to her chicken, 'that a recent study showed that a minimum population of a million people is required to provide the average person with twenty interesting friends. I wrote it down.' She nodded towards a scrap of paper lying on the table on which she had, indeed, written it down.

'A *million*?' he said.

'Un-hunh.'

'So someone in, say, Offaly could never have twenty interesting friends.'

'I'm glad we don't live in Offaly,' Heather said.

'But do they mean twenty interesting friends at one time? Or over so many years? And do they mean you have to live in a population centre containing at least a million people, or that you would just have to have met a million people in the course of your life?'

'Meet a million people?' She looked at him. 'Could you do that?'

'Well, I guess it depends on how you define "meet". Jimmy told me that there are times in your life when you no longer know any of the people you once knew. You've replaced them all with new people.'

Heather's brow furrowed bluely. Suddenly, she was all earnestness, a dense bundle of sincerity and expectation. 'Do you have twenty interesting friends?' she asked.

His heart did something like melt or contract or expand. He wanted to tell her that he had a million friends and that every one of them was interesting. He wanted to be omnipotent and reassuring. He wanted to find the designers of *Spermicidal Maniac* and take them tightly by the throats until their eyes bulged.

'It depends what we mean by "friends",' he said, 'by "interesting", and indeed by "at once". And am I average?'

She screwed up her mouth and thought about this. He should have just said yes.

He stared at her hands. There were moments so clearly

innocent of the future they seemed cordoned off from time. Heather, five years old, in a blue dress and looking up at him with love. Or standing in a field with his father, the world awash in a tangerine light. Or with Gillian in the south of France, 1999, talking about Y2K, before Gillian knew the guy existed, let alone had fucked him. But you hardly ever knew such moments for what they were until it was too late.

Heather had been with them in France that year. They'd rented a boat and the three of them had taken a five-day cruise on the Canal du Midi. Heather had sat on his lap, steering on the easy stretches, sounding the klaxon, gleeful with astonishment inside the locks, never tiring of the trip's magnificent monotony. It was there, within the forced intimacy of the boat, under the shade of the chestnuts and the plane trees, that he and Gillian had made the decision not to separate.

They'd come home to Dublin on a high, full of post-holiday fantasies of relocating to France – property was cheaper, weather was better, so was the food, and they both spoke rudimentary French. Gillian could learn to write Java and maybe he could get some work as a consultant. They'd even thought of olive farming. But there had been the question of leaving Grace alone in Dublin, and of Damien's mother too, who wasn't long widowed then, and the idea had evaporated within a few weeks of their being home.

And then the guy had come over from London to work in Gillian's office. If they had moved to France, things would have been different. Not just that, but everything. Maybe she'd have fucked someone in France, though. Maybe it had to happen. Or maybe not, because he'd have been different there too, and maybe she wouldn't have needed to. Not saying it was his fault, but still.

He looked at Heather. She had finished eating and was

staring blankly at the screen, her plate forgotten on her lap. Her blueness, he noticed, was more a royal blue than a blueberry blue. What did the choice of blue, per se, say about her psyche? Blue was the colour of melancholy, was it not?

Would he have described her as unhappy? Not exactly. Happy? Not that either. They were categories that seemed no longer to apply. They were too simple, too naive. When he asked her about drugs, as he did periodically, she said with a note of irony (either because he was foolish to expect an honest answer or because she couldn't bear the fact that an honest answer chimed with what he wanted to hear), 'Reality is the new escape.'

He figured it was an anti-drugs slogan she was pastiching.

'That lady phoned,' Heather said, lifting the plate from her lap and setting it on the coffee table next to his.

'What lady?'

'The one who came the other day to meet Grace.'

'Theresa? What did she say?'

'Just wanted to talk to Mum.'

Damien put his plate on the table and picked up a pillow and hugged it to his chest. Gillian was looking for home help a couple of days a week. They had allowed Grace to stay in the house alone for short periods – she insisted she preferred her own company to that of strangers and refused to discuss their bringing a professional carer into the home – but it was becoming unsafe. She had taken to turning the oven and the iron on, and leaving them on, without ever having used them.

'Theresa was nice, I thought.'

'Grace didn't like her,' Heather said. She looked at him, her eyes wide, a slight smile turning up the corners of her lips.

Grace had told Theresa to her face, 'We don't want you here,' then accused her of only pretending to be whatever she was so that she could get inside the house and steal things. Grace was obsessed with people trying to steal things.

'Grace won't like anyone,' he said.

Heather picked up the remote and ran her thumb over the buttons, staring at it and not saying anything.

'How's Emile?' Damien asked, setting the pillow aside.

Was she blushing? It was hard to tell with the blue.

'Fine,' she said, and didn't elaborate.

He didn't quite understand the relationship. But then courting wasn't what it used to be. He wanted to ask more, but Heather wasn't inviting it. She'd just raised the volume. It was time for *NY25*, which meant no talking. She tucked her feet up under her.

Dr Harding was sitting in the chief surgeon's office. The chief surgeon was telling him about a case of what was being called Reactive Dementia Syndrome.

'Reactive Dementia? What's the reaction to?'

'Thirty-five-year-old male with a brain tumour. It should have been a routine surgery. But the implant was obstructing the removal of the tumour. So, they remove the implant, thinking they can either put it back in when they're finished or, if not, the guy can get along without it but with his brain intact and the tumour gone. Problem is, they can't put the implant back. It's too close to the traumatized area and they decide it's an unnecessary risk. As the days go by following surgery, then the weeks, everybody starts to realize that this guy, the guy who had the tumour, has slipped into a kind of dementia.'

'Days he couldn't remember his own name. Didn't recognize his wife.'

'Like Grace,' Heather whispered, sneaking a glance at Damien.

Dr Harding leaned forward in his chair, his elbows on his knees. 'Could it be a result of the tumour?' he asked. 'Or the operation? Could they have botched the operation?'

The chief surgeon shook his head. 'The dementia appears to be a result of the removal of the implant. If he hadn't lost the implant, he'd never have known his faculties had completely atrophied.'

'So the moral of the story is . . .'

'Don't remove your implant.'

Dr Harding looked at his superior. It was obvious the chief surgeon knew more than he was letting on about Dr Harding's activities, but not quite enough to make a proper accusation.

'But why this guy?' Dr Harding asked. 'Why hasn't this ever cropped up before? It's not like this is the first removal.' There had been car crashes where head injuries had necessitated removals, and there had been instances of incompatibility and implant rejection. Dementia had never once surfaced.

'The explanation that's being offered is that he'd used the implant every waking minute for the past twenty years. He seems to have had it in place from the time he was fourteen.'

'Fourteen? That's illegal.'

'Yeah. That's Mnemon's loophole. That and the fact that he never turned it off. According to his wife, anyway.'

'Do you think he can be rehabilitated?' Dr Harding asked.

'Hardly.'

He leaned back in his chair and eyed the chief surgeon. 'How can you be so sure?'

'He's dead. Slipped out of the hospital yesterday and threw himself in the Hudson.'

'Threw *himself* in the Hudson.'

The chief surgeon looked sceptical. 'It's what NYPD is telling us.'

Dr Harding closed his eyes and sighed. His hands were a steeple in front of his face.

'Bill.'

Dr Harding opened his eyes.

'Sometimes it's tempting for a surgeon to play God. It's a temptation that should be resisted.'

Heather uncurled her legs and put her feet on the table, nearly landing her heel in a smear of curry sauce. 'Did Mnemon kill the guy?' she asked, her excitement tinged with irony, as though she weren't really dying to know.

'Dunno,' Damien said. 'You know those multinationals.'

Dr Harding was sitting in his living room, drinking a beer. His mobile rang. Mitya's name came up on the caller display. He didn't answer. He was fingering a scrap of paper with a number on it. He pressed the phone to his forehead and shut his eyes tightly.

Damien looked at Heather. She was biting her lip now. Her eyes were wide. He was pretty sure she was in love with Dr Harding. Was that okay? Dr Harding must be forty, at least.

The camera cut to Claire, walking with her daughter Marie in some very trendy area of New York. Marie, who didn't know that her mother was a Refusenik, had stopped to look in the window of Box Top, one of the shops that sold boxes for holding disks. Some boxes were plain, utilitarian, for work-related stuff, memories of conferences, business trips, classroom seminars, facts. Others were ornate – pink-cushioned or bejewelled for a girl's first romance; house-shaped for the birth of a baby; a little church for wedding memories; a model ship for memories of a cruise.

Claire's mobile trilled; it was a text from Dr Harding, asking her to meet him.

Next thing, Claire and Dr Harding were sitting in a half-circle booth in a smart little bar having a drink.

He was telling her about Reactive Dementia Syndrome. She looked stunned.

'I just think we should all wait,' Dr Harding said.

'This is an isolated case, though,' Claire said, without conviction.

'As far as we *know*, it's isolated.'

'What if we go public with it?'

'Well, you would terrify the people who have implants, so that they won't dare have them removed. As for those like . . . your daughter, people too young to have gotten it yet, who knows? They may not listen.'

'What about you?' Claire said. 'When were you planning to go for the operation?'

Dr Harding averted his eyes. 'I need a surgeon,' he said. 'I can't do my own. And so far, I don't have another surgeon I can trust.'

Claire looked at him. 'You know that's a credibility problem with the group. You're planning to remove several implants, teaching people how to get along without them, but you've no immediate plans to get rid of your own.'

'And now I'm saying I think you should all wait. Until more is known about this thing.'

'You know,' Claire said, 'sometimes I think we're like a bunch of ants trying to stave off a tidal wave. And then I wonder if what we're fighting is really as bad as we make it out to be. Plato thought writing would spell the end of memory and wisdom.' She shook her head. 'Maybe we're as wrong as he was. Maybe in a hundred years, our ideas will be as laughable. So I hang out in *pause*, like it's some great act of civil disobedience –'

'Claire . . .' Dr Harding's arm was resting behind her on the seat. Their lips were almost close enough that they could kiss.

Heather tensed on the sofa.

Dr Harding moved his face that much nearer to Claire's, but instead of kissing her, he whispered something in her ear.

Slowly, Claire pulled back from him. Her eyes were cast down. Her forehead was nearly touching his.

'I'm scared,' she whispered.

'I'm scared, too.'

Their profiles blurred in a still frame and the credits rolled.

Eight

Although she had set off for Spain alone, it was the way Damien had said to her at dinner, the night of their first date, *I could go with you* – the way it had made clear that whether she took him up on the offer or not, he'd be there for her when she returned – that allowed the journey to appear, at last, survivable.

In the three weeks between that first date and Gillian's departure, they had courted, in a chaste, old-fashioned sort of way, nothing like what she'd imagined or desired at the party the night they met when she'd whispered in his ear and felt the edgy elation of knowing they'd be lovers. But they hadn't become lovers and it was all because of Spain. Gillian knew about how sexual desire and proximity to death went together, but in this case it didn't seem to be so. (She figured that a happy complicity between the two required that the death, or deaths, be fairly fresh, or at least have taken place nearby.) Once she knew she was going to Spain, she felt her desire for him contract, her body tensing, anemone-like. The trip was a threat and Damien was a threat and her body was merely policing its borders.

She thought it best to treat Spain like a holiday. She would take two days in the city, then three in the mountains, then three at the sea before flying home again, the visit to the scene of her parents' deaths nestled in the middle as though it were just another item on a frolicsome itinerary.

But even before she'd checked into her Barcelona hotel – a small place that attempted to overlook the Arc de Triomf –

she knew the plan was absurd. She called the car rental firm and in her present-tense dictionary Spanish changed the date of her pick-up from Wednesday to Monday. After a distracted stroll up La Rambla and then the Passeig de Gràcia to see the Gaudís, she slept badly, and early the following morning set off for the Pyrenees.

She stopped on the way for coffee in a village called Ponts, about sixty kilometres from her destination. In the plaza, there were trees she'd never seen before, forlorn, supplicant, their bare arms raised to the sky, the small tufts of leaves at the top like fists they were shaking at God.

She continued on the main road until she saw a sharp right turn with a sign that said 'Tírvia 2km'. Tírvia was the last village before the site of the accident. She took the turn and the road was immediately twistier. As she climbed higher in the glaring sun, her anxiety increased. She had a feeling of unreality and hardly trusted herself to be operating a vehicle. The car was a left-hand drive, which didn't help. Unused to having half a car on her right and afraid to come too near the edge of the road, which was not always bounded by a guard rail but always gave way to a cliff, she kept drifting towards the middle, wanting to hug the mountain for safety.

Every inch of the road seemed a death trap and she felt a creeping sense of having been betrayed. How could they have done this? How could they have come here and taken such an obvious and unnecessary risk? The road wasn't even paved then; there'd have been *no* guard rails. For years Gillian had seen the accident as the result of a tragic and cruelly improbable coincidence, but now what struck her as improbable was the fact that anyone survived this road at all.

Grace and Martin had given Gillian the details – as much as they knew from what the Guàrdia Civil had told them – some years after the accident. What had most likely happened, according to the first driver to come upon the scene, was that her parents' white SEAT had come round the bend just as a small cascade of medium-sized rocks was loosing itself from the mountain. Her father, judging by the tyre tracks in the dirt, had swerved first towards the mountain – thinking, surely, to avoid the tumbling stones, as he would have pressed close to a wall to avoid a dripping eave. Then, realizing that such a position would be deadly were a car to come from the opposite direction, or else simply losing control, he had swerved hard to the right. Too hard, for that sudden turn had sent them over the precipice.

The steering wheel was slippery with the sweat from her palms. As Gillian rounded each bend, the road ahead of her swept into view, clinging to the mountainside, wispy and negligible as a hair stuck to some vast inhospitable surface. She was consoled only by the thought that to perish over a cliff edge while visiting the place where her parents had perished over a cliff edge would represent such a ludicrous degree of coincidence as to virtually cancel itself out as a possibility. Of second-order solace was the thought that if she were to die in the same way and place that they had, her death and theirs would be aligned in a symmetry so neat it could only indicate managerial intervention and thus an afterlife.

When finally she reached the stretch of road where the accident had occurred, she pulled off on to a small gravelly area not hemmed in by a guard rail. She wasn't certain of the precise spot where the car had gone over the edge but she knew it was a couple of kilometres beyond Tírvia. A little farther up the road was Burg, the nearest clustering of humans to her parents when they died. When in Ponts, making conversation with the man who'd served her coffee in the café, she'd asked how far she was from her destination and he'd counted out to her on his fingers the villages in succession: Sort, Rialp, Llavorsí, Tírvia, Burg, Farrera. The houses in Tírvia had all looked identical, as did the houses she could now see in Burg, as did those she'd seen everywhere in these mountains. Her sense of strangeness had been intensified by this fact; the simple act of telling one building from another was not for the uninitiated.

Gillian switched off the ignition and sat in the car. Should she walk up and down the road for a while? There was no hard shoulder; it certainly wasn't a road along which one might stroll contemplatively. In Barcelona, she had bought white roses and wrapped the stems in wet toilet paper to keep them fresh. She lifted the roses off the seat beside her, opened the door and stepped out, then moved around the front of the car to the side that faced on to the precipice. Keeping her hands, which clutched the roses, on the car behind her, she peered over the edge. She remembered a Hitchcock film where a woman was teetering on the edge of a cliff, and she thought how different women's breasts looked back then, like hard little pyramids that had been mass-produced and officially issued. The inanity of the thought made her laugh in a desperate way, the kind of laughter that contains no merriment and turns almost immediately to tears.

Feeling the first spasms, she reached quickly for the door handle, for she didn't want to be out here either laughing or crying without a handhold, and anyway that had been her plan all along: to grasp the door handle with one hand while, with the other, she flung the flowers as far as she could, a plan – as she was well aware – which would result in her assuming, briefly, the posture of a trick water-skier. But she had grabbed the door handle with the same hand that held the flowers, half crushing the flowers as she did, and saw that she'd forgotten to take the toilet paper off their stems. It was all a twisted and soggy mess.

She was crying harder now. She would have to pick the tissue off; she could hardly leave it on. She'd seen a roadside sign along the way that said 'No Abandonar Residuos', which she knew meant, basically, 'No Dumping'. Not only would she be tossing her *residuos* out into the wild, but the flowers would be prevented from fanning out in that tragic airborne way they always did in films just before thudding evocatively on the lid of somebody's coffin. Worse again, perhaps, was that the toilet paper itself wasn't even from her hotel room; she'd picked it up in a medium-filthy petrol station outside Barcelona and it seemed crude or insulting to be tossing *that* in her parents' direction. On the other hand, leaving the wet toilet paper on would enable the flowers to fly farther, due to the added torque or whatever it was called.

Gillian turned towards the precipice and peered over, still gripping the handle of the passenger door, which she'd been careful to lock before getting out. There was nothing much to see. Stone, grass, more stone, something that might have been broom, scree, patches of green that appeared delightfully neat and smooth, like suburban lawns set down in the middle of scrubland, then another even tinier road running parallel to the one she was on. In her mind she saw the SEAT somersaulting down the slope, her parents (no seat belts then) tossed like dice about the car's interior, their expressions wildly inappropriate: happy and handsome, their smiles frozen and incongruously composed.

The image made her momentarily dizzy. With her back against the car, she slid down to a sitting position. As she began to peel the toilet paper from the stems, setting the bits of it in a small lumpy pile to the side, it occurred to her that someone could be watching, indeed, that she could be all of Burg's live entertainment for the day. She peered up over the bonnet of the car and looked around. Someone *was* watching her: a cat. It was standing on the same side of the road, eyeing her with a pitiless poker-faced stare. Fuck you, she thought, fuck you, and started to cry again. She cried and cried into her fists, still clutching the roses, their thorns making small bloody cuts in her skin that she didn't immediately notice.

When the tears finally abated, Gillian surveyed the vast emptiness in front of her, then glanced over her shoulder. The cat was still there, not three metres from her now. As she stared, its head twitched to the right, towards some life stir imperceptible to Gillian's own relatively crude sensory equipment. It brought its gaze slowly, imperiously, back to rest on her and, lowering itself to the ground, lolled on to its side and proceeded to squirm against the gravel.

Toss the flowers and get the fuck out of here.

Gillian pushed herself to her feet, as though mildly arthritic. A few pieces of gravel that had embedded themselves in her bottom dropped to the ground as she rose. With no further ceremony (not that there had been much so far), she kissed the roses and flung them over the edge of the precipice, forgetting to grab the door handle as she did and teetering for a moment from the momentum of her throw, her commemorative stance, finally, that of a discus thrower.

The roses, deprived of their toilet-paper ballast, didn't go far. They did fan, however, landing scattered on the slope at skewed angles. Broken-necked and desultory, they formed an almost shocking tableau, looking as though they themselves might have been thrown clear of some more delicate disaster.

Gillian found them uncannily beautiful, and it seemed to her that she'd done something right after all.

She started the car and continued as far as Burg, where she could turn around. She had intended to go all the way to Farrera, which looked like the end of the line, or the highest village anyway, but now she wanted nothing more than to be down the mountain and off this road.

The return journey placed her on the inside lane, next to the mountain, and she began to relax slightly and take notice of her surroundings. She'd always imagined cocoa-coloured hills, a terrain that was treeless and whipped by wind or time into successions of mousse-like crests. Instead, she'd met a landscape green and rolling. The hillsides were covered in trees that from a distance looked bushy and soft, like in paintings of the Lake District. Much farther away, the slopes of the higher elevations were still filmed with snow.

She had booked into the hotel in Llavorsí for three nights, thinking she might go walking, lunching in cafés, poking around medieval churches, picnicking in the spring sunshine – all because she'd believed, ridiculously, that she would feel her parents' presence here. But she wouldn't do any of those things. Nor would she enquire at the office of the Guàrdia Civil to see if anyone who'd been on duty that day was still around. She would not attempt to track down the man who had come upon the scene and reported it. She would not introduce herself in Tírvia or Burg or Farrera and ask for the story of that day to be recounted.

That evening she sat on the terrace of her hotel. In front of her, the Noguera Pallaresa flowed swiftly. It was seven o'clock and still warm and she was drinking a glass of cheap but smooth red wine. Earlier she'd seen three people, two young men and a woman who'd come in from rafting, their wetsuits peeled halfway down their bodies so that they hung like thick skins they were shedding. They'd been chattering to each other in their odd state of undress; they'd been happy and, for a moment, Gillian had been happy for them.

She knew that in another context, were she not hauling this particular history around, she would have found it all beautiful: the villages fastened on to the hillsides; the houses of flat, stacked slate, the dizzying precision of such architecture, its strange rough elegance; even the funny phone box in the café in Ponts that had gobbled up all her coins and then failed to connect her to Damien. But under the circumstances, she found the place oppressive.

She drank too much wine before bed and felt queasy as she lay down. She slept fitfully, listening to the nightingales, not sure she was hearing right when she heard them first, finding the fact of birds singing in the middle of the night surprisingly distressing.

When dawn came, her first thought was that she should go straight to the airport, pay whatever exorbitant fee the airline would inflict on her and just leave. The five days ahead of her looked now like an endurance test.

She phoned Damien after breakfast, to say hello. She didn't plan to tell him of her loss of heart. Though they hadn't said as much, she knew they'd both believed she would return from her journey telling tales of catharsis, having put some demon to rest.

She told him a bit about the day before and said she'd likely spend the remaining days at the coast, and he said, 'Why don't I join you?'

'Join me? Here? In Spain?'

'Why not?'

'How?' she said.

There was a pause, then he said, 'I was checking . . . on the flights. I might be able to get to Barcelona by tomorrow night. I can meet you there and go with you to the coast.'

She swallowed.

'You sound sad,' he said.

The man at the desk was trying not to look at her. She tucked the mouthpiece under her chin and took deep breaths to calm herself. She was afraid that if Damien knew just how sad she was, and how badly she wanted him here, and how – now that he'd suggested it – there was no way she could survive the next few days without him, the vastness of her need would cause him to panic and withdraw his offer.

She made a murmuring sound of agreement.

'Is that good?' he said. 'Is that okay?'

'That's good,' she managed. 'That's really good.'

Damien flew in late the following afternoon and they caught a train to the coast. Gillian couldn't bear to be in the city. She needed fresh air and space. From the moment she met him at the airport it was clear he didn't care where they went; he was here only to console her.

Sant Pol de Mar was one of a handful of beaches listed in her guidebook. The book had described it as small and unspoiled and full of rocky coves for private swims. But what had swayed her was a multilingual brochure she'd picked up at the car rental place. The brochure's English text read:

Sant Pol's appearance, joined with its great urban offer, draw approximation and awaken the affection of many people. The sea combs the clean and cared sand, allowing bathers to enjoy their long amusement hours.

Diners, the brochure explained, could look forward to 'a variety of wisely mixed autochthonous products'.

They would go to Sant Pol. Its cared sand had already awakened her affection.

On the train, she couldn't relax. The view out the sea side was disheartening. Though it was warm, the day was wavering between clouds and sun, and as they travelled through this first stretch, the sky was grey and the water looked cold and Gillian wondered had it been a mistake, Damien's coming all this way. Too dramatic a gesture for such early days.

And then, within minutes, everything changed. The clouds retreated and the sun was surrounded by light years of blue sky. She nestled closer to Damien, her head in the crook of his neck, her limbs going loose like a rag doll's.

The nude bodies began to appear. Not many of them, and not clustered, as at a single nude beach, but merely dotted among the other bathers, who were scarce enough themselves. Gillian had seen topless women on the continent. But here were people naked in full view of the train, and no one was paying any heed. Only she and Damien seemed to have noticed. She felt his attention stir, a slight lifting of his drowsiness. She felt his thigh pressing against hers.

She saw only one man clearly, and then only from behind, as the train was still gathering speed out of the station at Arenys de Mar. The others had been mere fleshy blurs, their nakedness almost comical as it flashed past, but this man was stunning, standing looking steadily towards the sea as though anticipating a ship's return, one hand resting easily on his lower back, his fingers splayed slightly and pointing downward. Gillian sighed heavily. She and Damien hadn't been to bed yet. Her lips were parted. She kissed his neck softly, the tip of her tongue tracing a small circle on his skin.

At Sant Pol, they checked into a hotel on the edge of town, overlooking the sea. In the mornings they made love, then showered and went to the dining room for long breakfasts of sausages and cheese and bread and coffee. Before heading to the beach they wandered the town, watching the people and the cats. Gillian tried to count the cats the first day, but soon lost track and gave up. The cats were all skinny and too alike to tell apart and anyway made her think about the cat she'd hated, the one who'd watched her disdainfully on the road to Burg.

The old men were as interchangeable as the cats. All squat and balding and sienna-coloured.

'They all look like Picasso,' she said. 'Or is it the same one we keep seeing?'

'It's the same one,' Damien whispered, pulling her closer to him as they walked.

In the gardens of the houses, they saw birds of paradise and lemon trees. Flowers climbed the walls and giant aloe spread and swelled like blooms of algae. They drank wine at midday in a cool dim bar with Formica counters and had their lunch outdoors under the shade of an ancient tree, its long branches and thousand leaves spreading a canopy over the restaurant garden.

'Delicious,' he said. 'I don't think I've ever had autochthonous products quite this wisely mixed.'

When everything shut up in the afternoon, they went to the beach. As they lay on their sides on the blanket, face to face, she trailed her fingers down his chest to the top of his bathing trunks and back up again, speechless and contented.

She knew this was the finest thing she'd ever felt, and she

knew that Damien was undergoing a similar awakening. The impulse was to somehow fix the feeling, establish its precise coordinates and cordon it off from anything that threatened it, so that she could point to it at any moment and say that it existed and was theirs. But her thoughts about the future were tentative and unvoiced because she was beset, as she had been since the age of five, by the superstitious belief that anyone she loved too much would one day, and without warning, disappear.

He hadn't disappeared. Not in the way she'd imagined he might. There was no real drama, just a slow, insidious dilution of feeling, so that years later they found themselves discussing separation, without (it seemed to Gillian) knowing exactly how they'd arrived at that point. She wasn't in favour of it. She wasn't lying that night in France, when they'd sat up till all hours on the deck of the boat, talking, and she said she still believed they had a future together, that she still wanted them to have a future together. And yet, just after that, she'd had the affair. She felt mocked by the timing. It was as though Jonathan had been sent to test her faith, and she had failed.

She'd been working in on-line research for six years by then. Some days she'd look up from her desk and feel a not always fleeting despair at the fact that this was how she was passing her life. The weeks flew, despite their uniformity: each Monday, a staff meeting; project assessments every Wednesday; the weekend beginning and then as quickly ending; each Monday, a staff meeting.

She had started thinking about changing jobs, but anything she seemed qualified for was too similar to the job she had. When Damien asked her what she wanted to do, the best she seemed able to come up with was, 'Something . . . different.'

She was unable to explain that it wasn't just the job, it was a lack of purpose, because she wasn't sure what her definition of a purpose was. She worried about sounding drifty and unfocused; *female*.

He'd been travelling a lot in the few years leading up to that point, and her own life had become work and home again, work and home again. Many nights, it was just Heather and her, and sometimes Gillian loved it and sometimes she didn't. When she complained about how much he was away, Damien would explain, yet again, that he had to see first-hand the kind of projects going up. He complained about the travelling, too. But whenever he was home he seemed restless and preoccupied. It was as though he'd got used to being always on the verge of leaving. She began to resent the role she was playing – always in one place, where he could find her, always waiting for him.

She never suspected him of cheating on her. Hardly anybody suspected anybody of cheating (except, oddly, those people whose partners didn't cheat), and yet loads of people did cheat which meant that a lot of people were walking around deceived and she might well be one of them. Still, she didn't think so. It wasn't in him to complicate his life. At heart, he was straightforward, loyal in a way she found sometimes moving and sometimes lumpen. But loyal nonetheless, which meant that when she rang his hotel room in Cornwall or Prague or Washington DC, he never once sounded suspiciously distracted.

Gradually, her complaints about his absences had begun to ring hollow, then she'd pretty much given up complaining. When she'd hinted to Grace that things felt stale, Grace had smiled thinly and said, 'You mean it's taken this long? You got a good run.'

'So it's not a crisis?'

'I wouldn't think so,' Grace said. She said it thoughtfully, not dismissively. 'It's a phase.'

'Maybe it needs to be a crisis,' Gillian said.

Grace arched her brows, a look of gentle admonition. 'When there's not enough to worry about,' she said, 'we go looking for things.'

Gillian didn't think she was looking for things. She wasn't looking for someone else, either. But when he showed up, it was as though she'd been waiting for him, without even knowing it herself.

In the beginning she'd thought she could manage it, that it would be as simple as keeping a secret, one someone else had told her. She believed there were kinds of loyalty that were bigger than staying in the same bed all your life.

She met Jonathan at the office. Though she'd noticed him the day he arrived, and noticed, after that, that she took pleasure in seeing him around the place, it didn't immediately occur to her that he could ever be anything more to her than he was just then: a pleasant male presence, an object of mild curiosity. Nor did it occur to her that he might have noticed her in the same way. She'd come to assume, without quite realizing it, that her fourteen years of married life had rendered her not so much undesirable as unthinkable.

He was Vietnamese, though he'd lived in London since he was a child. He was thickset, not heavy but compact, strong. He was forty, the same age as Gillian. He'd come from head office in London for six months to fill in for one of their department heads who was on leave following a kidney transplant.

'My divorce just came through,' he told her, the first time

they really talked, which was about three weeks after he'd started. Five of them had gone to lunch at a little Italian café on Abbey Street, but the others had hurried off after eating, leaving her alone with Jonathan for the last bit of the lunch hour. They ordered coffee.

'I wasn't planning to get out of London,' he said, 'but as soon as they asked me, I knew it was the right thing to do. A change of scene. Clear my head.'

'That makes perfect sense,' she said.

'Let's hope so.' He smiled, barely, then leaned back in his chair, squeezing his eyes shut for a moment and rubbing his palm against his forehead. 'It's been a long year.'

When he opened his eyes again, he found her staring at him. She didn't look away immediately and neither did he. Later, every time she went over what happened, she always suspected that if only she'd looked instantly away, she'd never have ended up in love with him.

Over the next several days, they made a point of bumping into one another around the office. Each conversation was slightly longer than the last. At a staff meeting, they exhibited a mutual and slightly exaggerated deference. They exchanged jokey and tentatively thoughtful e-mails. The encounter in the lift was accidental.

Gillian was already inside, on her own, when Jonathan slipped between the closing doors. They both got a bit of a fright when they came face to face. He leaned against the wall perpendicular to her wall and looked at the ground, which allowed her to admire the way his left hand was resting on his hip, his jacket held back by his wrist like a curtain drawn aside. She wanted him to look up and see her looking at him – it would have been the thing to do, would it not? – but he kept his eyes to the floor and when the little *ding* went to signal their arrival, he motioned for her to go first, still without taking his eyes off the floor, and it dawned on her that she'd got it terribly wrong. He wasn't interested at all.

Outside the lift, he put his hand on the long handle of the glass door, on the other side of which their colleagues were milling to and fro, but he didn't open it. Instead, he turned to her and said, 'I'm working a bit late tonight. Do you think you could stay on for a few minutes? I'd like to talk.'

At 6.29, when almost everyone had cleared out, she got an e-mail asking her to meet him in the second-floor canteen. *The canteen?* His office would have been private, the little wine bar down the street would have been private, even the street corner would have been, in a way, private, but the canteen was a dreadful, soulless, wide-open place. She felt a queasiness that signalled shame. She saw herself sitting across from him, laminated cartoons of steaming espressos on the walls (which bore no resemblance to the plastic cups of instant coffee between them), as he told her she'd have to stop with the suggestive chatter; people were starting to talk; she was married; he was embarrassed; he felt subtly harassed by her pointed, carnivorous stares . . .

She sat for a moment wondering what to do. Then another message popped up.

Hurry, it said.

She hurried, though not so much as to arrive before him, or enough even to meet him on the way; that would disrupt the choreography. She took the stairs, slowly. Her legs felt unreliable.

When she entered the canteen, she didn't see him. The place had the peculiar phoney desertedness of an ambush.

Then he peeked around the corner of the small self-serve kitchen area, where employees made coffee and tea and kept their muffins and soya milks and takeaway salads.

'I'm in here,' he said, and disappeared again.

He had just filled the kettle and was setting it back on its base when she poked her head in the door. He turned around to face her, his hands resting behind him on the worktop. The look on his face surprised her. He looked sad. Sad and tired. But then he did have a certain post-divorce batteredness about him. It was one of the things she found so attractive; it tempered his handsomeness, which might otherwise have been too solid and self-assured and probably had been when he was younger.

Okay, she thought, maybe he just wants to have tea. Have tea and talk about his divorce. Or maybe that was the price of admission, listening to his woes. But then he held out his hand to her and, when she took it, pulled her gently, closer to him and embraced her, didn't kiss her, but just held her, like someone who was saying goodbye might hold her. Gillian felt wooden in his arms. Did kissing not come first any more?

His hand crept up over her shoulder and his fingers spread over her ear and up into her hair, his hand moving around the back of her head. He kissed her hungrily, his breath grazing her lips and cheeks and neck like little gusts of hot wind; his tongue creating small pockets of moisture under her ear and in the hollow at the base of her neck. She felt a physical delirium she'd forgotten she was capable of.

She drew back from him and looked quickly out the door.

'Is someone coming?' he asked.

She shook her head.

In the moment of anticipation before Jonathan took her in

his arms again, she felt rich, richer than she had in a long time.

He pressed his forehead to hers and asked her would she come to his apartment sometime, tomorrow, anytime, whenever she could, and she said she'd figure out a time because she wanted to, she really, really wanted to.

The kettle had boiled, and steam was filling the corner behind him.

'My back is getting warm,' he whispered.

The next day, at lunch hour, they made love in his company apartment in Smithfield, in the small boxlike bedroom, under the grey-white light from the window. Afterwards, as they lay there whispering and looking at each other, she watched his face with fascination. It had been so long since she'd been with anyone other than Damien, she'd forgotten the phenomenon: how intimacy takes a face you'd thought familiar and reveals it, making you realize you knew nothing of its variations, its angles and shadows. She felt like crying, for a variety of contradictory reasons. First out of sheer pleasure, then out of sorrow over the fact that this pleasure was outside of her life. Out of regret over what she'd done, then out of regret that she couldn't do it all the time. Out of the simple fact that pleasure passed, which was after all what made it pleasure.

In the taxi back to the office, she felt the power but also the vertigo that comes with deceit, and told herself not to mistake for love things that weren't love.

His name, Gillian discovered, wasn't really Jonathan. It was Tran Nghiem Toai. His parents had changed it when they'd brought the family to London in the seventies, after the war.

'It was *what*?' she said.

He laughed. 'Tran Nghiem Toai. Is that so funny?'

'It's funny when you call yourself Jonathan Tran.'

'Can you imagine English schoolboys getting their tongues around Tran Nghiem Toai?' He shook his head.

'Were you sad?' Gillian asked. 'To lose your name?'

'Oddly enough, no. I was still young enough that it seemed like an adventure.'

She met him two or three times a week, usually at his apartment at lunch time. On the weekends he took himself off to scenic spots around the country – the Ring of Kerry, the Antrim coast, the Burren – and came back so full of wonder she felt as though he were speaking about places she'd never seen.

He was relieved to be out of London. He said he felt he could breathe again.

'The divorce was so ugly. I forgot what it's like not to feel that knot in my stomach all the time.'

'So coming over here was a good decision?'

'It was a good decision,' he nodded, ignoring her double meaning.

Gillian noticed herself taking on his mannerisms – the way he put a palm to his forehead when thinking or clasped his hands and rubbed them together. She felt as though he was with her, even when he wasn't. Their relationship acquired a rhythm of its own that almost qualified as comfortable. She was surprised, and oddly offended, by how logistically easy adultery was turning out to be. Damien's apparent obliviousness angered her. And over time, she became angry with Jonathan. He appeared to her insufficiently disturbed, though she told herself that happiness was relative. He had been extremely unhappy in London, so naturally he felt good now in comparison. Still, she couldn't help feeling at times like she was little more to him than a bridge back to the world.

She brought it up one evening, hoping he would refute it. They were drinking orange juice at the table in his kitchen. From the window, she could see the chimney tower that people climbed to get a view of the city. She could see the big lights, scooped white rectangular sheets high above the grey brick walkway; they made the place look like a deserted film set.

'Dublin,' she said, 'and everything about your stay here is just a passing through, isn't it? None of this will stick.'

'What do you mean "stick"?'

'I mean when you go, you'll go. It's all temporary, the apartment, the car, the position . . .'

He stared at the floor. He knew what she was getting at. 'You want me to invest everything in this.'

'I didn't say anything about everything.'

'You're married, Gillian. It would be masochistic.'

'What if I weren't married?'

'If you weren't,' he said easily, 'I'd be dating you.'

'*Dating me*? Sweet Jesus.'

That made him laugh. She hadn't meant to be amusing, but she liked it when he laughed. She leaned towards him and ran her tongue slowly over his lips and he stopped laughing and kissed her with an intensity that seemed to come out of nowhere. (She had only to rest her hand on the inside of his thigh, sometimes she'd only to look at him. But as quickly as he tensed, he could relax again, so that the desire was woven seamlessly into their exchanges. It was there for them to take or to leave and sometimes they took it and sometimes not, as though they had all the time in the world.) His tongue tasted of orange juice and made her think of the orange-juice ice pops she made for Heather. She wanted him to meet Heather, she had a notion about orchestrating an accidental meeting between the three of them, but she hadn't mentioned it yet.

Leaning back again, he said, 'I think you want me to fall apart.' He said it almost playfully, without accusation. 'I'm trying to piece myself back together and you want me to fall apart.'

'No, I don't.'

'I don't want *you* to fall apart.'

She knew he meant it kindly, but it seemed to her an admission of half-heartedness.

The next time she brought it up, she tried to sound a little more offhanded.

'I don't know,' she said, shrugging. 'I just wonder if I'm, you know, something generic to you.'

They were sitting at the kitchen table again, where they often ended up after making love, hungry or thirsty. They had good times at that table, goofing around and talking about serious things and spoon-feeding each other whatever leftovers Jonathan dug out of the fridge. She had developed a huge affection for his impersonal little kitchen. Its blandness seemed to her complicit in their affair, inviting them to imprint themselves upon it.

He was wearing boxer shorts and a white vest, smoking, one heavy half-bared thigh crossed over the other, like a New Yorker in a gritty art-house film. Someone up to his eyes in debt. He blew the smoke straight up towards the ceiling, then brought his gaze level with her own.

'*What?*' he said.

'If I'm like . . . a salve.'

'A *salve*?'

'To help you get over the divorce.'

'Ah. Well, if you're a salve, then I must be a symptom.' He was mocking her now. Pretending he was putting himself down when what he was really suggesting was that her marriage had been in a bad state long before he came on the scene. They'd already had the symptom argument.

'That's insulting,' she said.

'And I'm not insulted that you refer to my feelings for you as a salve?'

'I didn't say your feelings were a salve. I said *I* was a salve.'

He didn't answer. She closed her eyes. She hated how she sounded. She was becoming needy and joyless.

He took a drag of his cigarette and thought for a moment. 'You want me to ask you to leave him so that you can say no. Why?' He looked sideways at her. 'So that you can feel you did the right thing? You're doing the right thing anyway.'

'I am?'

'I mean,' Jonathan said, 'you're not going to leave him whether I ask you to or not.'

'How do you know what I'd do?'

He crossed his arms over his chest and let his head fall back. He was staring at the ceiling again. 'We just go round in circles.'

'We go round in circles because you won't say what you want. Saying what you want doesn't mean that's what we have to do. It just means we're being honest.'

'And I'm telling you,' he said, bringing his gaze back to rest on her, 'that I would only talk about what I wanted if I knew that I could follow through on it, or we could.'

'What's that?' she laughed. 'Some branch of stoicism?'

He didn't answer. They sat there looking past each other. Finally, she said, 'Do you know what I want?'

'I do,' he said softly. 'But it's not that simple, it's not as simple as you and I sitting here, falling in love with each other.'

She looked at her hands in her lap. 'So this is as good as it gets.'

He reached over and stroked her cheek. 'I don't know how good it gets,' he said.

Nine

In the window of the No. 7 bus, Heather couldn't see much of her face – just two ghostly eyes and a nose and a mouth, floating unattached in the glass – but she could fill in the details. Her eyes were brown and her hair was darker brown, straight and thick. Her face was pale and a little flushed, like a baby's. There were tiny hairs she'd discovered down the sides of her face. She didn't think the hairs were plentiful enough to be noticeable, but she was keeping an eye on them.

Looking at her reflection, Heather wondered why Emile liked her. She wanted to ask him, but she was afraid that if he couldn't think of some good reasons right away, he might realize there was none. She wasn't beautiful, and she didn't think she was particularly clever or sophisticated, and Emile was all of those things.

But you heard about that happening, really wonderful people loving people who didn't seem half as wonderful, like there was some secret glow that only the wonderful person could detect, which made them seem even more wonderful for being able to see what no one else could and made the not-at-all wonderful person seem confusingly wonderful for having managed, by such mysterious means, to win the love of the genuinely wonderful.

Of course, there was no evidence that Emile loved her. Heather knew he didn't have a girlfriend, and that she was the girl he spent his time with, but if she was his favourite girl and yet he still hadn't shown any sign of wanting her to be his girlfriend, then maybe he wasn't the kind of guy who liked girls. It was hard to imagine. She had never known a boy her age who didn't like girls. In fact, she had never known any man of any age who didn't like girls, unless you counted famous guys like the Milkmaids, which she didn't. When Heather thought about it, about Emile doing it like the guys in the waterfall photo were doing it, she felt both distraught and tentatively curious; sometimes she tried to picture it and sometimes she tried hard not to picture it. On the other hand, maybe Emile wasn't like that at all. Maybe he was just hanging out with her till he found the girl he wanted to be his girlfriend, at which point he would stop calling her. It was hard to say which possibility was worse.

She got off in Ballsbridge and crossed over to Anglesea Road, where Emile lived in an old red-brick house with loads of rooms and staircases and hallways going everywhere. The house was full of exotic objects from other countries. There were colourful rugs hanging on the walls, and old black-and-white photos that showed men in complicated costumes on horseback.

Heather went round to the back door, where she could see into the kitchen. Emile was on the computer. She knocked on the glass and he looked up and motioned her in. When she opened the door, he said, 'Hi! Just a sec.'

She went over and stood behind him. He was playing the Amazon Jungle game, his favourite at the moment, where you were some kind of paramilitary commander guiding an expedition into the Amazon to find oil or special plants for medicine or a particular shaman who had some secret knowledge you needed. Sometimes there was a coup or your equipment got sabotaged or people got kidnapped. You got points for negotiating their release. You got points, too, for getting whatever it was you wanted without wreaking environmental havoc.

Right now Emile was piloting a helicopter over a convoy of trucks. He preferred the oil version of the game. His father had worked for an oil company in Egypt, which was where he was from. Emile's mother was from Dublin, but had been in Cairo teaching English. That was where they'd met, and where Emile was born. Somehow his mother had then convinced his father to move from sandy, sunny, exciting Egypt, where they actually had one of the Seven Wonders of the World, to rainy, grey, unexciting Ireland.

Emile stopped the game at Level 3, stood up and put his hands on Heather's hips and kissed her once on each cheek. Emile could do this because he was part French. Heather liked his double kisses – they made her feel like they were an exotic couple who went round in their dressing gowns and drank coffee by the poolside every morning, pecking each other's cheeks at every opportunity. But it was not something she would ever try with any of her other friends.

'Hi,' he said.

'Hi.'

Emile rubbed the back of his neck and twisted at the waist in a long, lazy stretch, giving Heather a chance to admire his torso. He looked like one of those statues you saw in Italy (or was it Greece?), the ones that were missing an arm or a leg or even a head but looked totally sexy anyway. 'I was playing for, like, two hours,' he said.

'Really?'

'Un-hunh. I found this plant called . . . I forget, some Latin name, and it cures some kind of blindness.'

Heather watched Emile's long lashes fan up and down. 'You can finish the game you were in,' she said, letting her head loll to one side to indicate her total lack of enthusiasm for this idea.

'I've had enough,' Emile said, shaking his head.

'What time is the thing on?' she asked. She'd come over so they could watch a DTV programme on plastic surgery, which was something they both found luridly fascinating.

Emile looked at his watch. 'It's already started. C'mon.'

They went into the sitting room and Emile pointed the remote at the huge wall screen and a man appeared, being propelled slowly through a tube.

A voice-over was saying: . . . *plastic surgery as we know it will have become obsolete. Laser beams will make minor and periodic adjustments in your features according to a profile created by you, with the assistance of your personal Controlled Ageing consultant.*

'Your CA consultant will be a combination doctor / graphic designer,' a guy in a white coat said. He was sitting behind a desk. He had one of those nasally New York accents.

'Is this the end of ageing?' an unseen interviewer asked.

'Not at all. Everyone will age. But it will be a painstakingly managed process, rather than the sort of hit-and-miss patchwork job it is now. On an interactive package, you will be able to fiddle with the possibilities till you get a spec you're happy with, which you will then present to your consultant for implementation.'

'But people do that already.'

The nasally man smiled and shook his head. 'With CA, there'll be no more scalpels or injections. It will be totally non-invasive. And you won't get this unpleasant post-plastic surgery effect that you see now.' He motioned towards some photos tacked up behind him – people whose eyes were hidden by thick black bands, like they were criminals, and whose skin looked weirdly taut.

'Look at their necks!' Emile said.

Their necks were lined and seriously saggy, like Grace's neck.

'Expensive, no doubt?' the interviewer said.

'Of course,' the man in the white coat said. 'At least to begin with.'

The voice-over came back. It was deep, and slightly quavering: *So what will this mean to those on the lower end of the socioeconomic scale? A new apartheid? Some think so.*

A sociologist from London spoke with great earnestness: 'If this technology comes into effect, there will be a deepening of class divisions, which will be immediately apparent to the eye. The poor will go in for the swipe all right; they just won't go as often. Certain neighbourhoods will end up the repositories of such classic visages as "weather-beaten".'

An inset photo showed a weather-beaten man.

'These people will be seen as the essence of who and what we really are, deep down; they are *what we mean*. We won't want to be them, but neither will we want to be without them. They will acquire a kind of inverted chic. Everyone will want to know someone who has aged . . . *naturally*. We already see individuals such as the prototypical sea captain – rugged, mid-fifties, his life etched into his face – in Gap ads.'

A rumpled man came on. He had loads of lines in his face and certain sections of it drooped like they'd been tugged on for ages. He was sitting in a lab. Heather thought at first they were going to digitally enhance him to demonstrate how CA would work, but it turned out he was an American novelist.

'The really interesting thing will be the backlash,' he said, with a crinkly smile. 'Suburban youth rebelling. Because people will begin to practise CA at earlier and earlier ages. Parents will look too close in age to their teenagers; teenagers will be appalled by the vanity of their parents. Rising up . . .' – he lifted his hands in the air – '. . . youth will decide to age. Think of it! What else *could* they do when they looked in the mirror and couldn't tell themselves from their parents?'

Heather and Emile looked at each other.

'Oh my God,' Heather said.

'What if we looked older than our parents?' Emile's eyes were wide with the contemplation of it.

They burst out laughing.

'You could date my mother!' Heather said, and immediately regretted it.

Emile's smile froze and he turned back to the TV. 'What is this?' he said.

It looked like a freak show. It was a sepia photograph of about a dozen people of various ages clustered around the outside of a house no bigger than Emile's kitchen. Their faces were smudged with dirt, but the smudges looked strangely fake, maybe because Emile and Heather had only ever seen smudged faces in the movies. They wore ill-fitting clothes – shirts whose sleeves were too short and trousers that didn't touch their shoes, if they had any shoes. The children's bodies seemed not quite right, as though someone had pieced them together from a stick-on game and put the wrong limbs on the wrong bodies. The adults looked either stern or stupid. Everybody's eyes were too close together.

Then the screen split and another family came on. They were in colour. They were all clean and wore nice if rather boring clothes. The grandparents looked happy, though they had wrinkles and their skin was paler and their bodies looked like you could snap them if you tried.

From our contemporary vantage point, the people in the first photo look a little odd. But this is an American family from the

1930s. Nothing but diet and more comfortable living conditions have been responsible for the differences we see between these two families. So what will we look like if – or is it when, as some experts predict? – Controlled Ageing becomes as commonplace as applying make-up or tinting our hair? Will the family in the second photo look as strange eighty years from now as that 1930s family looks to us?

The programme was over. Emile muted the volume and got some leftovers from the fridge. Heather liked eating at Emile's. When they lay around on bright embroidered cushions munching kofta and falafel and baba ganoush, it was like they weren't in Dublin at all.

They talked about whether or not it would be a good idea for people never to look old.

'But wouldn't it be bizarre,' Heather said, 'like say if Grace looked really young now even though her brain was getting . . . old.'

'That would be bizarre, all right,' Emile said. 'At least now when people look old, you sort of know what to expect, like that they'll be slower or hard of hearing.'

'Yeah. It's like having L plates on the car.'

'Exactly,' Emile said.

Heather sank a little lower in the sofa. 'Grace tried to drive to the shops the other day and nearly killed someone on a bike.'

'She did?' Emile stopped chewing and looked at her. His shoulders slumped in sympathy. He liked Grace. What was not to like? She hardly had opinions any more, and when she got angry it was more like when a child gets angry, nothing you could dislike her for. She was small and frail and, like the grandparents in that photo on TV, she looked as though you could snap her in two and that made you want to protect her from snapping in two accidentally. Plus, Emile had seen photos of Grace from before Heather's mother started dressing her in orange Velcro trouser suits and said, 'She looks so much like my grandmother. She looks totally French.' It was true. She was lean and had worn scarves and interesting layers of wool.

'Yeah,' Heather said. 'Then she just pulled over and wouldn't get out of the car. They phoned my mother, and my mother came and Grace was, like, blaming her.'

'Blaming your mother? For what?'

'Dunno. She blames my mother for everything. It's her latest phase. I think because my mother wants to get someone in the house to help take care of her, she's freaking. She thinks my mother has this big plot against her.'

'A plot to do what?' Emile asked.

Heather shrugged. 'Who knows.'

'Poor Grace.' Emile went back to spreading baba ganoush on a triangle of bread. 'I didn't know she could still drive.'

'She's not supposed to. Now we have to Grace-proof the house, like we have a new baby. Hide all the washing-up liquid and stuff, so Grace won't drink it.'

'Hide the car keys, too,' Emile said.

Heather looked at the bite of falafel that was left on her plate. 'We already did.'

'It's sad,' Emile said. He pushed his plate aside and wiped his hands on one of the linen napkins he'd brought out. 'It's sad when you can't do stuff any more.'

Heather nodded. It was sad, all right. It was so sad she felt like crying, though in truth she couldn't say if it was for Grace losing it or for the fact that Emile still hadn't kissed her.

Ten

Having to wait is now seen as a sign that something's malfunctioning in the system. We believe that waiting should have been eradicated by now, at least in the First World. Waiting = communism, Depression-era bread lines, humanitarian disasters, etc.

Gillian chewed on her pen and stared at what she'd just written. It wasn't quite right. People still waited for things (*A new pair of glasses while you wait!*), but the understanding was that the amount of time one would be expected to wait would fall inside the boundaries of what was currently deemed bearable. How was it, she wondered, that everyone in a particular culture had more or less agreed on how long they were willing to wait for any given thing? Was it a bottom-up or a top-down decision? Last week, during a brief flurry of intellectual energy, these questions had begun to percolate and resemble the basis of a lecture – the one she was still hoping to deliver at the gender and self-help conference. She could see the connections taking shape. Women, after all, had traditionally been the ones who waited, often for men, who were at sea or at war or just at the office. But what happened to that capacity when patience was no longer considered a virtue but a sign of disempowerment? Can waiting and agency coexist? In an ever-accelerating world, how can women reclaim the right to wait?

These reflections had seemed fascinating a few days ago, but now that she was back home and trying to flesh them out, her interest was flagging. Instead, she was trying to decide what to say about the new sign Elspeth had affixed to the door of their office.

Abandon hype, all ye who enter here.

Gillian didn't care for it. But then she didn't care for much of anything right now. She suspected she was depressed. She was worried enough that she'd asked Grace's neurologist about it. He'd suggested it might be the strain of looking after Grace.

'It's estimated that up to 50 per cent of caregivers are battling depression,' he'd said. 'And there is such a thing, you may have read about it, called caregiver's dementia.'

Dr Saroyan was a tall slender man with round glasses. His beard was like a euro sign lying on its back. Gillian trusted him, but she had balked at the idea that she might be suffering from caregiver's dementia. It sounded like she was trying to piggyback on Grace's proper dementia.

Saroyan had tipped his head slightly and suggested she might benefit from an antidepressant.

'So I seem depressed to you?'

'Well . . .' he'd said, 'a mood stabilizer might allow you to think a little more clearly about how you're feeling. And what you're feeling.'

'But if I go on an antidepressant, then won't I be feeling something other than what I'm really feeling?'

He'd smiled and stroked his euro. She and Saroyan had come to regard each other with a wry affection. 'Think of it this way. It's like the difference between trying to patch a sinking ship while you're in it, and being helped to tow it ashore, then dealing with the problem from there.'

Gillian had been taken aback. 'Do you see me in a sinking ship?'

'Not at all,' he'd said, with a matter-of-factness she had found reassuring. 'And, anyway, a sinking ship doesn't necessarily go down. There are a number of ways of being rescued, or of rescuing oneself. It's a matter of finding the best way in the given situation.'

'But if I'm not *in* a sinking ship . . . ?' Gillian had persisted.

He'd held up one hand. 'Let's not get stuck on that image.'

Gillian had thought for a moment. Finally, she'd said, 'I'd prefer to leave it for now.'

'It's your choice. Only you know how you feel.'

But of course that was the whole problem. She didn't know how she felt. All she knew was that she could no longer judge how happy or unhappy she was, how happy she should be, or how happy anybody else was.

What is patience? she wrote, and underlined it twice. *A choice we make, or a thing we either have or don't have?*

QUOTES TO KICK OFF:

1. *'Patience is nothing more than the art of finding something else to do.' – Anon.*
2. *'Waiting sharpens desire . . . It separates our passing enthusiasms from our true longings.' – David Runcorn*
3. *'Quickness has disappeared . . . We now only experience degrees of slowness.' – James Gleick*

Gillian dropped her pen on the desk and began massaging her temples. Degrees of slowness. She felt slow, though not in the way Gleick meant it. He meant we had lost patience with things that didn't happen instantaneously. (Gillian could still recall Grace, no longer wonderstruck over this high-speed miracle called the Internet, but drumming her fingers on the table, waiting for something to download, and saying, 'It's so bloody slow! All of Dublin must be on-line.') For Gillian, the opposite seemed true. She'd been on a two-day week at the Farm for nine months now and what her re-immersion in the real world was making clear to her was that she'd become somewhat institutionalized; she felt out of sync with the world, which appeared faster to her than ever. Gadgets and appliances were becoming obsolete before she'd entirely got the hang of them. She used to poke randomly at the buttons on the VCR until one of them – she never had known which – would spur the thing into action. And then the big clunky VCRs had been replaced by sleek flat DVD players with what seemed like far too few buttons to cover the range of things they could do, or no buttons at all but just slightly raised lines on a remote with tiny odd cave-painting-like symbols above them that everyone but her apparently knew the meaning of. Or the way that things that were 'off' now had a light on to indicate their off-ness. When had that happened?

One day you walked into a public toilet and found that the act of flushing such toilets manually had been consigned to the dustbin of history. Gillian had been perfectly happy flushing public toilets with the toe of her shoe and, as far as she knew, other women had, too; in fact, having to flush the toilet after themselves was so far down on the list of women's grievances, Gillian didn't think she'd ever heard it voiced. But now the toilet flushed itself, and if it hesitated you never knew why because no guidelines had been issued. You had to do a little dance then in front of the toilet bowl, or sit down and stand up again, trying to fool it. Same with the sinks. Same again with the hand-drier. It should have made the news: ALL ACTUAL TOUCHING OF SURFACES IN PUBLIC TOILETS TO BE ERADICATED.

She looked at her watch. In an hour she was picking Grace up from the day centre and taking her to town. Heather would join them after school. The outing was Gillian's attempt at a bit of homemade Rem Therapy: they were going for fish and chips. When Gillian was a child, Grace used to bring her for fish and chips at Forte's on O'Connell Street. Forte's was gone now, but they could go to Beshoff's, on the same street. Gillian knew not to expect much. Grace was moving beyond the logic of stimulus and response. Over the past six weeks, she had gone rapidly downhill. She was no longer behaving according to the Alzheimer's timeline Gillian kept in her desk drawer. The symptoms had begun appearing and disappearing faster than Gillian could develop strategies to cope with them. The latest was something called expressive aphasia, which meant that Grace couldn't even find the words any more in which to ask her day's supply of questions. (It was one of the things that made Gillian weepy when she was alone, the thought of Grace greeting each day with a little satchel of questions she'd packed.) Instead of saying, 'Where are we going?', Grace had begun pointing to the road ahead and saying, '. . . where? . . . where?' Instead of saying, 'I've never been to Seapoint' (her capacity for revisionism was startling), she'd begun to say simply, '. . . no . . . no . . . not Seapoint . . .', as though it were a place of punishment they were threatening her with.

Gillian had held off, briefly, making the appointment with Saroyan. It seemed like the kind of temptation she should resist, bringing Grace in after each new descent, only to have Saroyan look past Grace and right at her, as if to say, *What is it you're expecting to happen?* She was afraid she was being unrealistic, insufficiently accepting of the disease cascade, or just losing track of what was 'normal'.

On the caregivers' website she'd taken to visiting, a lot of people advised against forcing reality on sufferers – *Thank her when she brings the dirty dishes to the bedroom!* Gillian understood the rationale, but the collusion could have an unsettling effect.

Beware of what they call reality distancing, Sylvia from Boca Raton had written. *Don't worry, it isn't neurological, but it's real. It's a psychological condition induced by stress, your nights of interrupted sleep, your 24/7 on-call status, and the weird way you end up entering into somebody else's very unreal version of reality. I'm not suggesting we force reality on the person we're caring for, I'm just saying be prepared for a little 'reality-distancing' yourself.*

The MRI had come back last week. It showed lots of little bright spots throughout Grace's brain, and here and there in clusters. They were the cause of Grace's sudden decline – mini-strokes, hundreds of them, that had assaulted her in the dead of night or maybe in the light of day, as she'd sat in the passenger seat or in front of the television, oblivious to the damage being done.

They got a table near the window so they could look out on to O'Connell Street. Gillian had ordered cod and chips for all of them and a pot of tea, because that was exactly what she and Grace used to have. Now Grace was staring at her plate, looking slightly pained. Gillian thought perhaps her pad needed changing, but Grace had gone before they'd left the house and she ate so little, it was a wonder she produced anything at all.

Heather said, 'This is yummy,' raising her eyebrows as she chewed to indicate enjoyment and looking at Grace, who was seated beside her. Grace turned to look at Heather, blinking a few times.

'He's nice,' Grace said to Gillian, meaning Heather. Grace

was going through a phase of being particularly fond of Heather. Several times a day she would look at her and say, 'He's nice.'

Heather smiled at Grace and gave her a few quick affectionate rubs on her curved back with the hand that wasn't covered with grease. 'Don't you want some, Grace?' she said.

'Don't like,' Grace said.

Heather looked at her mother.

'You don't have to eat it,' Gillian said. 'I just thought it would be nice because you and I used to come for fish and chips.'

Grace was sitting forward and low in her chair. Her hands were in her lap. Her chin nearly touched the table top. 'Who for chips?' she said.

'You and I came for chips. The two of us.' Gillian motioned with her hand.

'Not for me,' Grace said, shaking her head. 'Never ate you.' Then she turned to Heather. 'You too,' she said.

'Me too what?'

Grace shook her head, more vehemently now, and didn't answer.

'That's Heather,' Gillian said.

Grace stared at Gillian, perplexed. 'But who is he?' she said.

'She's my daughter.'

Grace lapsed back into silence.

'I,' Heather said, pointing to herself, 'am *her* daughter. *You*,' pointing at Grace, 'are her . . .' She looked at Gillian.

'Mother,' Gillian said. She had decided some time ago that she would simplify matters by becoming Grace's daughter.

Heather nodded. 'Mother,' she repeated.

Grace turned to Heather and smiled at her, as though they'd just been introduced. Heather smiled back. She understood the seriousness of Grace's condition, but she was still young enough to derive pleasure from adults acting goofy.

Gillian put her hand on Grace's arm and looked at Heather. 'When I was a girl, Grace used to bring me to the city. I loved it; I thought it was so exciting.' She turned to Grace. 'Sometimes when you had things to do in town, you'd collect me after school and take me with you to the shops, and afterwards we'd go for a treat, for fish and chips . . .'

Heather was looking encouragingly at Grace. Grace was staring blankly at Gillian, neither pleased nor displeased. Gillian tried to smile. It was pointless. If she could accept the pointlessness, she might be able to enjoy the afternoon, but she felt abandoned, knowing that Grace no longer shared a history with her (or at least no longer knew she did), knowing that their most important day at Forte's had been wiped from Grace's record – the day Grace promised she would never leave her, by which she meant she wouldn't disappear the way her mother and father had.

It was the afternoon of Gillian's Story Day debacle. Gillian was eight years old. Her teacher, Miss Donaghy, had phoned Grace at lunch time, to fill her in, and when Grace picked Gillian up from school that afternoon, she didn't take her home but brought her to a matinée. She said nothing about Story Day until after the film, when they'd gone to Forte's.

Gillian loved the words 'fish 'n' chips' (she had seen them written like that somewhere) almost as much as she loved the things themselves. She liked to say the words, and if she could combine saying the words with eating the things, well, that was about the best of all. She sat there at the speckled laminated table, her head lolling on her neck, her upper body rocking forward and back in a steady autistic rhythm, alternating between a chip and a bite of a fish, and saying in a deep voice, *fiiish'nnn'chips, fiiish'nnn'chips, fish'n'chips-fish'n'chipsfish'n'chips*! What Gillian couldn't get over was the way someone had made three words into one. Who had done it, and who had let them? At some level, she intuited that this was a rare example of playfulness in the otherwise terribly un-fun grown-up world. Maybe it was a sign that being grown-up would not be as awful and serious as she feared, but there'd been so little additional evidence for such a conclusion that she did not hold out great hope. Instead, she rocked in her chair intoning *fishnnnnnchipsfishnchipsfiiiishnchips* until her aunt said, 'Sweetheart . . .'

She brought her rocking to an abrupt halt and stared at her aunt with what she believed was a theatrical intensity, but was really just the dumb look kids assume when they sense a serious subject about to be broached. She swallowed her fish, which had suddenly grown dry in her mouth.

'Miss Donaghy told me you read a story today.'

Miss Donaghy? How had she done that? This was another thing about adults. They had a line of communication somewhere up in the clouds. This wasn't the first time Gillian had noticed information about her having been mysteriously exchanged between them.

'We all did,' she said. She wondered was she in trouble, for writing the story or for crying, or both.

Miss Donaghy had given the assignment – 'Something,' she'd said, her eyes sparkling, 'something unique to you, a part of you you'd like the whole class to learn about . . .' – and Gillian had written a story called 'The Girl with No Parents', a just-the-facts account of the day her aunt and uncle told her about the deaths. The tone was that of a thriller: *It was a suny morning in Dublin the day they told me about the acident. I was eating melan in the kichen with Aunt Grace. The phone rang and Aunt Grace picked it up . . .*

As she'd read her story out to the class in a monotone cadence, she'd made a point of looking up occasionally from her page, and what she saw confused her. She had expected, at the very least, undivided attention, but what she saw instead was a sea of wriggling bodies, girls fiddling absentmindedly with their various appendages – twisting the tips of their noses, tugging on their lower lips, poking their fingers into their ears – their vacant gazes directed at the ceiling or the floor or their desktops. Dotted in amongst the squirming masses were three or four girls who sat utterly still, staring right at her, chests resting against the desk edges, mouths slightly ajar, heads lolling to one side, in what was either rapt attention or its exact opposite. When at last Gillian reached the end of her story, she did not return immediately to her desk, but allowed for a moment of post-performance hush.

Gradually, the silence registered and the girls looked up at her, one by one their little eyes fastening on to her, but not really on to *her*, just on to the thing at the front of the room that happened to be her, the latest object presented for their distraction. And she knew by the look of them that they hadn't been paying attention.

The tears had come out of nowhere, like one of those burps that sometimes took Gillian by surprise, leaping out of her throat like a small sour animal. She'd pulled her shoulders in, ducked her head and trudged resentfully towards her desk.

Miss Donaghy had called on one of the other girls and told the class to continue. She took Gillian out into the hallway and stroked her arm and said, 'I know, I know. But you're very brave and we're all extremely lucky to have heard your story.'

Miss Donaghy thought Gillian was crying about her parents, but really she was crying about the flop her performance had been. The most awful and important moment of her life had failed to hold the attention of her listeners, and if *that* didn't do it what would?

'Sweetheart?' Grace was looking at her. 'Miss Donaghy said the story was about your mum and dad and that you were upset.'

Gillian didn't say anything. She stared at the shiny brooch on Grace's bosom and tried to remember what she'd heard about something called hypnosis. It had to do with staring at an object for a long time and then like magic you could do tricks or be somebody else for a while.

'Did the other girls say something to upset you?'

Gillian's mouth was open. She shook her head.

'The girls didn't say anything?'

'No.'

'So it was the story? The story made you sad?'

Gillian nodded. She wished they could go back to eating their fish 'n' chips. On the other hand, she wanted to tell Aunt Grace everything she felt, even the things she didn't know how to tell, because she thought it might make a difference in the real world, the one outside her head. But she was confused, because these people – her mum and dad – well, she was already forgetting them, not forgetting they'd ever existed, but forgetting what they felt like or sounded like or moved like. She was sad when she thought of them, but the sadness was often distant and vague, like something she knew but couldn't feel, the way she knew now that she'd felt sad at the pictures today (when the puppy had got kidnapped and the little girl was crying on her doorstep) but didn't feel sad any more. The problem had something to do with the fact that she couldn't hold her parents in her head. She couldn't see them the way she could see Aunt Grace and Uncle Martin in her head when they weren't around, or her bedroom when she wasn't in it, or Miss Donaghy on the weekends, when she wasn't at school. When she asked her head to make a picture of her parents, she got only a picture of a picture: the one Aunt Grace kept on the mantel at home, alongside other photos of other people they were supposed to love.

'You poor pet,' her aunt said.

Sometimes Gillian felt sad because that seemed to be her job and it was easier to just do her job than to try to figure out why it was her job or whether it would always be her job. But it wasn't like that today. Today she really was sad because Aunt Grace was sad, and Miss Donaghy had been sad, and nobody had listened to her story, and that had made her very, very sad.

'There's something I want to tell you, dear,' Aunt Grace said. 'What happened to your mum and dad, you don't have to explain that to anyone. You know what happened, and I know, and your Uncle Martin knows, and anybody who loves you knows. But you don't have to tell the girls in your class how it happened, or anybody else . . .'

Gillian stared at Aunt Grace's pretty blue brooch and nodded.

'The other thing is this,' Aunt Grace continued. 'Your mum will always be your mum. And your daddy will always be your daddy. They're in heaven now. They're your mum and dad in heaven.'

Gillian nodded. Many times she had been told they were in heaven, but as it was apparently not a place you could travel to in a train, the information was as good as irrelevant.

'And Martin and I are your dad and mum here.'

'In Dublin?' Gillian said, looking up at her aunt.

'Well, yes, here in Dublin. Here in . . .'

'In Ireland?'

Aunt Grace smiled. 'In Ireland,' she said. 'And if you ever want to call us that – I mean, if some girls in school ever ask you where your mum and dad are and you don't want to tell them the story that makes us sad, you can tell them that Martin and I are your daddy and your mum. And that won't mean that we've forgotten your real mum and dad. We'll never forget them. I'll make sure of that. But if it ever makes things easier, you can say that, okay? What I've just said.'

Aunt Grace reached over and stroked the side of her head and smiled in a way that wasn't happy. 'As you get older,' she said, 'this will all get easier. That's the good thing. Do you understand what I'm saying?'

She looked deeply into Gillian's eyes, and Gillian looked back into Aunt Grace's eyes. Aunt Grace was trying to tell her something. Gillian didn't know what it was, not exactly, but she knew that Aunt Grace was very, very kind and so whatever she was trying to tell her must be nice. She never yelled at Gillian, even when she was angry, and she had a lovely garden with all sorts of bright flowers and she made cakes and jumpers and she and Martin said things that made each other laugh and Gillian knew that this was not the way with all parents.

Aunt Grace looked like she was waiting for her to say something. Gillian couldn't speak. She was feeling anxious, more and more by the second, as though someone were pouring it into her. When she was smaller, she used to imagine that her mother and father might miraculously reappear. Not dead after all! A mistake! They'd been kidnapped, or had been hit on the head and given amnesia; they'd got lost in Russia or China or somewhere else vague and unimaginably vast.

These hopes, though, had slowly turned into fears. There was a period in between fantasizing about their miraculous return and full acceptance of the impossibility of that when Gillian had had nightmares of her parents coming back to claim her – strangers who would snatch her away from the loving arms of Aunt Grace and Uncle Martin.

Now she was a big girl, too big to believe that any more, but the anxiety hadn't gone away.

Finally, she said to Grace, 'Will you go away?'

Aunt Grace looked puzzled. 'When?' she said. 'Go away where?'

'I don't know,' Gillian said. 'Just away . . .'

Aunt Grace sighed; her shoulders drooped as though someone had just let the air out of her. She shook her head. 'Of course not, darling.'

Then she took Gillian's hand, which was greasy from the fish and chips, though Aunt Grace didn't seem to mind because she didn't let go and even wrapped her whole hand around Gillian's greasy one and squeezed it and didn't say *use a serviette*, and Gillian considered this marvellous and inexplicable.

'I'm not going anywhere,' Aunt Grace said, and shook her head again. Then she smiled, and this time her smile looked a tiny bit happy. 'Sure, where would I go?'

Eleven

He found her wedged behind the bedroom door, lying on her side, her skinny legs bent neatly at the knees. She looked as though someone had folded her up and placed her there carefully, like an extra chair that was in the way.

There was no one else in the house. It was Sunday and Gillian had left for Meath after lunch. Heather was in town. Damien had been downstairs in the study and hadn't heard Grace fall. When he'd come up to check on her he had thought at first she was only 'hiding'. She'd been doing that lately, curling up into a ball and tucking herself into odd places – the corner of the sofa or the floor of her room between the dresser and the bedside locker. He and Gillian were pretty sure Grace thought she wasn't visible and had decided they would pretend not to see her; they figured hiding was a sign she wanted to be alone.

'Grace?' He leaned over her. 'Are you okay?'

Grace didn't move. This was not the crouching readiness that characterized her bouts of hiding; it was the stillness of something inanimate.

'Grace?' he said again. Already his breath was coming fast and his heartbeat had quickened. He put his hand on her shoulder and repeated her name. His voice sounded quivery and high-pitched.

In order to see her face, he had to pick her up and turn her towards him – she was so light, where was the dead weight, he wondered (for he knew by her eyes she was dead). As soon as he put her down on the bed, he saw that his hands were shaking and he grasped her calves to still them, but it seemed an almost violent gesture – her calves were disturbingly thin and his hands so large by comparison.

Damien had never been with a dead body before, or not one that had so recently been alive (his father was dead seven hours by the time Damien reached the house in Mayo), and he wasn't quite sure what to do, though he knew that ringing Gillian should be high on the list. He needed to collect himself; he didn't want to upset her more by saying it in the wrong way, whatever the wrong way was, because he knew that whatever words he chose to use, she would remember them for the rest of her life.

His eyes were resting on Grace's red slipper. It had been on her right foot when she was lying behind the door, but had fallen off when he'd lifted her to the bed. It was a delicate embroidered thing, like a ballet slipper. Damien couldn't tell if the left one had fallen off when Grace collapsed (it looked as though she'd just lain herself down and, very gently, curled up and died) or if she'd been only halfway through putting the slippers on, but in either case it meant that she'd been planning to come downstairs. To think of it. Grace had had a plan. Right up to the final moment, the mind was organizing and arranging, preparing for the next moment and after that the next, keeping going.

He picked up the two slippers and held one in each hand. The *agitated purposeful wanderer*. That was (or had been, he corrected himself) Grace's 'wandering category', according to the nurse at the day centre. She'd started out as a *reminiscent wanderer*, a title both he and Gillian had thought rather nice. It sounded poetic; it sounded almost like a choice.

Though Damien's eyes were shut tightly, the tears had

begun to squeeze through. He was crying for Gillian, for himself, for Grace, of course, for the fact that anyone ever had to grow this small and this lost. He was crying from relief, too. Because he felt a tension easing, a pressure he couldn't have put a name on but had been aware of for some time. It was the atmosphere Grace had introduced into the house. The way she'd skulked about, a phantom presence. He would look up from his desk and find her standing in the doorway of the study, watching him, and he'd get a fright. What he saw on her face unsettled him. The incipient madness. The way she no longer attempted to mask her deterioration. She was too stark a reminder of too many unpleasant eventualities, and he'd look at her in the doorway – stooped, listing to the left, the blank stare almost like a challenge – and he'd see a shell that seemed to contain no one at all.

He wiped his eyes with the heel of his palm. He had a passing thought that he might feel Grace's hand on his back, stroking him, comforting him. He had sat with her on this bed before, nights Gillian was in Meath and Grace was feeling anxious or insomniac. The odd night he'd stayed with her until she fell asleep. Not as often, he knew, as he might have.

It was twenty past five. He had to phone Gillian, phone her before she phoned him, which she usually did around this time on a Sunday, just before she had her first session with the new guests. The phone was in the other room. They'd taken the extension out of this bedroom after the time Grace had believed its ringing was the smoke alarm. His mobile was down in the office. He didn't want to leave Grace to phone Gillian (although it would be equally odd to phone Gillian with Grace lying dead behind him). In fact, he didn't want to phone Gillian at all. He and Gillian had talked about the end, and she'd said, 'Wherever she is by then, whether she knows me or not, she won't die alone.'

And now she had died, and he'd been right there in the house and hadn't been with her.

At least he'd been home, though. If it had been tomorrow, only Theresa would have been here – she had started a few weeks ago – and though she might have stuck closer to Grace than he generally did, Grace often didn't recognize her; she would have died in the company of a stranger. He wondered then if she'd known she was dying. Or had she just felt faint before collapsing? Either way, why hadn't she called to him? Made a thud, at least, as she fell? He would have been up in a flash, he'd have held her. It occurred to him that he should lie to Gillian, tell her he'd been there beside Grace, just like they'd promised they would be, that Grace had squeezed his hand and looked into his eyes and that she hadn't been alone.

But then Gillian would say: Why didn't you ring an ambulance?

One lie would necessitate another, and on it would go. No. It was a stupid idea. It was overwhelmingly complicated. Anyway, Gillian hated coddling; she hated false comfort and denial. She was afraid that if she accepted protection, she'd begin to believe in it, and if there was one truth in her life, it was that there was no such thing as protection, not against the things we really wanted to be protected from.

Damien swallowed. He was suddenly extremely thirsty. (Did crying do that?) He was still clutching the slippers and he became aware of the dampness of them, from having been pressed against his face as he wept. The silk had been soft on his skin. The slippers smelled of talcum powder. Grace had stopped perspiring months ago.

He turned and set the slippers on the bed beside Grace's

hip. She appeared infinitely more dead than she had when he'd last looked at her, just moments ago; she *felt* more dead; her deadness was now filling the room, as though requiring an increasing amount of oxygen for its expression. Were there degrees of deadness? Was there a determined number of minutes that you got to spend with someone who'd died before they really seemed dead to you? A period of time that corresponded to something real – not the soul leaving the body, Damien didn't believe in any of that, but something else, something more material, like a smell you didn't even know you were smelling or some slight shift in the atmosphere due to a change in energy, a message that reached the brain, a communication that had once served an important purpose, eons ago, transmitted by the dead and received by the living, a message that said: *I'm gone for good*, or *You go on ahead without me*, or maybe, *Bury me, please* . . . Animals got the signals, didn't they? That's why they got spooked. Dogs around a dead dog, same for cats. They say animals don't know they're going to die, but they know what dead is when they see it, they know it isn't sleep.

He stood up quickly – before inertia set in again – and left the room without looking back. It was five-thirty. Gillian's session started at six. She could ring any time now. If she got to him before he got to her, he'd have to say Grace was asleep, otherwise it would sound appalling: *Grace? Oh, she died, I just haven't had a chance to ring you.*

He went into their room and sat down on the bed. He thought of the minutes of a certain kind of life that was left to Gillian – a life in which Grace still existed – and that the exact number of those minutes, to a point anyway, depended on when he called her. He tried to imagine his stalling as a gift to her.

Then he closed his eyes and rubbed them and thought of Grace. Curled tightly in a corner of the sofa or waiting placidly in the passenger seat of the car; burying Martin and raising Gillian and sitting out in the back garden, her face to the sun; the pink cap she wore swimming and the scarves in winter; the red Mini she drove years ago and the first time he ever met her, and it all seemed to amount to so little and at the same time to very much.

He lifted the receiver and slowly tapped in the number of Gillian's mobile, his hands shaking, like they had the first time he'd phoned her.

Twelve

Their first day in France, they woke to rain. From the breakfast room of their hotel, they could see it teeming on the promenade. They sat there, their eyes wide as they sipped their coffee, staring out at the deluge, trying not to take it as a sign of anything.

They were staying in Menton, on the French–Italian border. Damien had insisted they get away after the funeral. He'd made all the arrangements, with encouragement from Elspeth and Heather. A team spirit had grown up around the holiday, as though they were sending Gillian on a sponsored walk. She hadn't been enthusiastic. The effort involved in travelling had appeared enormous. It was enough to do the simplest things since Grace's death, since the moment she'd said *hello* and Damien had said *hi*, then hadn't spoken, and she'd known something was very wrong.

Damien finished his coffee and suggested they go to the aquarium in Monaco. Gillian immediately agreed and they both felt relieved at having a purpose and a destination. By the time they gathered their things and dashed out to the rental car, the rain had been reduced to a surmountable impediment, and their anxiety transformed into a spirit of adventure.

The aquarium was packed because of the weather and because it was Sunday, and they took their place in a fat snaking queue that was shuffling from tank to tank. Inside the first tank, turtles and sharks occasionally bumped into one another, looking as though they were simply too lazy to steer clear. Gillian was pointing to a blue-and-green fish about the size of her hand that was banging its nose repeatedly into one of the rock formations.

'It must be to do with food,' she said to Damien. 'He seems to be pecking. But it looks like it hurts.'

A middle-aged woman beside her, in a clear American accent and without taking her eyes off the tank, said, 'Maybe he's self-harming . . .'

Gillian turned to the woman and frowned.

'I'm only joking,' the woman said quickly and smiled, then added reassuringly, 'I'm pretty sure he's feeding.'

Gillian nodded and turned back to the tank. A brown-and-white spotted fish that looked like a handbag darted through the water.

The woman disappeared. Damien and Gillian shuffled along again, stopping at each tank to note whatever idiosyncrasies its inhabitants exhibited. Damien liked the shrimpfish, which were long and thin and swam vertically, in a synchronized group, bobbing up and down about the tank. They seemed sad to Gillian, stuck in their impoverished loops, as though riding the same lift for the rest of their lives.

'Look,' Damien said, 'it says they are "sociable and harmless".'

'Sounds like you,' she said, and touched the small of his back.

He tilted his head in front of the glass and stared. 'Should I take that as a compliment?'

The American woman turned up again at the shark eggs' tank, where the shark embryos wriggled around inside translucent pods hanging from what looked like the branch of a tree.

'What's that film?' Damien said. 'Where everybody comes out of a pod?'

Gillian tried to remember. 'I know the one. We saw it. Ages ago.'

'*Invasion of the Body Snatchers*,' the American woman said.

'That's it.'

The Mediterranean morays were revolting. Their heads were rising out of some plant life, and at the end of their snouts, their mouths opened and closed incessantly in a futile beseeching motion Gillian found intensely depressing. They were like a gruesome bouquet out of a nightmare, something gone suddenly animate as you held it in your dream-hands.

'Oh look,' Damien said, from over on her left. She was almost afraid to look after the cluster of morays. 'The sea-horses.'

She went and stood beside him, watching the tiny mythic creatures propelling themselves from vine to vine. They curled their tails in turn around each vine, as though they were monkeys gliding in slow motion between branches. The fins on their backs fluttered like tiny delicate fans as they moved. When they came to rest, they collided gently with one another as they alighted on the vines, gracefully jostling for space. They were as calming as the eels were disturbing and Gillian stood watching them for several minutes, transfixed by their peculiar elegance.

When she and Damien finally moved on, she found her energy waning. The autistic to-ing and fro-ing of the fish was getting to her; their colours and shapes were beginning to appear distressingly lurid. She was feeling the weight and airlessness of being underground. Or underwater. Whichever they were. Both, maybe.

'Shall we go?' she said.

'I've had enough,' he said, though she knew he could have stayed another hour.

They climbed the stairs to the gift shop, where they bought postcards and tinned anchovies and fish-shaped chocolates. The rain had let up and as they stepped outside, Gillian saw the American woman again, getting into a taxi.

She'd have forgotten all about her – just as she was already forgetting the Cockneys with the camcorder and the Japanese men who'd shared her amusement at the silver squashed-nosed lookdowns – if she hadn't seen her again the next morning at breakfast.

Gillian was in the hotel dining room writing the postcards she'd bought the day before, an activity which caused her to reflect anew on the paucity of close friends in her life, or even casual friends. The demands of running the Farm weren't entirely to blame. As far back as she could remember, Gillian had been a loner, something she'd later attributed to the deep impression made on her when she'd told new friends or playmates that she had no parents – their blank stares of bewilderment or apparent indifference, and her subsequent conclusion that the experiences of each person were cordoned off from those of all other persons and that talking about experiences, or the feelings they engendered, didn't result in those things becoming a part of anybody else's life; if anything, it seemed to reinforce the knowledge that certain things in life were just yours.

So she'd become a 'private' person. That was what the grown-ups had called her. Grace would look at her and say teasingly, *You're a private little thing, aren't you?* And Gillian had liked that. It had made her feel she had important secrets that others envied and wished her to reveal. Being 'private' (even a *private little thing*) sounded rather grand, more grand than furtive or bewildered, which was how Gillian would have described herself had such words been part of her vocabulary. And the more people told her how private she was, the more private she felt obliged to be, not wanting to surprise or disappoint.

By the time she went to university, the habit of reticence was ingrained. One or two people she could really talk to was enough; seeking company for company's sake struck her as a waste of time, an indication of neediness. When it was pointed out to her that this was unusual in a woman, she'd felt fortunate. Needing less of others seemed a sort of insurance against pain, and against the foolishness with which many people carried on, their inner lives so easily disrupted by the actions of those they called friends.

Even so, running the Farm hadn't helped. She had no time to pursue new friendships. She couldn't even answer her e-mails. As for Damien, he had friends the way many men did: offhandedly, guardedly, lacking in the intense mutual sympathy and unqualified trust she considered to be the basic requirements of friendship.

She sifted through the remaining postcards. She had already written one to Damien's mother, and one to Heather, who was staying with Miriam's family. She chose one for Elspeth and Peter with a picture of writhing morays on it and was addressing it when the American woman walked in. They smiled in mutual recognition and exchanged hellos.

The woman sat at a table adjacent to Gillian's and ordered her breakfast in what sounded like impeccable French. Then, switching to English, she said, 'Did you enjoy the aquarium yesterday?'

Gillian looked up and saw the woman digging in her small

leather handbag. She almost thought she'd imagined the question.

'We loved it,' she said tentatively.

'Um,' the woman continued to dig. 'It's *so* great. I go there every time I'm in the area.'

The woman found what she was looking for, which turned out to be a blister pack of pills, and pressed with her thumb against the back of one of its pods. Gillian heard the sound of perforating foil and saw a two-tone purple capsule pop out on to the tablecloth. She slid her eyes back to her postcard. People were always popping pills in public, and she often wondered who was popping what.

The woman picked up the purple capsule and swallowed it with a gulp of juice, then turned to Gillian and said, 'I'm Katherine.'

Gillian introduced herself and sipped her coffee. 'On holidays?' she asked.

'I come here for a couple of weeks every year. My husband and I used to spend half our time here and the other half in London. He was from London.' The waiter set a café crème in front of Katherine. 'He died two years ago,' she continued. 'A month after he retired. Now I come back here for, I don't know, I have friends here, and I guess I come for sentimental reasons. We had a little place in Roquebrune, but I sold it last year.'

'I'm sorry,' Gillian said, 'about your husband.'

Katherine took a large swallow of coffee. 'It was bad timing. We had a lot of plans for after he retired. But I don't know what good timing would have been.' She managed a wry smile. 'Twenty years from now, maybe? Anyway. What about you?'

'I'm here with my husband,' Gillian said.

'Okay,' she said. 'Vacation?'

Gillian nodded.

'From what? Dare I ask.'

'Sorry?'

'What do you do?'

'Oh.' Gillian hesitated. There had been a time when she would have offered an elaborate, enthusiastic explanation of her work. This morning she just said, 'I run a kind of . . . clinic. To help people who want to slow down.'

'Wow.' Katherine leaned forward. 'And where do you do this?'

'In Ireland.'

'I see,' Katherine said. 'Tell me more.'

Gillian took a breath and forced herself to switch into brochure mode. 'To help them find ways of responding creatively to stress and overstimulation. To help them realize they have choices about how much information they take in, or take on. That sort of thing.'

'Wait a minute,' Katherine said, her eyes narrowing. 'Ireland. Slowing down. I've heard of you.'

Gillian wasn't surprised. 'Maybe,' she said, picking up her spoon and resculpting the terrain of foam that was resting at the bottom of her cup.

'No, I have. I'm sure I have. It could've been in the *Times* or somewhere. Wow,' she shook her head. '*That* must be interesting.'

Did Gillian detect a note of sarcasm? No, she didn't think so. She shrugged. 'Yes and no.'

The waiter reappeared and with a small bow presented Katherine with a plate of delicately cut and beautifully arranged fresh fruits.

'What?' Katherine said. 'You're not liking it?'

'It's not that exactly. It's just right now things are . . .' She told her about Grace.

'Oh, I'm sorry,' Katherine said, then nodded. 'You were close?'

'She raised me. Her and my uncle. My parents died when I was five. In an accident.'

Katherine looked pained. 'I'm sorry,' she said again.

Gillian shook her head. 'I don't mean to be so, you know, first thing in the morning.'

'No, no, no. Don't be silly.'

Gillian bit her lip. 'We were close,' she said. 'Yeah. She and my uncle were very good to me.'

'Well,' Katherine said, relaxing a bit, 'I guess you were lucky to have them.'

'I was a lucky girl, all right.' The old sarcasm was in her voice.

'I didn't mean –'

'No, I know, I'm sorry.' A wan smile. 'I'm tired, you know. I'm just tired.'

'You're grieving,' Katherine said. 'I can see that.'

'You can?'

'Sure,' she said gently. 'But that's okay.'

Gillian looked around the breakfast room. 'I know. I just didn't think it was,' she shrugged, 'noticeable.'

Katherine looked puzzled. 'What's wrong with it being noticeable?'

Gillian shook her head and tried to smile. 'You know, I feel like I need about a year off.'

'What would you do if you took a year off?'

'I don't know,' she said. 'Grieve?' They laughed. She watched Katherine spear a thin crescent of melon. 'Oh, I don't really want to take a year off. I just want to feel . . . I don't know. It's like I'm in a bubble. Everything's sort of muffled. Like somebody's packed cotton wool around my brain.' Gillian was surprised to hear herself saying all this to a stranger; it wasn't like her, though she knew it was often easier to confide in strangers. They couldn't check up on you afterwards.

'I'm not depressed,' she added, because she figured that was Katherine's next question. It was a question a few people had asked. 'It's not that.'

Katherine nodded, looking sympathetic. 'I understand,' she said.

'You do?'

'Of course I do.'

Katherine was staying with friends in Cannes that evening, then going back to London the following day. They exchanged e-mail addresses before they left the breakfast room – 'I must come to your place sometime, to slow down,' Katherine had laughed – and Gillian went for a short walk along the promenade before going back up to the room, where Damien was sitting on the balcony reading the *Herald Tribune*. It was unseasonably warm for October, and they packed a picnic lunch of cheese, bread and fruit, and spent the afternoon at the long sandy beach at Cap Martin. Unlike the day before, the skies were a deep, searing blue. The air was autumnal, but it held the heat, the last of the season. This was Gillian's favourite time of year, when the heat was dry and spent, and yet possessed an intensity that felt like the accumulation of a summer.

They spread their blanket on the sand and went straight to the water. The French found it too cold for swimming now, but she and Damien were used to the Irish Sea. From the road, looking down, Gillian had seen the dramatic shift in the sea's tones – from the milky blue swathes close to shore to the darker opaque depths, the border between them as clear and striking as if it had been drawn upon the water.

Damien took off in a smooth crawl, swimming parallel to the shore. She remembered the first time she'd seen him swim, more than twenty years ago at Sant Pol de Mar, and how surprised she'd been at his ease in the water. Gillian herself had swum from an early age; Grace had taken her, sometimes forcibly at first, from the time her parents died – *You'll thank me later*, she'd say.

Her feet found the bottom and she dug her toes in, trying to root herself like a reed, letting her body sway gently with the water and keeping her eyes on Damien. He'd stopped swimming and was floating on his back now. Occasionally he let fly a single emphatic kick, sending a high celebratory plume of spray into the air. Out of nowhere, she felt the force of her various disloyalties: the affair; the amount of time she'd spent pondering a life with someone else; the disdain with which she often regarded his work; and all the ways that she had closed herself off from him over the years.

Something had to give, and she wanted it to. She wanted to say she was sorry in a way that was so fresh and sweeping that it would propel them into some new way of seeing. But she wasn't sure how and, anyway, knew enough by now to understand that grand gestures were rarely what was called for. What was needed instead was a series of infinitesimal shifts she wasn't sure she had the energy or the vision to undertake.

She felt a sadness filling her, a large, wide-ranging sadness that had to do with the sheer wonder of the physical world – its heft and colour and light, its oceans – as well as with the way all the people she'd loved as a child had ceased to inhabit it. (When she'd taken the trip to Spain all those years ago, she had photographed deserted plazas and uninhabited landscapes – the places her mother and father had passed through on the way to their deaths. Later, when she'd had the photographs developed, she'd stared at each one for a long time, trying, in vain, to inscribe her parents on to the emptiness.)

She knew she should swim over to join him – it was one of those gestures worth making – but he looked happy how he was, and instead she called to him and waved and began making her way towards the shore.

Thirteen

He felt bad for thinking it, but he wished she'd be on her way. It wasn't just that he needed to get on the road, it was that the goodbye was drawing out to the point of awkwardness; he was running out of sheepish grins.

The airport was busy, even at seven in the morning, and the Passengers Only queue doubled back on itself several times, intestinally. She was wearing a dress, dowdy and unflattering, the kind that if it weren't for his mother Damien would have assumed didn't get made any more. In amongst the other passengers in the queue – the neat families of four and the futuristically angular Chinese students, the business heads with their lightweight laptops ready for screening and the gangly slouching teenagers – his mother looked not so much old as solid in a way that was outdated and a little bit defiant.

She'd stayed with them in Dublin the night before so he could drive her here this morning. She was going to Francis's for Christmas. It was her first trip to Seattle, first time west of Chicago, where she'd gone with Damien's father to visit cousins in the summer of '95, his last trip abroad.

When she wasn't looking he checked his watch. He was hoping to be in Kill by ten and back in Dublin before rush hour this evening. His mother was staring ahead, gravely, impassively, at nothing at all. He could see her legs, momentarily, through the confusion of other legs, her thick ankles. He thought about deep-vein thrombosis.

She'd be twelve hours in the air. Gillian had given her some travel socks last night, only to discover she already had two pairs, donated by neighbours. His mother searched him out again and caught his eye. She was doing this periodically, making sure that he was still there, each time sending him a communiqué of sorts – a thin smile or a raised brow, a frown of exaggerated impatience, and once, fleetingly, a look of such world-sorrow he felt the bottom drop out of his morning. It was the whole welter of her – all the things she'd never done but wanted to, and whatever she regretted or was ashamed of, how much she had or hadn't loved her husband, whatever her fears were and how deeply she knew she was alone in the world and even how well she knew that everyone was. And then he realized: she's crying. Not much, just a few discreet tears, enough to require the brief attention of her index knuckle, drawn tenderly in turn under each eye.

As she entered the security zone, he gave her a smile of apology, for large, unspecified and impersonal wrongs, an apology on behalf of the world, that it should be the kind of place it is. A middle-aged man on a high stool sitting at a grey podium checked her boarding pass and spoke to her, smiling, a sidewards half-shake of his head, a gallant and comradely flirtation, and Damien felt a gratitude so sudden and enormous it was for a moment the totality of him.

When his mother's turn came, she stepped, like everyone, both boldly and hesitantly through the rectangular maw of the metal detector, on the other side of which two smiling security agents – one man, one woman – waited as though to greet her, their scanners hanging from their hands like laser swords they might duel with for a laugh. They didn't raise them to his mother. She lifted her bag from the conveyor belt and was absorbed into the corridor's throng, and Damien turned away and headed towards the exit, feeling both satisfied and bereft.

It was still dark when he pulled out on to the motorway, and he felt the melancholy that came with being up and about before the sun was. He took the M50 as far as Palmerston and headed west from there. He hadn't grown up amidst motorways, and he still noticed their particular geometry – the smooth lift of the off ramps, or the wide curls of tarmac hiving off; the odd self-importance of them, allowing you to believe, for miles at a stretch, that it was a vast expanse of land you were traversing instead of a small island. Damien's family hadn't often come to Dublin when he was a child, but he did remember once, when he was eleven or twelve, travelling in the car with his father to meet an uncle coming off the boat: the two-lane roads, mostly empty, linking the villages, and the way the countryside seemed to roll right up to Dublin's door. Now the countryside was in retreat, contracting into the remotest corners. The tips of Cork and Kerry, the outer reaches of Donegal, the islands.

He managed to pass the new housing estates without really seeing them; that is, he didn't allow himself to lapse into disdainful musing on what it might be like to live in one or attempt to imagine alternative housing schemes that might have been or even to become momentarily depressed by the simple visual fact of them.

It wasn't until he got beyond Enfield that he began to feel any sense of space at all. The sky had gone a grey-yellow, and it was light enough to see clearly the trees and the bungalows. He felt sleepy from the fug of the car's interior. He lowered the heat and cracked the window and cold air shot in. It wasn't a bad morning. There was no wind; the trees stood absolutely still, what leaves there were looked delicately balanced on their branches. He didn't mind the barrenness of winter, and he loved the dawn. He drove for nearly an hour in an unusual state of calm. It lasted about as far as Longford.

He didn't know how concerned he should be about the meeting with Judith. When he'd spoken to her yesterday by phone, she'd said, 'Just a couple of hiccups we should talk about. I'll tell you when I see you.' She did mention that Sean, the poet-philosopher, was unhappy. Damien had immediately assumed he was looking for more money. Sean had turned out to be Kill's undisputed star attraction. Last month, when the village was voted the year's Most Innovative New Development in Ireland by the Heritage and Museums Association in the UK, special mention had been made of Sean, the only employee singled out for praise.

But apparently, Sean's unhappiness was not to do with money.

'It's deeper than that,' Judith had said.

And Damien had asked, 'You mean more deep-rooted or more profound?'

'Actually,' she'd said, 'the latter.'

His mistake, he thought, as he left the N5 and headed towards Castleplunket, had been in giving Sean that silly job title. To be dubbed the poet-philosopher had encouraged him to take himself far too seriously, whereas what Damien had intended was that Sean would wear his wisdom lightly, performing in a spirit of playfulness. Damien had, in the beginning, addressed Sean with mock reverence on occasion, but he wouldn't do that today. According to Judith, Sean was already feeling mocked.

*

She was waiting for him in her office, in her regulation blue skirt and jacket. Damien wasn't wild about the uniform. She looked like an air hostess.

'Good morning.'

'Morning,' Judith said. She set her cup of tea aside.

Before he even sat down, he saw a sheet with bullet points lying on her desk. He threw his coat on one of the chairs and turned the piece of paper so he could read it. Next to the first bullet point Judith had written: *Mairead*. Mairead was a sweet old lady from only up the road. She'd worked at Kill from the start.

'Mairead?' He looked at Judith. 'What's wrong with Mairead?'

'Sit down,' she said.

He took a seat. 'I'm down.'

She smiled. Affectionately, he thought. 'Would you like some tea?'

He shook his head. 'Tell me about the hiccups.'

'Okay.' Judith fingered the sheet of paper. 'Mairead's been telling . . . stories.'

'Yeah?'

'About her childhood in the laundries with the Sisters of Perpetual Kindness . . .'

Damien rolled his eyes. 'Let me guess.'

'About how much they enjoyed locking her in a dark cellar with the rats.'

'Lovely.'

'When she had no shoes.'

He cringed.

'She frightened two little girls the other day,' Judith said. Judith thought Mairead might be getting a bit dotty, in which case Damien would have to let her go. The thought of it put a knot in his stomach.

'I'll talk to her,' he said. 'What else?'

'Alexa.'

'What's Alexa's problem?'

Young Bryan, it seemed, had recently broken up with her, and Alexa, disconsolate, had come into the pub drunk the other day and let loose. 'Something to the effect,' Judith said, 'that nobody who worked in Kill gave a shit about it, that she herself couldn't wait to get out of here, and that all the money people were spending here was making "fat guys" in Dublin rich.'

Damien arched his brows. 'That sounds like more than a hiccup.'

'There was only a handful of people there,' Judith said.

He recalled with fondness Alexa's stripe of bare midriff. Did Alexa think of him as a fat guy? He wasn't fat, actually. She probably meant rich. 'Well,' he said, 'except for the bit about the fat guys, isn't that how people here felt in the fifties?'

'Authentic bitterness is not something we should try to cultivate,' Judith said.

'I was joking.'

'Matt said she was writhing with shame the next day.' Matt was the barman. He had put Alexa into a taxi and sent her home the night of her outburst. 'I think if I talk to her it might be enough. Unless you want to.'

Damien shook his head. 'No, no, you do it.'

Judith nodded. She sipped her tea. 'Sean might be a bit trickier.' Sean, Judith explained, was in love. With an American woman.

'Is he leaving?'

'Well,' Judith said, 'I don't know what he's doing. According to Matt, this American woman is going around saying we've taken advantage of him. She says we've set him up as the village idiot.'

'Village idiot? He's the poet-philosopher.'

'She says he's a wind-up doll.'

'And what does Sean say?'

'He hasn't said anything. Not to me, anyway.'

Damien leaned back in his chair and clasped his hands behind his head. There were no more bullet points. 'So,' he said, 'what's the good news?'

Judith bit her lip and smiled. On her desk was a small gnome of unidentifiable ethnicity. She was nudging it around with her fingertip.

Neither of them spoke for a while. Finally, Damien said, 'Well, how are *you*?'

'Fine,' she said. 'Grand, yeah.'

'Are you sure?'

'It's a change from Dublin, I'll say that.'

Damien nodded and thought for a moment. 'Any nice men around here?'

Judith shook her head, slowly and deliberately. She picked up the gnome between her first and second fingers, holding it by its neck like a cigarette. Judith had recently quit smoking. 'Doesn't matter, though,' she said. 'I'm detoxing.'

'Oh?' He drew back. 'Are we toxic?'

'No,' she smiled. 'I just meant having down time.'

Damien crossed his arms over his chest and looked at her. 'It's all a science now, isn't it?'

'I wish it were. The results might be easier to predict.'

He found Sean in Carroll's, one of the two pubs on the main street. He was sitting alone at a corner table with a pot of tea and some bread and jam in front of him, reading the *Guardian*.

'Can I join you?'

Sean looked at him over the tops of his spectacles and motioned towards the seat opposite, then poured himself a cup of tea. Damien had no cup, and Sean didn't suggest he get one.

Damien sat down. 'So, how's things?'

Sean nodded. 'Things is fine,' he said. He transferred two spoonfuls of sugar from the bowl to his cup and stirred his tea for an irritatingly long time, while Damien watched, wondering what it was to be newly in love at sixty-something. He looked sideways at Sean. He wasn't a bad-looking man. He had great hair, a thick white thatch, cut short, and his thighs and arms looked strong. He was an avid cyclist, and his face had a certain flush of good health. On the side of his nose, though, tiny veins flashed like purple lightning. His neck looked raw from that morning's shave, and his lips had thinned nearly to the point of nonexistence. A wattle of flesh hung from his chin. But a woman was in love with him.

'I hear there was a bit of a scene in here the other day,' Damien said. He'd decided the best approach might be one of solidarity. 'Were you here during Alexa's little outburst?'

'Yes, I was here,' Sean said, with what looked like the hint of a smile.

'Judith said there were some tourists in the pub. How did they react?'

'Oh, they were faintly scandalized, or pretended to be. Really, they were delighted to have got the anecdote.'

'Anecdote provision,' Damien said, 'that's our business.'

Sean stuck his chin in the air and said, '"It is the privilege and presumption of the tourist to take in the human misadventures of a foreign scene with the indifferent frivolity of a play-goer."'

Damien looked at him. 'Who said that? Or did you say that?'

'Henry James said that. I don't say anything.'

Damien shifted in his seat. His eyes strayed to the purple veins again. He'd never sat quite this close to Sean. 'What do you mean you don't say anything?'

'Whatever you say . . . say nuttin'.' Sean winked and gave him a half-nod.

Damien changed the subject. 'I heard you're having a . . . a romance.' He tried to sound pleased, but not greatly interested.

Sean spread butter and jam on a thick slab of brown bread and took a slurp from his tea. '"A chronic state of love can sometimes be caused by anxiety."'

Damien considered this.

'Thus spake Ovid,' Sean said.

'Sean . . .'

Sean stared straight ahead of him and said, 'They say we love others because the version of ourselves that's revealed is one of the few we can bear.' He turned to look at Damien. 'Whoever they are.' American twang: 'A panel of experts.'

Damien attempted a laugh. 'You don't use that voice with visitors, do you?'

'No,' Sean shook his head, 'I use this one.' Gazing at the far wall, as though reading the words from an autocue positioned there, he lowered his voice and said slowly, '"Vanity of vanities, all is vanity and a striving after the wind." Ecclesiastes.' He lowered his eyes to the table and contemplated his tea and bread.

Damien nodded. Ecclesiastes was okay. 'So how are things going, anyway?' He tried to sound enthusiastic, fresh, as though he'd just sat down.

'Pour moi?' Sean raised his eyebrows, which were thick and rather wild, and placed a hand over his heart.

'Yes, for you. On the job. Things going okay?'

Sean inclined his head, but continued to stare at the table. 'You know what Roethke said about seeing,' Sean said.

Damien pressed his palms to his temples and pushed his hands back through his hair. 'No,' he said, 'I don't.'

'"In a dark time, the eye begins to see."'

He's mad, Damien thought. 'And is this a dark time for you?'

Sean shook his head, to signal a change of subject. 'Here's a joke. A senior citizen,' he began, reverting to the American twang, 'was driving down 101 when his cellular phone rang. It was the missus. "Herb!" she said, "Thank Gad I got you! I just heard on the news that there's a car goin' the wrong way on 101. Please, Herb, be careful!" "Hell," Herb said, "it's not just one car. It's hunnerds of 'em."'

Damien forced himself to smile.

'I told that to your mother-in-law,' Sean said.

'You told that to Grace?'

'She laughed.'

Gillian had brought Grace here in the summer, and Grace and Sean had been instant soul mates. She'd planted herself beside him on the wall outside the pub, her two hands folded in her lap as Sean recited to her in its entirety Yeats's 'When You Are Old'. Grace had closed her eyes as she listened; her face was turned up to the sun and a little smile had played on her lips. She'd looked as though she'd heard in the distance some old dancehall tune from when she was a girl.

Sean picked up his teaspoon but seemed to have no use to put it to. It hung in the air as he said thoughtfully, 'She was a lady.'

'She liked you, too.'

Sean nodded. 'And how is your wife since?' he asked.

'She's okay.'

'They were close,' Sean said, meaning Grace and Gillian.

Damien pursed his lips. He wasn't here to discuss that. 'How are *you*?' he said again.

'"Me?"' Sean said, raising his hands and crimping his fingers into inverted commas.

'Yeah, you.'

Sean folded his hands in his lap and gazed once again in the direction of the window. '"A bore is a man who, when you ask him how he is, tells you."'

'So be a bore,' Damien said flatly.

It was not a tone Sean took to. Clearly, he had no intention of responding.

'Sean . . .' Damien said, attempting an attitude of appeasement.

'Mr McGarry . . .' Sean continued to stare straight ahead.

Damien was at a loss. 'Well,' he said, and clapped his hands on his thighs, 'if there's anything you want to talk about, you know where to find me.'

'Sir,' Sean said, by way of goodbye, puffing out his chest.

Mairead didn't seem to be around, and Judith wasn't in her office. The tea room and the shops were closed; the village was on winter hours, which meant nothing opened until one. Damien found Judith in O'Dwyer's, the other pub, with Matt. There was a bag of turf propped against a bar stool and crates of Coke stacked on the floor. Some bingo cards were lying on the bar. Judith and Matt were standing at the far end of the counter. The lower half of Matt's body was hidden, but Judith – and specifically the angle of her arm – was visible.

The wheeze of the door opening had alerted them and their heads were turned in Damien's direction but, like him, they were momentarily frozen with surprise. Though Matt and

Judith were looking him in the eye, and though he was returning their gaze, the attention of all three was concentrated on a single point at which not one of them dared to look: Judith's hand, which had obviously been exploring Matt's groin.

Damien cleared his throat. 'Morning,' he called.

Shifting her gaze to a spot on the floor, Judith retracted the offending hand. Matt slid behind the bar. Damien blushed. Neither of the lovers did.

After several seconds of silence, Damien said to Judith, his tone oddly jaunty, 'I'll talk to you before I head off,' then backed out the door.

He stood outside on the footpath. He was expecting Judith to come straight out after him – to explain – but he soon realized that wasn't going to happen. He could wait for her in the other pub, just across the road. But no, he didn't want to go in there; Sean would still be in there. He looked up and down the street, which was deserted. He felt suddenly ridiculous, unable to enter either of the licensed premises in Kill, wondering where he should wait while his employees finished having it off. Because (it was dawning on him) instead of wondering how best to minimize the embarrassment the scene had caused, Matt and Judith might be finishing what they'd started. His walking in on them had probably heightened their arousal. They were, quite possibly, just over his left shoulder – maybe in the alcove where the recycling bins were kept – rutting like dogs this minute, while he stood outside the door with his arms crossed over his chest like a fucking bouncer. He turned and walked towards the interpretive centre.

Judith's office was open, and he sat down to wait. He was trying to decide what to say to her. He was tempted to say something smart: *So that's what you meant by 'down time'*? He shouldn't be smart, though. Maybe something chummy but serious, and perhaps accompanied by a quick collusive wink, just to show he wasn't prudish or uptight. Something like: *Just be discreet*. Or, *Confine it to non-working hours*. Or maybe, *Remember, you're the figure of authority here . . .*

But everything he thought of sounded exactly like he didn't want to sound: parental, sober, maybe even jealous. And he wasn't jealous, not exactly, though the knowledge was having a disquieting effect on him. It wasn't that he harboured any feelings for Judith but rather that his discovery was making him feel, like so many things these days, deluded. The idea of himself and Judith as lovers, an idea he had sometimes entertained idly while travelling back and forth between Dublin and Kill, had not seemed to him implausible. There were nineteen years between them, a gap that was large, Damien conceded, but not so large as to be comical.

But Matt, who was twenty-seven years younger than Damien, had struck him – despite his hulking frame and the shadow of his beard by day's end – as a boy. The fact, therefore, that Judith was sleeping with him made Judith seem suddenly younger, and Damien, now that he had another man to compare himself to, much older. He thought of Alexa, who, he now recalled, had openly fancied Matt at one stage. This made him feel worse. For while Matt was certainly a suitable object of desire for the sixteen-year-old Alexa, Alexa – whatever the claims her exposed midriff occasionally made upon Damien's mind – was really not an appropriate object of desire for Damien. And it was this relay of lust, in which Damien saw that his would-be lover's lover's would-be lover could not be his lover, that made him feel decidedly redundant.

He crossed his legs and stared at Judith's tea cup (it was rimmed with a pale rose shade of lipstick), then at her coat hanging on the back of the door, the furry collar that probably looked quite fetching when she gathered it to her neck, its soft hairs tickling her skin. Should he have made a play for Judith himself? He was pretty sure she had resorted to Matt only because eight months in Kill had skewed her standards. Kill's isolation, its prevailing atmosphere of unreality and the aphrodisiac taboo of boss–employee sexual relations were the causes of Judith's going native, not anything to do with Matt per se.

But he'd never have made a play for Judith. It would have been foolish for a number of reasons, not least because Judith had been doing a good job and he wouldn't want EI to lose her if things went sour between them. Even if Judith weren't in charge, though, he wouldn't have attempted it. As often as Damien thought about other women, he hated deception. Maybe it was the moral high ground, or else the belief that if he crossed that line himself his marriage would be effectively over – not because Gillian would find out, but because it would be an admission on his part that he no longer saw her own betrayal as an aberration. The idea of their entering into some tacit arrangement in which they tolerated one another's infidelities depressed him intensely.

But Judith. He looked at his watch. She was taking her time, anyway. Maybe she wasn't coming straight back to the office. Why did he assume she was? But surely she knew he wanted to talk about Sean before he left. What the fuck was she doing? And how long, he suddenly wondered, had she been doing it? There she was telling him there were no men around when in fact she was itching for him to leave her office so she could get over to the pub for the twelve o'clock quickie. It wasn't acceptable, this sort of carry-on. He'd have to say something. Maybe Jimmy would know what he should say. They had talked about Judith last week – they'd agreed she was probably feeling a bit isolated down in Kill in the dead of winter – and Damien had known what Jimmy was thinking, or thought he had. Jimmy was thinking how easy it would be for Damien to sleep with Judith (if she were willing) under cover of trouble-shooting at the village. Jimmy was thinking of Judith all alone down in Kill, twenty-nine-year-old Judith, with her long black hair and her exceptional breasts and her isolation. And Damien had known that if he said nothing, and said it in a particular way, Jimmy's suspicions would only grow.

But now Judith was fucking Matt. And that wasn't the worst of it. The worst of it was that while Damien had believed that Jimmy was half-suspecting him of sleeping with Judith on his jaunts to Kill, Jimmy might actually have been wondering how to puncture his illusions before he made a fool of himself.

What was it Sean had said? *Vanity of vanities* . . . something something something.

Fourteen

Instead of working on their project to do with the problem of Internet grooming, the four of them were just wasting time, talking about how, years ago, before Heather was born, her father was supposed to go to Belfast with this guy he worked with but then decided to take his own car. The guy had had a fatal accident on the way.

'He rolled the car. It was like this.' Heather pressed her palms together.

'Wow,' Miriam said.

'I don't believe in fate,' Heather said. 'My father was just totally lucky.'

'I believe in fate,' Miriam said.

Heather could feel Cormac looking at her. He looked at her a lot. 'I saw your father on the nine o'clock news,' he said.

Miriam turned to her. 'When was he on the news?'

'A few weeks ago.'

'What did he do?' Roger asked, gazing dopily at the sea of triangles he had doodled in his notebook.

'He won an award,' Cormac said, in a way that made Heather feel proud.

'For work,' Heather added. 'For this village he designed.'

'Oh,' Miriam said.

'Yeah,' Cormac said. 'We went to Kill during the summer. When my brother was over from New York with his family.'

There was a silence. Then Miriam said, 'How . . . did . . . you . . . like . . . it, Cormac?'

Miriam thought Cormac was dull, but she was encouraging Heather to encourage him.

'You never know,' she'd said.

'You never know what?'

'He likes you,' she'd said impatiently.

Heather hadn't told Miriam about being in love with Emile. It wasn't just that Miriam might mention it to him, then get angry with Heather for getting angry with her, saying something like, *That's what's wrong with you – you think he can read your mind. That's why you've never got off with him.* It was also the way being in love made Heather feel, like she'd joined a special society, and it was obvious that people who weren't in the society didn't understand because they said things like *getting off with him*, which wasn't at all how Heather thought about Emile.

Cormac was talking, he was talking and looking at Heather. '. . . my brother, too,' he was saying again. 'We'd a great time. We played bingo with these Americans. It was totally hilarious.'

Heather smiled. God, she thought, he is so dull.

'Oh-*kay*,' Miriam said, opening her folder. 'Enough excitement for one day. So the first part is we have to say what Internet grooming *is*.'

'It's when you comb your hair while you're on-line,' Roger mumbled.

'Exactement, mon ami!' Miriam was doing French, and she was always throwing French words around.

'C'mon,' Cormac said, 'we have to take this seriously. It is so fucked, what happens. My brother works with this guy whose nine-year-old daughter was groomed by this fifty-seven-year-old pervert who was *married*. He came to her school to pick her up . . .'

Everyone in the group was looking at him.

'So what happened?' Heather asked.

'The police got him. But the girl was going to go with him because he'd told her he was like her long-lost uncle and they were going to surprise her parents.'

Miriam was staring at him. 'That seems not very smart of the girl.'

Cormac looked at her, a look of offended disbelief. 'She was nine, Miriam. Didn't anyone ever ask you to keep a secret when you were a kid, so they could surprise someone?'

'I'm just saying,' Miriam said.

Roger, who never looked anyone in the eye, lolled his head to one side and said, 'We could use it as, um, what do you call those things that are like an example but they're real . . .'

'Case studies,' Heather said.

This time Miriam didn't say, *Exactement!* She just jiggled her foot and chewed on the end of her pen.

Cormac said, 'Yeah, a case study, that's a good idea. So we could figure out how we could've helped the girl at the very beginning when the contact started.'

'Or help her know she shouldn't go with anyone unless she checks with her mum,' Heather said. She felt bad for thinking he was dull a minute ago. He wasn't dull; he was sensible. He watched the news and he cared about little children and he stood up to Miriam, which hardly any guys did because Miriam was pretty and had big breasts. When Cormac looked up from his notebook, he caught Heather watching him. She blinked and slid her eyes to the left, but she could feel Cormac still looking at her.

Cormac, she had decided last week, was going to be the one. He didn't make her feel like Emile did – in fact, there were moments when talking to Cormac made her miss Emile more than ever – but she was trying to approach this rationally. And the conclusion she was coming to was that maybe it was just too much to ask, falling in love with and losing your virginity to the same person. In fact, statistically, it was probably quite rare. So maybe the next best thing was losing it to someone who cared about children and kept up on current events. Cormac seemed grown-up, and that was important. Because Heather was not an experienced girl. The sum total of her sexual activity had been three snogging sessions, one of which had involved hands groping around her bum and her breasts. She had got just about zero enjoyment out of those sessions.

It wasn't that she'd never felt sexual pleasure. She'd felt it while sitting in the whirlpool at the health club her family had joined last year and while looking at the photo of the two guys shagging under the waterfall and in chemistry class leaning into a lab table, the corner of which hit her directly between the legs. But two of the three situations had arisen in public and so did not lend themselves to further exploration. And she had yet to make the connection between looking at a photo and self-administering arousal. She knew that men did it – wanking was what all those magazines were for – but she wasn't sure if women did it too, or what was supposed to happen if they did.

'I should write our ideas down too,' she said, leaning over to look at Cormac's notebook. As he pushed the notebook to the right so she could copy it, she felt the static electricity from his arm, the little hairs on it reaching out to communicate with the little hairs on her arm.

Fifteen

'Hallmark offers greeting cards for a hundred and five familial relationships. One hundred and five!' Elspeth said. 'This is true.'

People shook their heads; a few looked worried, wondering if there were some 'familial relationships' they'd rather not know about.

'Buy blank,' she said.

There was chuckling.

Elspeth was pacing back and forth in a slow flattish arc in front of the group, like a caged animal looking out at those who looked in at it.

'You're standing in front of a rack of toothbrushes in Tesco – size, shape, curvature of handle, angle of head, colour, bristle and, of course, price. And you're asking yourself if your teeth are worth five-eighty-nine, or is Colgate playing on your fears?'

She turned on her heel.

'Maybe the no-frills straightback at two-sixty-five would be just as effective. Those optional extras are only gimmicks and you're not going to fall for that. This isn't rocket science. But is dental care really where you want to skimp? What's three euros when the alternative is toothlessness and ulcerated gums? Okay, get the Oral-B Navigator and be done with it. The red Navigator? No, the one you're replacing is red, and you like to alternate. There's a nice teal. You reach for that.'

Elspeth's hand stalled mid-reach. Her face darkened.

'Oh. They only have the teal in soft and hard and you need

medium. They've got the medium in yellow. Yellow's okay. It's rather cheerful, for those dark winter mornings. But look! There's the teal in the Aquafresh TripleAction Medium, and with a nice racing stripe up the front. But the Aquafresh doesn't have the up-and-down bristles, like the Manhattan skyline, which was the very thing that had sold you on the Oral-B, imagining how well those taller bristles could sneak into the in-between places . . .

'And around and around you go, staring at the options until you notice that something's happened to your decision-making faculty. The choice itself has degenerated into non-sense, like a word does when repeated over and over again. You pick a toothbrush, but now the choice is made in exasperation. Where is your intuition at this point?'

No one said anything. They thought it was a rhetorical question. Maybe it was. Elspeth didn't seem eager to cede the floor.

The toothbrush spiel was new. Gillian hadn't heard it before. (She didn't often sit in on Elspeth's workshops, but since coming back from France she'd been trying to immerse herself in all aspects of the Farm, in the hope of rekindling her enthusiasm.) It wasn't bad, Elspeth was getting her point across, but she was doing it in a fairly dizzying manner. Maybe that was the point. Marrying form and content. Was that terribly clever, or did it simply intensify what they were trying to help alleviate? Elspeth's style had changed, too. She was no longer acting as facilitator of a forum for the open exchange of ideas. She was less Socratic now, more like a motivational speaker.

'How about this for an idea?' Elspeth said. '*Ask your dentist*. Then just buy it. And waste no more time dithering over toothbrushes. One of the keys to making good decisions is to make only those decisions that count.'

Gillian looked at Katherine, who caught her eye and smiled. Katherine had arrived on Sunday. Gillian hadn't even twigged her name on the list, probably because she'd forgotten her surname, thinking of her only as Katherine from Menton, one of a number of people she kept meaning to e-mail.

Katherine had greeted her with a warm, delicate hug and said: 'I was curious when I read about it, and even more curious after I'd met you.'

Gillian's relief at seeing Katherine had surprised her, making her realize just how excluded she'd been feeling at the Farm, how sidelined by Elspeth, who had, over the past year, assumed a proprietorial air over the place. She felt the urge to guard her new friend jealously, as though Elspeth might steal her, charm her, dazzle her, the way she did everyone.

She and Katherine had sat next to each other at dinner Sunday night, but hadn't got a chance afterwards for a proper, private chat. On the second night, when the guests went their separate ways after dinner, the two of them sat up in the kitchen, drinking peppermint tea. Gillian found herself talking about Grace's illness.

'I thought you said she died of a stroke.'

Gillian sipped her tea. 'It was, in the end. But she had Alzheimer's.'

'Aah.' Katherine nodded. 'And that's why you were worried.'

'Worried about what?' Gillian looked up.

'About . . . well, when we first met, you said you felt foggy, like you had cotton wool in your head. When my husband died, I felt the same. For months. I couldn't remember things.'

'Did I say I was worried, though?' Gillian didn't recall having said that.

'Not in so many words. It was the impression I got. But I'm sorry. I might've picked you up wrong.'

Gillian swirled her tea gently around her cup. 'I read this thing recently,' she said, 'about how if you read a lot of stuff on-line, it can make you remember less.'

'Really?'

'Yeah, because remembering something depends a lot on context. But if the context is the same for a lot of the information you're taking in, meaning your computer screen, then you're less likely to remember it.'

'Interesting.'

'So is it the world or is it us?'

Katherine's eyes narrowed. 'What do you mean?'

'I *am* worried,' Gillian said, staring into her cup. 'But maybe I shouldn't be. Maybe it's normal, feeling slow.'

'Grief, depression, memory trouble. They're all linked. Stress, too. Stress is no good for the brain,' Katherine said. 'As for Alzheimer's . . .' She rolled her eyes. 'Big hereditary factor. My mother had it, and one of my grandmothers had it. My mother used to look at me when I was over having dinner with her – during a lull in the conversation, what I thought had been a pretty coherent conversation – she'd look at me and put her hand on my arm like this, just like she was going to say, *Could you pass the salt?*, but instead she'd say, *Would you mind telling me who you are?* I never got used to that. It was like being erased over and over and over again.'

Gillian sighed. 'I know the feeling.'

'I'm sure you do.'

'I remember one day I went to Grace's house to gather her things after she'd moved in with us, and I found these notes stashed in kitchen drawers, in the bedside locker, in the desk in the study. They said things like *Check oven is off before bed* and *Water garden every day.*'

Katherine winced. 'So she knew what was happening?'

'She was going to manage it with Post-Its, I guess.'

They stared at the table and considered this. Katherine picked up the tea pot, and while refilling Gillian's cup said, 'I'm on medication.'

'Oh?' Gillian remembered the purple capsule. 'What kind of medication?'

'Well, they can't come right out and say it – not yet, anyway – but what everybody hopes is that it's an Alzheimer's preventative. All they can say now is that it's been shown to help people with Mild Cognitive Impairment, which means maybe, down the road, those same people don't get Alzheimer's. Technically, I shouldn't be on it. But my doctor knows I've got Alzheimer's in the family, so I'm at risk. I told him how I was feeling . . .' Katherine tapped her head. 'I took the tests. I have a bit of what they call Age-Associated Memory Impairment. He prescribed it as a possible preventative. It's legal, it's just off-label.'

'And does it work?' Gillian asked.

Katherine sat up. 'I definitely feel sharper,' she said, her eyes going wide.

Gillian leaned back in her chair and ran her finger slowly round the rim of her cup. 'What do you mean sharper?' she asked.

'Well, I often think of it like this, that it feels like the difference between having a hangover and not having a hangover. I feel like I remember feeling when I was younger. Not so fatigued or fuzzy any more.'

'But do you remember things you couldn't before?'

'For instance,' Katherine said, 'you know when you go to a movie and a week later you can hardly remember anything about it?'

'A week? How about the next day!'

'Well, I remember the movie. It's like being able to fill in the blanks. They don't even feel like blanks any more.'

Gillian was looking at her new friend intently.

'At work, I don't have to reread stuff I read the day before. Even if I did read it on-line . . .'

Gillian managed a smile.

'I remember appointments without having to check my calendar incessantly. I remember people's birthdays! And their kids' names and whether their mother or father has already died –'

'Oh!' Gillian put a hand to her mouth. 'Do you do that, too?'

'You say, "So how's your mother doing?" and they look at you –'

'And say, "My mother died two years ago."'

'"Don't you remember the card you sent?"' Katherine shook her head and smiled wryly.

'You know,' Gillian confided, 'the latest thing for me is sometimes when I'm watching telly and the ads come on, and I'm sort of zoning out and suddenly I realize that I can't remember what it is I'm watching. I try to remember and I just draw a blank, and I have to wait for the programme to start again.'

Gillian chuckled, but Katherine didn't join her. Instead she said, 'That's a little worrying.'

'You think that's worrying?'

'Oh, I don't know.' Katherine waved her hand dismissively. 'It could mean anything. Being very preoccupied. Or like you said, you've been exhausted.'

Gillian looked around, as though trying to locate the source of her exhaustion. Turning back to Katherine, she said, 'This drug, does it have side effects?'

'Diaxadril? A few. A little tummy discomfort sometimes – crampy, you know. And sometimes a slight . . . warmth . . .'

'In your head?'

Katherine laughed. 'In my body. It's hard to describe. Ever been on antidepressants?'

Gillian shook her head.

'Well, it's not so different. A little shaky, a little sweaty. Nothing major. Just like you've had too much caffeine. Except antidepressants mute you. Diaxadril wakes you up.'

Gillian didn't think being sweatily, shakily alert sounded pleasant at all. And yet Katherine didn't look shaky or sweaty. 'What about in your head? Does it feel . . . busy?'

Katherine thought for a moment. 'It's like those first hours of the morning – you know the best ones for work –'

'Fewer as I get older,' Gillian laughed.

'– well, it's like that time of day all day long.'

'That sounds a bit tiring.'

'Only because we've got used to feeling sluggish. We've forgotten what it's like to have mental energy. Listen,' she said, 'ten years from now, we'll think back on this conversation and laugh.'

'What do you mean?'

'I mean Diax will be tame in comparison to what'll be out there. It'll go mainstream even before that, though, as soon as enough time passes without anybody going postal on it or dying of blood clots. Because everybody wants to be sharper. Diax will reach the tipping point and *bang*, suddenly half the people you know are on it, and the other half have been on it or are about to go on it, and you won't know when you're talking to someone whether they're on it or not. But the chances will be pretty good. Like Prozac in the nineties.'

'You think so?'

Katherine shrugged and opened her eyes wide, almost playfully. 'Maybe.'

'Do you ever . . .' Gillian held her teaspoon like a pen and ran it along a shallow groove in the wooden table top. 'Do you ever remember things from way back?'

'Way back . . . when?'

'Like, things you'd totally forgotten?'

'What?' Katherine said, drawing back. 'You mean like repressed memories?'

'No! I just mean, you know, normal things, just childhood things or . . . I don't know . . .'

'Oh.' Katherine's expression was sad. 'I know what you mean,' she said, 'and, no, I haven't. I don't think it works that way.'

'Yeah, I just thought . . .'

'I know.'

Gillian shook her head, casting out the idea.

Sixteen

The rumour was that Sean had holed up in Brittas Bay, in the summer home of his American lover, and was writing a memoir of his brief career at Kill. He had walked out of the job just before they'd closed the village for the Christmas holidays. Damien believed the rumour. In the Weekend section of this morning's *Irish Times*, there was a half-page feature under the headline:

From Tin Whistler to Whistle-Blower

The whistler-blower was Sean, though whistle-blower was a bit strong in this case (and Sean had never been a tin whistler). The journalist, Gerry Murphy, was profoundly disturbed by Kill. He claimed that the village was emblematic of EI's drive to commercialize every element of Irishness, 'including the poor sheep, who are herded up and down the street at intervals for no other purpose than to beguile city-dwelling tourists with romantic notions of rural life'. He said that old people were propped up around the village 'like garden gnomes'. He called Kill the equivalent of a minstrel show. 'The reduction of Irish to a game of bingo is an insult to those who have fought to keep our language from dying.' He quoted a lecturer at Maynooth University named Tully who said that while his children had enjoyed Kill, he had felt 'ashamed'. And he quoted Sean extensively.

Damien passed the paper to Gillian. 'Journalists,' he said,

'are people who spend their days pretending to be passionately alarmed about situations that are basically harmless, while mostly ignoring what is genuinely dangerous.'

She frowned and took another bite of toast. 'Who said that?'

'I just did.'

He watched her as she read, trying to detect something – outrage, incredulity, derision (directed at Gerry Murphy, not at him); he needed her to help him laugh it off.

When she was finished, she didn't look up straight away.

'It's a bit over the top,' he offered, to get her started.

'Well . . .' she said, '. . . he makes some, you know, interesting points.'

'Like what?'

'Like . . . for instance . . .' She scanned the paper. She sipped her coffee. 'For instance this business of not being allowed to talk about anything contentious. That's interesting. How we try to comfort visitors by offering a certain, what's the word he uses, *neutered*, neutered version of ourselves . . .' She trailed off, staring hard at the paper again.

'What else?'

'Or like this bit.' She ran her finger down the page. 'Where is it? This bit about the bingo game.'

'Jaysus.' He shook his head. 'That is so precious, that attitude. Like we can't have fun with the language, like it has to remain connected in our minds with misery –'

'You know that's not what he's saying.' Gillian folded the paper and put it aside. 'He's just pointing out that there are wider issues involved.'

'I realize that.'

'Well, to me, I'm sorry, that's interesting.'

'Is that what you always thought?' he asked. 'Or are you jumping on the bandwagon?'

'It's hardly a bandwagon.'

'You didn't answer my question.'

She sighed and tipped her head away from him, scratching the now elongated side of her neck, which did not, he was sure, itch. 'Okay,' she said, 'what is your question?'

She was brittle lately, distracted. *She's gone*, she'd said the other day, with a puzzled matter-of-factness, as though she'd only just discovered Grace was missing.

Damien stared into his coffee cup. What was his question? He pointed to the paper and tried to sound unconcerned. 'Do you think he's right?'

'I was only there once,' she said.

'And you enjoyed it.'

'I'm not saying it wasn't enjoyable.'

'But what? You felt "ashamed"?' He wasn't serious. He was making the accusation so that she could refute it out of hand and reassure them both of its absurdity. But she didn't refute it. She scratched her neck again.

He sat forward. He was almost laughing. 'Did you?'

'No-oh,' she said. Like he was bullying her. 'I felt . . . ambiguous.'

Heather had announced her vegetarianism the previous week, inspired both by the New Year and by a programme she'd seen about intensive farming, rows of pigs in cages where they couldn't even turn around.

Now Damien was watching her load her plate with mashed potatoes. Three, four, five scoops. Mashed potatoes and nothing else.

'Take some beans,' he said.

'I don't like beans.'

'Take them anyway.'

Gillian looked down at her own plate. Heather took five beans, extracting them one by one from the dish.

Damien sighed with irritation, then took another bite of lamb. 'This is good,' he said to Gillian.

Gillian kept chewing and said 'Uhm,' by way of agreement.

He turned to Heather. 'Lambs get to run around.'

'Don't,' Gillian said, with the slightest shake of her head.

He caught her eye. When she looked down again, his gaze moved to her ear, then her neck, where it sloped into her shoulder. He wanted to touch the back of his hand to the side of her breast, he could see the shape of it, just; she was wearing a V-necked shirt of some synthetic but flattering material. It wasn't tight, but it clasped her at the sides. It clung, casually, as though having blown up against her in a breeze.

To his left, Heather said, '*Yeah-ah*. Then they get their throats slit.'

Gillian put down her fork.

'This is a discussion we should have later,' he said to Heather.

'Why not now?' Heather asked.

'Not while you're wearing leather shoes.'

Gillian bowed her head and smiled.

Heather pressed another square of butter into her diminishing mountain of mashed potatoes and didn't look at him. 'What does it mean a parody?' she asked, wrinkling her nose. 'Exactly.'

That was Sean's word. This was Heather's revenge. She'd read the *Irish Times* piece, too.

From the time I started at Kill, I felt odd. I'd been hired to play myself. I was told, in so many words, to exaggerate certain aspects of my personality. I knew about EI's visitor survey list, the one we used as a guideline. And yes, it made me uncomfortable. Did I feel like a parody at times? Absolutely.

'A parody is making fun of something,' Damien said.

'What's anecdote provision?' Heather asked. She was doing this thing with her neck now, like a chicken. He wasn't sure she even knew she was doing it. Her body was like that these days, full of absentminded pointless movements, as though controlled by a capricious puppeteer. He wondered should he worry, was it some kind of disorder shaping up? But more likely it was the age, hormonal restlessness, a self-consciousness that resulted, paradoxically, in behaviour that called attention to itself. With the hand that wasn't holding the fork, she pulled on a piece of her neck as she stretched and retracted it.

'Anecdote provision' was another accusation of Sean's, taken utterly out of context. Damien had said, he remembered clearly – *Anecdote provision, that's our business* – but Sean had known he was being facetious.

'It means,' he said, helping himself to more lamb, 'doing funny things so people can tell stories about it later.'

Heather slid him a look. She was not going to persist with her revenge.

His mother had rung him that morning. She had wanted to know if he'd done something wrong.

'Recently?' he'd said. 'Or ever?'

It became a bandwagon. The first sign that the trouble with Kill had entered the collective consciousness came in the form of a sixty-second radio slot. He and Gillian were lying in bed reading the papers and waiting for the midnight headlines when one of those plaintive and sermonizing voices sounded that could only mean *The Way We Live*, the nightly feature in which an ordinary citizen talked about his life-changing moment in the Congo or urged you to pay attention to small birds when they landed on your windowsill.

Tonight, *The Way We Live* was about Kill. Damien looked up from his paper and stared at the far wall as the speaker described how disturbed she'd been, when visiting the village, to see the elderly 'being made use of like this'.

He brought his hands to his face and moaned as the woman continued.

'Ireland is the success story of the European Union. We have much to be proud of. But do we need to take the older members of our society, those who depend on us for care and love, and put them at the service of the tourist industry? Traditionally, visitors to our country have been able to enjoy the wisdom and humour and gentleness that these people possess, because we Irish have always taken a genuine pleasure in interacting with foreigners. The great Irish writer Sean O'Faolain said, "The art of living in Ireland is the art of conversation." But what will become of the pleasure of conversation, now that it has a price tag attached? Shouldn't we say: *Stop!* Before it's too late?'

'Stop!' Damien said. 'Stop . . .' The music that wasn't quite music came on, signalling the news headlines. He switched off the radio.

Gillian turned her head on the pillow to look at him. 'One of the guests at the Farm asked me how I felt about the scandal.'

'The *scandal*? Is it a scandal now?'

'That was her word. And if it's any consolation, I think she was being sarcastic. She thought the piece in the *Irish Times* was rather funny.'

'So she didn't consider it scandalous?

'Not at all. She was from New York. She said, "What's all the fuss? It's a job. You put on your uniform, you go to work, you come home, you take off your uniform." She couldn't understand.'

'Good for her,' Damien said.

'I figured you'd like that.'

'Hey,' he said, staring at the sheets, 'I thought you didn't read papers at the Farm.'

'I read about you,' she said, in a tone impossible to interpret.

The next time Kill made the news, it was as the topic of Maurice Keegan's weekly *Irish Times* column, headlined 'The New Ghettos'. Keegan, after musing on the criteria EI had employed in selecting Kill – low degree of technological saturation and third-level education, ageing population – wondered if perhaps EI viewed those in the heritage-designated areas as the 21st-century version of 'defectives': 'the kind we used to hide away in institutions, but have now discovered we can market.'

Keegan suggested EI's plans weren't ambitious enough. 'Why not zone the entire island of Ireland (with the consent of those in the six counties) "The Past"?' he asked. 'As the country is small, and as the network of motorways continues to spread in all directions, it could become the world's first drive-through country, saving both tourists and locals a lot of work.' The government, Keegan argued, could assist in this process of 'past-urization' by outlawing mobile phones, conspicuous consumption and battery-operated milk frothers, and by taxing Gore-Tex and Polartec while subsidizing wool and tweed. It could initiate forced relocation to the countryside. 'With foresight and dedication,' Keegan wrote, 'we in Ireland could achieve a level of backwardness of which we could be truly proud.'

He closed by saying, 'McGarry is married to Gillian Harmon of Moilligh Farm, known for her championing of *stable temporal reference points*, pockets of time in which we are meant to turn our backs on change. One wonders if McGarry has taken too many leaves from his wife's book.'

Damien phoned the Farm from his office that afternoon. Elspeth answered.

'I saw it,' she said.

'You seem to do nothing up there but read the papers.'

'I know. And they're so much more fun to read when you have to hide them.'

'I can imagine,' he said. 'Sorry your name got dragged through the mud.'

'Gillian's name.'

'You're supposed to say it wasn't the mud.'

'Fuck them,' she said. 'It'll blow over.'

'I suppose it will.'

'Of course it will,' she said. Then, her voice conspiratory, 'Is it true you encourage smoking at Kill?'

'*What?*'

'So it's more like the fifties?'

'Jes*us*. Of course not. Anyway, what do you mean more like the fifties? Lots of people still smoke, sweetheart.' It was true they had applied for an exemption to the workplace smoking ban, based on the fact that the village was a 'historical zone'. And it was true they supplied empty boxes of Woodbines for employees to put their Silk Cuts in. But they had never encouraged anyone to take up smoking. 'Where did you hear that?'

'I don't even remember,' Elspeth said. 'Forget it.'

*

Damien was delighted, the following Monday, to see a letter to the editor vehemently disagreeing with 'The New Ghettos'.

'As a "defective",' the man had written, 'I live in constant terror of being given a job where I will be required to perform the odious and demeaning task of sitting around all day chatting amiably to holidaymakers, and I can only pray for the return of back-breaking manual labour, the deadening repetition of the assembly line, and the all-night nixer of taxiing young vomiting drunks from one nightclub to another . . .'

Damien smiled and laid the paper on his desk.

Just before lunch, he received a call from the producer of *Ireland Tonight*, a live weekly television programme in which a panel of guests was arranged to disagree about a particular topic. Next week, the panel would be discussing EI's current strategies for tourism development in Ireland, a subject made topical by the recent media attention on Kill and the fact that a former employee of EI's was now writing an account of working in the village. (Sean's rumoured memoir was now an established fact; his book deal had lately been noted in the *Irish Times* books pages.) To Damien's relief, Sean was not going to be on the panel. It seemed he was in America.

'I believe he's got a friend there,' the producer said.

'I believe you're right.' Damien was sitting at his desk, tapping the rubber end of a pencil on his desktop. Through the glass wall of his office, he could view the more public terrain of the third floor: a labyrinth of chest-high panels, covered in what looked like industrial carpet and notched into each other in rearrangeable configurations. At the far end of the room, an accordion-style screen was rising, disappearing into a cleft in the ceiling, revealing an alcove where four people were just finishing a meeting. It was as though their bed sheets had been yanked off. Damien looked away. Whatever happened to walls? Why this desire in corporate culture to ape the minimalism of noodle bars? Bring back wooden panelling. Upper management needed to hide sometimes, and drawing the venetian blinds was not the same.

'So who's going to be on?'

'Chris Tully from Maynooth, Breege Hanlon from the *Irish Times*, and Tommy Geraghty, the Roscommon TD. And you, we hope.'

'E-mail me the details,' he said.

When he'd hung up, Damien turned his full attention to the pencil he was still bouncing, enjoying the slight *boing* of the pinkish nub on the hardwood and thinking, not for the first time, of the fact that it wasn't easy to get pencils with rubbers any more.

Three people near the far window were rearranging a section of panelled cubicles, their movements hasty and purposeful, as though they were effecting a scene change. The staff were free to rearrange the panels in order to facilitate temporary working arrangements, but Damien suspected they also did it to signal severed or newly forged alliances. Office policy did not allow anyone to change the position of cubicles other than his or her own, but changes could, nevertheless, leave 'innocent' desks in radically altered surroundings. Damien suspected the policy was meant to give staff members an illusion of agency and to keep office life feeling fluid and creative, but it seemed to him that the changes were merely disorienting, like the rearrangement of foodstuffs in the supermarket. Gillian was right. Unnecessary reorganization was upsetting. He felt no need for it. He'd had the same dozen knick-knacks and photos in his office since he'd moved into it eight years ago.

He looked down at his legs. They were parallel to his desk,

the right one draped nonchalantly over the left. He liked the look of his legs in this particular position, and today they were especially reassuring as he was wearing a new charcoal-grey pair of Hugo Boss trousers. The mirror was a different story. He didn't care for what he saw in the mirror. The past year or so had brought unpleasant changes. A dryness had crept into his complexion. Slight hollows had formed under his eyes. His hairline was undeniably in retreat. And just lately, his lips seemed to have thinned and four evenly spaced and fairly definite lines had appeared, descending from just beneath his lower lip.

He held the pencil like a baton, then a chopstick (recalling, wistfully, Glorianna's hairdo; he hadn't called in to her in ages), then drummed it quickly against his thigh. There really wasn't any way out of appearing on *Ireland Tonight*; even if there were, he didn't think he'd take it. The only reason he was having to defend this project was because it had proved so successful. Kill had made a lot of people happy, and that was nothing to be ashamed of. The only person capable of causing him to feel shame, it seemed, was Gillian, whose lack of blind faith in him he was unable to forgive, and whose approval, after all this time, meant more to him than anyone's.

Otherwise, his detractors could go, as Elspeth suggested, fuck themselves. The self-appointed guardians of the nation's soul quibbling over what was 'real', what was 'Ireland', holding to the notion of ideal holidaymakers who settled down in the evenings with tomes on the Famine or the 'Northern question'. What the guardians didn't want to admit was that real tourists had neither the time nor the inclination to keep straight the Collinses and O'Connells and Connollys, the GAA, IRB, IRA, UVF, UDA, RIC, RUC and the GPO, or to remember things they couldn't even pronounce (*Cumann na nGaedheal?*). Instead of worrying about the details being fudged, they should be happy such people remembered to drop by at all when they could be snowboarding or petting elephants or just sitting around some place where the sun was shining and beer cost fifty cents. No, he wouldn't have skipped the *Ireland Tonight* appearance. He was almost looking forward to it.

Seventeen

Heather's parents didn't know Cormac was coming over. Her mother was at the Farm till tomorrow night, and her father had gone to the TV studio for his *Ireland Tonight* appearance. He wouldn't be home before eleven. That gave Heather three hours with Cormac, which should be more than enough time. She hadn't told her parents about Cormac because they would have asked a million questions, had a big discussion about it, then probably said, *We don't know this boy. Why don't you invite him over tomorrow, for dinner, and we can meet him?* An official presentation ceremony was exactly what Heather didn't want. Cormac would think she was trying to get some big relationship thing going, and he would get either very serious or very freaked out.

Then her parents would have asked what happened to Emile, a question she didn't want to answer. Even if she knew the answer, which she didn't.

When Cormac arrived, Heather showed him the house and they spent a few minutes messing with Barney, scratching his big wide belly, until Barney righted himself and strode off as though he'd suddenly remembered he had somewhere else to be. Then Heather took Cormac into the kitchen and they sat at the table drinking Red Bull and she told him that Barney had been Aunt Grace's cat but that Aunt Grace had died of Alzheimer's.

Cormac nodded, like he knew all about Alzheimer's.

Heather felt as though he was waiting for her to elaborate,

so she said the most interesting thing she could think of just then, which was, 'Once she flunked her therapy class.'

'Flunked therapy?'

Heather nodded. 'Therapy to help her remember things. She couldn't keep up with the group, so they moved her down to the next one, where people forgot more things.'

Cormac frowned. 'That must've been . . . sad,' he said.

'Yeah.' Heather sighed, feeling sad herself now. Thinking about Grace was making her think about Emile because Emile had known Grace, whereas Cormac never had, and back when Grace was alive, Heather had still believed that Emile might actually love her. She missed Grace and she missed Emile and she missed the days before she'd settled for Cormac.

Maybe Cormac could tell she was getting sad, because he changed the subject. He told her about the trip his family had taken last summer to Bilbao and how it had made him think he wanted to be an architect. Heather said she thought she might like to be a journalist.

'What kind of a journalist?' he asked.

Heather hadn't actually given a huge amount of consideration to the journalist thing. She bit her lip. Her arms were crossed like an X in front of her, and she noticed that her posture was very slumped; she was practically folded in half. She thought they should go into the sitting room because it didn't seem like anything was going to happen in the kitchen. She straightened herself and said, 'Like one who goes to foreign countries and reports on what's going on there. I think it'd be cool to interview normal people, like about their lives, instead of just politicians or whatever.'

'Like places where there are wars?'

'Yeah,' she said. 'Maybe. Sometimes where there are wars. Not all the time, though.'

'That would be cool,' Cormac said.

Then they both looked around the kitchen until Heather said, 'Wanna watch some TV?'

They went into the sitting room. She picked up the remote and aimed it at the box and when she turned around Cormac was sitting on the sofa. She sat down next to him. Cormac was sort of big – heavier than Emile – so when she sat next to him, the slope his weight caused in the sofa made her slide a bit closer to him.

He picked up the *RTE Guide* and their heads were touching while they pretended to read the listings. Cormac's thigh was pressed against hers, and Heather was feeling the way she felt when she looked at the photo of the two guys under the waterfall. It was a kind of nervous impatience, but for what, exactly, she still wasn't sure.

Now Cormac's hand was on her thigh underneath the *RTE Guide* – gently squeezing in a way that felt nice – and his breathing was a bit heavy and his head kept twitching in her direction, like he had some kind of problem, but then he turned his head, and then his whole body. His shoulder was pressing into hers and his right hand had replaced his left on her thigh and just like that they were kissing.

It was bizarre. Heather had thought she'd have to suggest something, or explain to him why he was here, but no, all she'd had to do was sit beside him and next thing she knew, they were kissing, exactly as she had planned. The only explanation was that Cormac had planned it too. Heather wasn't sure how to feel about that. On the one hand, it was convenient – it saved her having to suggest it; it saved her the embarrassment of Cormac having to say he liked her but he didn't *like her* like her – and it made her more interested in him because it meant he was cleverer than she'd given him credit for being.

On the other hand, it meant that Heather hadn't been as crafty or as mysterious as she'd thought. Cormac had known what she was thinking, he knew things he'd never been told, things he had no business knowing. She was tempted to push him away, just to teach him a lesson – who was *he* to have a plan? – but that would be stupid, she'd never get to enact *her* plan then, and anyway, she was liking the feel of the soft-rough tip of his tongue on her tongue and the way his hand was moving up her thigh and wedging itself gently between her legs.

They stopped kissing for a moment and she emitted a gargley sigh. There was a moment of embarrassment and she wondered should she sigh again, as a corrective, more smoothly this time, but Cormac hadn't seemed to notice. He was too busy lowering the zip on her jeans. He tucked his finger inside the top of her knickers and started moving it like a pendulum, back and forth across her skin. Heather had closed her eyes, but she was watching it all on some kind of inner screen like it was a programme on telly, wondering what was going to happen next. Was Cormac going to slide his hand all the way inside her knickers and if he did, what would she do? That was the funny thing about this programme: even though she was in it, she had no idea what she would do next, and in fact was quite surprised when she found her hand going in search of his thing. She'd never done that before. Once a boy had put her hand there, on top of his trousers, but she'd moved it away and he hadn't put it there again. Cormac was wriggling his arse so he could lower his jeans a bit and that was when his thing appeared out the vent of his boxers. When she touched it, he made a sound like a tiny hiccup. She almost did, too; it felt strange, the top as smooth as a light bulb and the other bit covered with loose skin like an old person would have. What was it like, she wondered briefly, to have this thing between your legs all your life? This thing that was like nothing on your body, that was like it came from somewhere else, from an animal, maybe, and was always going from pulpy to hard to pulpy again?

He slid his hand between her knickers and her jeans and started moving his fingers in circles against her. So now she was touching him but he wasn't touching her, not directly. That didn't seem right. Weren't their activities supposed to match? Where they touched each other and which clothes they took off or left on? But just as she was puzzling over this discrepancy, a funny thing started happening, a thing that felt like she had a lava lamp in her belly. She decided to move her hand to his shoulder, not because of the discrepancy issue (which she'd completely forgotten about), but because the business in her belly was commanding all of her attention and she was afraid of mishandling his thing.

She went rigid, which seemed the wisest course of action under the circumstances. Otherwise, with all that was going on, her body would start doing odd things, undulating, bucking, writhing. She'd look like a complete nutter. Cormac would wonder what her problem was. So she went rigid, like she did at the dentist's when she was waiting for the first whirr of the drill on her tooth.

A kind of itchy heat had developed between her legs. This, Heather liked. It made her want to rub up against his thing, which she suddenly was dying to touch again, to squeeze, to wrap her hand tightly around it, his *dick*! Cormac's! Not just anyone's, for in that moment, she wanted to cling to Cormac in the oddest way, to crawl inside of him and never come out, that was the answer to any kind of loneliness she'd ever felt, but suddenly, with no warning, Cormac stopped, the circling motion stopped and she nearly blurted something out – *keep doing it!* – but thank God she didn't and thank God he started doing it again. Why had he stopped? His wrist was at a funny angle, maybe he was getting a cramp or something. She tried to care, but couldn't, because there was a pressure bearing down on her belly, no not her belly, somewhere lower, a place she didn't even know the name of, it was like someone was in there blowing up a balloon and it was getting bigger, bigger than her below-the-belly area could possibly accommodate, and the lava lamp was going *glunk-glunk-glunk* and the itchy heat was getting itchier and she suddenly lost control of her eyelids (what did her eyelids have to do with it?), they were flitting, quivering, like in a film they'd seen in school showing someone during REM sleep, and Heather bowed her head slightly in case Cormac should stop breathing in her ear and decide to look into her eyes, and the angle of her head together with her quivering eyelids made her feel possessed, like a girl in a horror film, but what could she do? She didn't know how long this feeling was going to go on or how long she could hide it from Cormac. She could tell he had no idea what was going on, which kind of scared her because if she didn't know and he didn't know and if neither of them knew how long it was going to last –

Just then several darts of something moved through the bit below her belly, like small animals chasing each other, then a hot thick liquid seemed to fill the area from her neck to her knees. The small animals came to rest.

Cormac's fingers, meanwhile, completely ignorant of the havoc they had just wreaked, continued to play softly over the outside of her knickers. And these fingers, the fingers that only a moment ago had seemed magical, omnipotent; the fingers that had held the key to Heather's inner being; the fingers that had somehow possessed a knowledge of her body even she didn't have; these same fingers were now tickling her, irking her, making her feel queasy. She wanted to push Cormac's hand away, but she suspected that would be rude. It occurred to her that she might get away with removing his hand if she accompanied this move with a return of her own hand to his thing, and she duly effected this manoeuvre. The problem was, she now had no interest whatsoever in his thing, which was still resolutely hard and seemed suddenly rather stubborn and dull-witted. She felt an aversion to it that was in inverse proportion to the devotion she had felt to it only moments ago. In fact, Cormac himself was beginning to seem dull-witted. It was so obvious that it was over and yet he clearly didn't realize it was over, just like he hadn't realized he was making her have an orgasm, for Heather was pretty sure that was what she'd just had. She'd seen it in films. But in films the woman was usually doing it when she had an orgasm. After about ten seconds of shagging, the woman would start moaning and writhing and then the man would too. Nobody ever moaned or writhed when someone was just touching them outside their knickers. Heather thought maybe she wasn't normal, or maybe an orgasm can only happen when you're doing it and what she'd had was a mere preview, in which case she was nearly frightened to think what a real orgasm might be like.

Her hand was resting motionless on Cormac's crotch. She scooted away from him on the sofa. He pulled back and looked at her. 'What's wrong?' he whispered. His voice was funny, gargley like hers had been. He cleared his throat. 'What's wrong?' he said again.

She looked around the sitting room, which was dark but for the glow of the TV. The sound was turned down. He had muted it just after they'd started kissing. That seemed like ages ago, like it had happened in another life, the life in which she had wanted Cormac to be sitting beside her on the sofa. Now she was living a life in which she kind of wanted him to leave.

After clearing her own throat, she said, 'I'm just a bit worried about my mother coming home.' She checked her watch and tried to look nervous.

'I thought you said she was spending the night in Meath.'

Cormac was wriggling his arse like he had before, though this time to get his jeans up. He looked to Heather as though he now felt self-conscious about his thing, which she'd sneaked a glance at while checking her watch, just before it disappeared back into the vent in his boxers. It was still hard, she'd noticed, but now it was also sort of curved. She felt suddenly sorry for it and, by extension, sorry for Cormac. But with every second that passed, she was more certain of the fact that she wanted him to leave.

She stood up. 'I know, but my mother . . .' Heather scratched her head. 'She's a bit unpredictable. Because then later she said she might come home tonight. Because of my father being on TV. Or something.'

Cormac looked blankly at her.

'So I'm actually not sure,' she said. 'Sorry. I just forgot. I got, I got . . . carried away.' Where had that come from? Apparently it was the perfect thing to say, for Cormac stopped looking aggrieved and gave her the tiniest, the sweetest of smiles.

Cormac is sweet, she thought.

But she still wanted him to leave.

He looked at his watch. 'It's only ten to nine,' he said. 'We could listen for the car.' Then added hopefully, 'You could get carried away some more . . .'

Heather experimented with a new smile, one she'd never tried before. With this smile, she attempted to convey to Cormac that she would really like to get carried away some more but that it was just too risky.

'My mother is . . . since Aunt Grace died, she's just really, I don't know, like she'll just all of a sudden not want to deal with people. So I think she will probably come home.'

Cormac nodded. 'Yeah,' he said. 'That's cool.'

'It is?'

He shrugged. 'I guess.' Now Cormac sounded like it wasn't cool. And it wasn't, Heather knew. Okay, so she didn't know much about sex, and what had happened to her tonight had never happened to her before, but intuitively she knew that what she was doing was not cool. Especially as she had no intention of making it up to Cormac, of picking up where they'd left off, because she was in love with someone else, which also wasn't cool but seemed not nearly as uncool as asking Cormac to leave while his thing was still hard, while he still had that look on his face.

Cormac straightened himself up and Heather walked him to the front door, making a point of checking her watch on the way in order to substantiate her concerns. When Cormac hesitated in the open doorway, Heather thought there might be things she should say. Things he might like to know. Like how he'd made her feel, like what his fingers had done to her (because he still had no idea and that seemed cruel). She thought she should tell him about the moment she'd wanted to cling to him, to be closer to him than she'd ever been to anyone. Of course, Heather had no idea how a person would go about describing such a feeling, and even if she did know she would have been far too shy to attempt it.

*

After submitting to Cormac's goodbye kiss, Heather wandered around the house for a few minutes. She wasn't sure what you were supposed to do at a time like this. There was something about sex and smoking, but Heather didn't smoke. She was tempted to call Emile – not to tell him, of course; he didn't know Cormac was coming over; he didn't even know Cormac existed – but Emile was out to dinner with his family. They were celebrating his sister's one year of not being a drug addict. His sister said she was celebrating the fact that if she stayed away from drugs one day at a time, she'd never end up in Benidorm again.

It was almost nine. *NY25* was on in two minutes. She got a glass of cranberry juice and a packet of chocolate Hobnobs and curled up on the sofa, in exactly the same spot where she'd been sitting with Cormac.

The opening shot was of Mitya standing by her window in a one-piece red jumpsuit, looking out at the rain and crying. She had the remote in her hand and she started clicking on it. Her disk showed Dr Harding walking away in the rain, down the footpath in front of her house. She had watched him through the window, the same window she was standing in front of now. It must have happened only moments ago. There he went down the footpath. And again. And again. And again. Mitya was a glutton for punishment. It was clear Dr Harding had finally done it: he'd dumped her.

'Hah-hah!' Heather said, lifting another Hobnob from the packet. 'It's about time!' She didn't feel at all sorry for Mitya. Mitya needed to get a life.

While Mitya stood there watching Dr Harding walk away, Dr Harding was already at a meeting with the Refuseniks. There were only four of them there – Claire and Mymar and a minor Refusenik named Kurt. Dr Harding was holding up a disk.

'I don't know who sent this,' he was saying. 'And I don't know how she knew to send it to *me* . . .' He looked around at the group.

'Bill,' Claire said, 'if you think anyone here has blown your cover –'

He held up his hand. 'I'm not suggesting that.'

'How do you know it's a she?' Mymar asked. Mymar looked nice tonight. He had on a crisp white shirt that contrasted nicely with his Slovakian ruggedness. Maybe he knew Dr Harding had dumped Mitya and that he needed to smarten up if he was going to have any chance at all of winning Claire.

'Once or twice, a hand appears in the frame. It belongs to the person recording. I'll slip it in. You'll see.'

Dr Harding dimmed the lights and popped the disk into a small machine on the table. A screen on the wall lit up, showing five people at a board meeting, not including the person recording.

'There's Johansson from Mnemon,' Claire said.

'And Wylie from the National Security Commission.'

The woman who'd sent them the recording was giving them a good look at everyone. Whoever she was, she knew when she walked into that meeting that she was going to be passing on the disk.

'Christ, Bill, what have you got here?'

Heather wondered when the Refuseniks had started calling Dr Harding 'Bill'. Had she missed an episode? The one where Dr Harding said, 'Call me Bill'?

Litigation is hitting Mnemon hard, a man on the wall screen was saying. *You all know that.*

'Mnemon lawyer,' Dr Harding said, from somewhere in the dark. 'His name's Graves. The woman is Johansson's PA. The other guy is a Security Commission lawyer.'

Graves was referring to the people who claimed that viewing reproductions of memories was causing them trauma. They'd accused Mnemon of psychological recklessness. Mnemon had responded by placing disclaimers on the packaging: *The contents of these disks will be re-creations only. Mnemon accepts no responsibility for viewer reaction.* But still, they had lost a couple of huge class-action suits. Heather found that subplot kind of boring. She was more interested in the steaming underclass and in who was going to end up shagging who.

As you also know, Graves went on, *we have a back-up copy of every moment that has ever been recorded on Mnemon disks. We have back-ups of back-ups. We have the mother of all hard drives. But as it stands now,* he went on, *the government – you – has to subpoena individuals if you want access to memory disks. The ACLU is a pain in your ass. In exchange for the introduction of legislation protecting us from the growing tide of class action trauma suits –*

And other such nonsense, Johansson chimed in.

– we're willing to do a deal on access to our banks.

The National Security Commission people looked interested. *Tell me more,* Wylie said.

A woman's hand appeared in the lower left-hand corner of the frame. She was wearing a wedding ring. Her hand was delicate and pretty; she had a French manicure.

You'd be dealing directly with us, Graves said. *Bypassing the courts. We're offering you sole direct access. Obviously, it's a completely confidential arrangement.*

Dr Harding clicked the machine off.

'When was this made?' Claire asked.

'It's dated three weeks ago,' Dr Harding said.

'We've never had proof like this.' Mymar shook his head.

Kurt said, 'There's two places people feel hit – their pockets and their privacy. We show people this, they will turn on Mnemon in an instant.'

'We show people this,' Dr Harding said, 'and that woman is dead.'

Mymar and Claire nodded. They'd already figured that out. Only a lower-level Refusenik wouldn't have got it straight away.

Cool, Heather thought. It was crunch time for Dr Harding. Breaking up with Mitya was a sign that something big was coming, but Heather hadn't foreseen this.

'Do you think we could convince her to go public?' It was Claire.

Dr Harding stared at the table. Maybe he did know who the woman with the French manicure was and just wasn't saying, Heather thought. Maybe he loved her, or she loved him, and that's why she'd risked everything to send him the disk. Maybe he was lying to the Refuseniks, to Claire. But he loved Claire. Could he love both Claire and the French manicure at the same time?

'At this point,' he said finally, 'I have no way of knowing.'

'We had a meeting last night,' Mymar said. 'Everybody feels we should go ahead with Colombo.'

Dr Harding's cheeks filled with air. Then he let the air out slowly and put his head in his hands. Colombo was the site of one of Mnemon's biggest memory banks. It was in Sri Lanka, which was underneath India. Mnemon had set up there because they didn't have to pay people very much and the government would do whatever Mnemon told it to, as long as they gave some dark men with sunglasses enough money. All the places where Mnemon had memory banks had exotic names and dark men with sunglasses: Dakar, Quito, Bangalore. But the main one was in Colombo. Heather thought it looked like a cool place – palm trees in the middle of the city and the sea right there, like you could just pop out of a traffic jam for a quick swim. There were always people hanging out on the promenade having a lovely time and when the evil Mnemon executives met with the crooked government officials to give them some more money, it was always on the patio of this swish hotel on the water and everybody looked relaxed and dangerous at the same time.

'We have people on the ground there like we've never had anywhere,' Claire said. 'We've got two Mnemon guards on our side. If there is one mission that has a chance to succeed, it's this one.'

'What about casualties? That place is on the go 24/7.'

Claire shook her head. 'There's always a gap between one shift ending and the next beginning, when the place is evacuated for security checks. Robots sweep for explosives. After Section A is swept, the guards go in and plant the bomb there. They'll have time to get out of the building before it blows. Bill,' she said, 'we will do everything in our power to avoid the loss of innocent lives. You know that.'

Dr Harding looked at her, but didn't say anything.

'Bill!' Claire slammed her fist on the table. 'They are talking about doing a deal that will give the government access to every corner of your mind, to your most private experiences and memories. Don't you think it's time we sent them a *message*? Look at what's at stake here! That woman risked her life to tell us this. What do you want to do? Hand out leaflets on the street corner?'

Kurt and Mymar were looking sympathetically at Dr Harding. 'We can't afford to sit on the fence, Bill,' Mymar said quietly.

The four of them stared at the table, all glum.

Next thing, Dr Harding and Claire were walking to their cars. Heather wondered why, if the Refuseniks' meetings were so secret and if they weren't even supposed to know each other, they were always strolling around the car park together.

'Are you all right?' Claire said.

'I'm not happy about Colombo.'

Claire looked puzzled. 'There's something else, though, isn't there?'

Dr Harding sighed. 'Yeah,' he said. 'It's just . . . stuff.' They leaned against Claire's car, facing each other. Their bodies were so close. 'Sometimes . . .' he said.

'What?'

'Did you ever . . . I mean, sometimes when I leave here at night . . .'

Claire looked at him. She looked at him like she knew, knew that he watched her when he was at home alone and knew that he wanted to confess it to her. But Dr Harding couldn't confess. Not tonight.

'Bill,' Claire said finally. 'Be careful.'

'I've made a back-up and put it in a safe deposit box,' he said.

Claire nodded. 'Good,' she said. 'But that's not what I meant.'

Dr Harding looked around the dark car park.

'You know who that woman is, don't you?' Claire asked. 'The one who sent you the disk.'

He didn't answer. Instead he said, 'Sometimes, sometimes when I go home at night, I watch things. Things from a long time ago. Or things I've seen during the day. People . . .'

He shook his head like he was clearing it, then gently slapped the roof of Claire's car, the way men do for some reason when they're saying goodbye. 'I'll call you tomorrow.'

When he got home, Dr Harding made himself a purple shotza, lay down on the sofa, and pushed a button to make a screen descend from the ceiling. He put the top-secret disk in another little machine and fast-forwarded it to the woman's hand and stilled it. From the look on his face, it was hard to tell whether he was trying to figure out where he knew it from, or if he knew where he knew it from and just liked looking at it, or if he'd never seen it before in his life but was falling in love with the woman who owned it. Whatever the case, Dr Harding looked sad. Heather wanted to curl up next to him on the sofa and make him feel better. She'd tell him that Claire loved him and that the woman with the hand wouldn't get killed and that nobody would die in Colombo. She'd assure him that the Refuseniks would win and human nature would be saved and that everything would be fine because it was only TV. She'd tell him that he was a hero. And Dr Harding would give her a big hug and return the favour. He'd say that Heather shouldn't worry because what happened tonight was all right, the thing with Cormac. He'd say that her mother would be okay, that she was only acting strange because she was sad but that sad stuff passed. And he'd tell her that Emile loved her, more than anything in his world, but that it wasn't easy for boys to show these things or to say them (Dr Harding knew this because he'd been a boy himself) and that if only she could be patient a bit longer, Emile would . . . Emile would . . . Emile would . . .

Heather couldn't even bring herself to bring Dr Harding to say it. She picked up the remote and switched over to *Ireland Tonight*.

Eighteen

Damien stood in the doorway of the sitting room, sipping a glass of whiskey, his gaze resting tiredly on Heather. He had just got home from the TV studio.

'You're up late,' he said.

'This is good.' Heather pointed to the television, not taking her eyes from it. 'It's about Pablo Escobar.'

She had slid so far down the sofa that her back was where her bottom should be and her head was where her back should be. Why was sitting up so difficult at that age? Barney was curled up beside her, his head pressed against her hip. Heather seemed to wear him at times, without quite noticing it. He'd taken to sleeping in her bed. After Grace died, Barney had exhibited undeniable signs of trauma. He'd moved through the house in a low creep, his belly brushing the ground, more like an iguana than a cat.

Damien leaned down and gave Barney a quick scratch behind the ear, causing him to curl tighter in upon himself, then dropped into the armchair next to the sofa.

The documentary was on TG4, the Irish station. The man being interviewed was speaking Spanish, the subtitles were in English, and the intermittent voice-over of the filmmaker was in Irish. It was difficult to follow.

'Are you getting all this?' he asked.

Heather nodded, which wasn't easy from her current position. 'He turned himself in and they thought he was going to prison, but he picked the prison, and it wasn't really a prison, it was a mansion. And they didn't figure it out for like a year or something . . .'

Damien took a swallow of whiskey. He stopped trying to follow the narrative and instead just watched the images on the screen as they came and went. There was Pablo, mucking about on the soccer pitch; there was a blood-spattered stage (some political rally cut short by the assassination of the candidate); a funeral procession and keening widows; there was a room with parcels of seized drugs, neatly wrapped and stacked but managing somehow to look hazardous. And there was Pablo again, grainy, sensual, looking pretty hazardous himself. He had a certain something. Even Damien, in his exhausted and preoccupied condition, could see that Pablo had presence. He should have been an actor, instead of what he was. Thinking about Pablo, Damien experienced a sudden wave of self-forgiveness, the kind that comes from recalling that there are countless other lives being lived and some of them are way more fucked up than your own. He glanced at Heather. He could see she was fascinated by this world of swarthy outlaws and palm trees and hidden airstrips; his reprieve from anxiety was brief. There were drug kingpins right here in Dublin, if that was what a girl fancied.

'He was a bad guy,' Damien said slowly, disappointed at this half-assed attempt to serve as the moral compass in Heather's life.

'Some poor people loved him because he gave them houses to live in and stuff, but he killed loads of people, too.'

'Mmm,' he said, glad to see that his daughter had the measure of Pablo Escobar. 'Did your mother ring?'

Heather shook her head. 'No. But your mother did.'

'Oh. What did she say?'

'Just for you to ring her tomorrow.'

'Did she watch it?'

Heather shrugged. 'Dunno. Did Mom?'

'I don't know. She was going to try.' Officially, they had no television at the Farm, but Elspeth had one hidden in her bedroom and Gillian had said she'd try to catch *Ireland Tonight*. But she hadn't rung, so she probably hadn't watched. Or maybe she hadn't rung because she had watched. He'd been hoping she might drive down tonight and come to the studio and go back to Meath early tomorrow morning – she had mentioned the possibility at some point – but the idea had evaporated and he suspected she hadn't been seriously considering it, anyway.

He couldn't read her at all these days. But he felt her veering away from him. He was trying not to succumb to the obvious suspicion: that she was seeing someone else. Instinct wasn't always such a sure guide. The time before he'd had no inkling – he'd known things were a little flat, but that was all. She'd been fucking the guy five months and he'd never suspected. It almost made him an accessory. How inattentive *was* he? And he hadn't found out because of any sudden and belated insight, but through sheer chance, and by that time it was just about over.

He'd been at a meeting over on the north side the day he saw them. As he and Jimmy were walking towards the car, they'd bumped into a guy who used to work at EI. This guy – whose name Damien couldn't even remember – told them he'd just seen Gillian. He was smiling at the coincidence, at the fact that he hadn't seen either Damien or Gillian in over a year and now he'd seen them both in the space of three minutes. When Damien asked where she was headed, the guy said he didn't know, he'd only seen her from across the road.

It had just come up to lunch hour. Gillian's office wasn't

far. Possibly, Damien thought, she was on her way to that French place on Capel Street where she'd mentioned sometimes going. He looked at his watch. He was already running late but thought, Fuck it, I'll surprise her.

Fuck it! I'll surprise her!

He still recalled clearly the instant at which that thought entered his head, probably because Jimmy was standing next to him and surprise was one of the things Jimmy had counselled. Jimmy knew about his problems.

You get into these straitjackets, he'd said. *She acts this way, you act that way . . . Surprise her. Be different. Allow her to be different.*

And there she was, being different. Right there in La Belle Époque. Standing inside the door, caressing the neck of some Asian guy while they waited for a table. Damien stood stunned on the opposite footpath.

His first impulse was to ring her on the mobile and say, *Look out the window. Right now.* Or maybe go in, straight up to her, and act surprised but not surprised, so she'd know she was caught. But was she caught? Was it what it looked like? He was trying to think clearly, to remain rational. Hadn't he, on occasion, caressed the neck of a female colleague, a quick comradely shoulder rub? He had. But what he'd seen in the window just now wasn't comradely. It was intimate. Proprietorial.

They got a table somewhere in the back and disappeared from view.

He went to a coffee shop on the opposite side of the street and a few doors up and ordered a toasted cheese sandwich (the most innocuous thing on the menu), which he watched congeal on the plate in front of him, untouched. He turned the pages of the *Irish Times*, reading indiscriminately, without retaining anything. It was the longest hour of his life.

When Gillian and the Asian guy finally came out (he wasn't wearing a ring, Damien noticed, as he sheltered ludicrously behind the *Irish Times*), they exchanged a few unhappy words – her hand inside his jacket, resting on his hip (Damien knew what he was seeing: two people who were used to touching each other) – before heading off in opposite directions. Well, he thought, at least they didn't look happy.

He followed the guy and was surprised – the day was full of surprises! – to see him, after having stopped for cigarettes, heading into Gillian's office.

But of course. They worked together.

Once Damien knew that much, he was able to find out more. He rang somebody one of his colleagues had used while fighting a dodgy insurance claim after an accident and by the time he left the office that evening he knew the guy's name, when he'd started in Gillian's office, that he'd come from London, that he was Vietnamese, and that he was due to go back to London next week. He'd been working in Dublin less than six months. Damien tried to console himself with that: months were not years, after all. A month was only four weeks, and how many times a week? Once? Twice? Even three times a week for five months (he gave it a month to get started) meant sixty times, and they probably didn't fuck every single one of those sixty times, so the total was maybe more like fifty (though he should add back the ten because the odd day they probably fucked more than once), which didn't make him happy but was better than the 288 times a two-year affair would have allowed them.

At the time, he had wondered if his and Gillian's having recently agreed not to separate had somehow encouraged her to do what she did, that it was a last rash act, a final self-indulgence before she settled down for life.

It wasn't long after the guy went back to London that Gillian had started talking about how badly she wanted out of that office. She was vague about what she'd do, and Damien had been a bit scared that leaving the office was some kind of dry run for leaving home, but he was more inclined to feel it was a sign that she was putting the whole business behind her. He'd tried to focus on the fact that with no persuading on his part, she had ended it. He had won, without even trying. And Gillian was different, at least for a while. Like she was holding on to him for dear life. He knew he could fuck with her head if he wanted to. He was angry enough. He could torment her by hinting that he knew about what she'd done without ever quite saying that he knew. But the danger in that was in going too far, pushing her to the point where she was left with no choice but to tell him, and then there was no controlling where it would go. So he'd said nothing and spent countless hours wondering if his ability to keep quiet was evidence of faith and maturity, or just an indication that he was far weaker or more apathetic than he cared to admit – that he was now living according to the dictum his father had lived by: *Anything for a quiet life*.

'Ew,' Heather was saying. 'Eungh . . .' He focused on the screen. Pablo was dead. The bloodstains looked like spilled ink.

He got up and went to the kitchen to refill his whiskey. The house had a way of being empty of Gillian that he was sure was different from the way it had of being empty of him, or of Heather, or of all of them. What he wanted right now was simply for Gillian to be here. The loneliness was almost a relief: a single identifiable emotion declaring itself in the midst of what had been, all night, a stew of anxieties. When he came back into the room, he said, 'So did you watch it?'

Heather nodded, looking up at him.

He sat down again. 'So . . . ?'

She pushed herself up the sofa until she was sitting almost normally. Barney slid into the hollow made by her hand and lazily righted himself.

'So how did I do?'

'It was, like, a draw.'

'A draw?'

'Yeah. You didn't lose. And sometimes the other people on the panel looked stupid. I liked what that lady said about living in the real world.'

'The lady in the audience?'

'The goat-cheese lady.'

A woman had shaken her fist at the lecturer from Maynooth and said, *Ye want the rest of us to stay pure, the likes of ye up there in Dublin with yer goat's cheese and what have you, but we've got to live in the real world too, and that means paying the bills!*

The audience had loved her. They'd applauded and called, *Good on ya, girl!*

'Tully's comeback wasn't bad, though,' Damien said. Tully had responded that parcelling off tracts of land for 'theme park simulation' was an odd definition of living in the real world.

'He was *so* arrogant.'

'He sounded arrogant?'

'Yeah,' Heather said, 'he was always smirking. Like when he was talking about the guys who speak Irish saying obscene things to women.'

Damien groaned. He had no idea how Tully had found out about that. Cathal and Eoin had been overheard raising their glasses to uncomprehending female tourists and saying, 'Seo fionnadh ar do ghabhal.'

Heather looked sideways at him. 'What did they say? Those guys?'

Here's to fur on your crotch.

Damien squinted and shook his head. 'I don't remember, exactly.'

'You don't?' She sounded like she didn't believe him. 'Anyway, that guy, Tully, he was trying to make Kill look bad by telling that story, but people just thought it was funny.' Heather paused before continuing. 'But, you know,' she said, 'the guy on your side, the TD, he was kind of . . .' She clenched her teeth and retracted her lips in an exaggerated cringe.

'Thick?'

She nodded again, this time reluctantly. 'He kept doing that thing with his throat.'

'You mean clearing it?'

'I don't know.' Heather's nostrils flared and her eyebrows leapt. Her face was alive with disgust. 'It was like, phlegm or something. And his face was purple.'

Damien smiled.

'The audience was on your side, though,' she said.

'I think you're right.' He slid down lower in his chair and rested the whiskey glass on his thigh. 'So you're not ashamed to know me?'

Heather picked a chocolate biscuit from a packet that appeared to have been torn open by a wild animal. 'No!' she said to the biscuit.

She meant it. He wanted to hug her. Her attitude had softened since their exchange over dinner after the *Irish Times* piece and his crack about not discussing vegetarianism while wearing leather shoes, perhaps because she hadn't been able to hold the moral high ground (sausages were her downfall) and he'd refrained from mentioning her numerous lapses. Or maybe she was just incapable of sustained nastiness where he was concerned.

Through a mouthful of biscuit she said, 'Emile texted me afterwards. He was watching it with his parents. They thought you got ganged up on but that you handled it.'

'I see,' he said. 'And what did they say about what we were discussing?'

'His parents?' Heather shrugged. 'Dunno.'

He pointed to the biscuits. 'Can I have one?'

She handed him the packet. He took a bite of chocolate Hobnob and washed it down with whiskey, instantly regretting it. It wasn't a good combination. He tried to disguise the mistake with another swallow of whiskey, larger this time. He felt that one in his brain. A slow wallop, a dull pleasurable *thrum*. His head was momentarily warm. He had the sudden urge to get drunk. But he had to be up in the morning.

He looked at Heather. She was holding out her hand for the Hobnobs. He handed them over and she extracted one from the tattered packet. Their gazes came lazily to rest on the screen. A greeny-blue satellite image, or a mock-up of an image. Rows of arrows stuttering downscreen. Areas of low pressure that looked like tufts of fur hovering over the Atlantic. Bearing down, as always, on the West of Ireland. The weather forecast could be oddly disconcerting. Something about its cartoonish simplicity made Damien feel insignificant in all the wrong ways.

Heather turned her head, eyeing him thoughtfully. 'Dad?' she said.

'Yeah?'

'What's Zapruder?'

Nineteen

Gillian pressed a capsule out of the blister pack and rolled it around in the palm of her hand. The capsule was two shades of purple, with a tiny white code imprinted on one half. She popped it in her mouth and chased it with several gulps of water (she was often thirsty since she'd started on the capsules), then dropped the pack into her bag. Gillian was more discreet than Katherine. She'd been on Diax for over two months now, and she hadn't told anyone. Her doctor was the only one who knew, and his knowing didn't take away from the unexpected thrill that had come with being on a drug.

She hadn't told Damien because she knew he wouldn't approve. Diax was only a year on the market and he was wary of drugs generally. Anyway, she hadn't believed that anything would happen; she had thought she'd be off it again in no time and so didn't see the point of getting into an argument over it.

At first, nothing much *had* happened. Gillian had noticed only the crampy sensation, a dry mouth and some occasional tremors. Sometime into the second month, though, she had begun to feel a new mental energy, an excitement, really, like the kind she used to feel when she was energized by a new idea or project, except now the excitement was there all day and didn't depend on any particular stimulus. She felt plugged in, attentive. When she thought of something she needed to remember, she didn't have to write it down; she just put it to one side of her mind, and when she went to look for it later, it was there. When people said, *Now what was I saying?*, she was able to tell them. There was never that awkward hesitation when introducing acquaintances whose names she definitely knew but had mysteriously forgotten.

Suddenly, Gillian knew why the Farm had never had a single guest under forty. It was because Deceleration wasn't really about respect for time or the earth or the needs of others. It was about individual mortality. When you accepted the fact that you had a limited life span, you wanted to start bargaining over the rate at which it played itself out. (She'd just read about a study that said vigorous exercise may add about two years to your life, but most of those two years will have been spent exercising.) What Gillian realized was that she'd created a cottage industry out of her own utterly ordinary fear of death.

She wept a little upon the realization. But she was prone to tears those first weeks on Diax. Not the heavy and despairing kind she'd cried following Grace's death, but tears of bittersweetness – tears at the sight of an elderly couple holding hands and tears when she saw mentally disabled children enjoying themselves. She was often moved, and she enjoyed the feeling. She was alive to the world, and suddenly she wasn't at all sure she wanted it to slow down.

She looked at her watch. It was nearly two. She was leading a workshop in ten minutes: 'Loving the One You're With: Monogamy in an All-You-Can-Eat World'. She gathered her things and headed to the main meeting room, where several chairs were arranged in a circle. There was a flip chart at the front of the room. On a fresh sheet she wrote:

Concentration is the natural piety of the soul – Malebranche

Then she turned a page over to hide it.

In ones and twos they filed in. Monogamy was one of the most popular workshops; hardly anyone ever skipped it. Gillian smiled at them as they took their seats, but said nothing. It was a rule for workshops that once you crossed the threshold, idle chatter ceased.

When everyone had settled, Gillian flipped the page on the chart, turned back to face the circle, and said, 'What does this have to do with monogamy? And what does monogamy have to do with Deceleration? I want you to keep these two questions in mind as a backdrop for today's discussion.'

She gave them a few minutes to jot down the questions and to record their immediate responses before continuing.

'The purpose of this workshop,' Gillian said, 'is not to promote or to discredit monogamy. It's to talk about how the choices we make with regard to our sex lives relate to the way we think about entitlement, about time, about natural resources, about quality and quantity, depth and surface, about other people, and about choice itself.'

There were nods of understanding around the circle.

She turned a page on the flipchart and spelled out E-N-T-I-T-L-E-M-E-N-T, then asked the group to share their associations with the word. She went through the entire list of topics in this way, and was about to announce a tea break when a man in the group – a Mr Phillips from London – said, 'This business about doing and not doing . . . it seems as though in the past, say, in Freud's time, everybody repressed drives, or so we're told. But now we're being taught all these new drives. Or maybe not new, but we're expected to act out on them. And if you don't act out, there's this feeling that you're not living life fully, properly.'

Rueful nods from several in the group. 'Go on,' Gillian said.

'Now you're told you have more to lose by *not* doing, whereas, in the past, *doing* was the risk.'

An American woman raised her hand. Americans were always raising their hands. 'It's like the line between fantasy and reality has been blurred, so you have this fantasy of something you want, and instead of being content with it as fantasy, you're encouraged to try and actually get it, or do it, whether or not it's appropriate or ethical or whatever.'

'You know what the difference is, though,' someone else jumped in, 'between now and the past, it's the democratization of that blurring. It used to be just the privileged classes who believed they had the right to indulge all their fantasies. The monarchy and the dissolute elite.'

Gillian was looking at Mr Phillips. His eyes were dark and almond-shaped and happened to be resting on her, as though he was still waiting for a response to his original comment. But Gillian wasn't able to respond. A wave of something, not quite a chill, had just moved through her. She felt a quickening of her attention, a nervous alertness. But she felt shaky, too, less substantial than she had a moment ago. She suspected that if she tried to stand, her legs might buckle underneath her.

She took a deep breath and looked at the floor, trying to ground herself. The others were talking on.

'– well, it's not as if you don't have a choice,' she heard someone say.

She looked at Mr Phillips again. There was something about him – his eyes, maybe, or the inflection of his voice (a certain London accent), or the tilt of his head as he spoke to her.

Someone else said, 'We always have a choice –'

Gillian closed her eyes. It was little more than a flash – Jonathan in the apartment, sitting on the small sofa in his customary position (right leg bent, knee up to his chin, his left thigh flat on the cushion and his arm draped over the sofa back) and looking up at her, the expression on his face one of bemusement. But it was as clear in her mind as if she'd only just left him, fresh the way an hour ago is fresh.

The room had gone quiet. Then a woman with a Donegal accent said, 'Pretending the culture is making you do it is such a lie. Why not just say: this is what I want and I'm willing to risk the consequences?'

(He held out his hand to her. *Sit beside me.*)

'– there are pressures that usen't to be there.'

She opened her eyes.

The Donegal woman said, 'So deal with them. When we have choices, we have to grow up and make them.'

Mr Phillips was still eyeing her, now less in expectation of an answer than in concern.

'I sat through five years of an affair my wife had, waiting for her,' a wiry man with a Belfast accent announced, deadpan. 'And when it was over, she left me.' The room went silent. Some said nothing out of respect for the speaker's pain, others because they were staring at Gillian.

(Jonathan slipped his arm over her shoulder. She kissed the soft smooth skin at the side of his neck.)

The man on her right leaned over and whispered, 'Are you okay?'

Gillian nodded and took a deep breath. She looked at the long-suffering Belfast man but couldn't trust herself to do anything more than nod again, compassionately, she hoped.

(*I missed you.*

Did you? Her finger traced a line along his thigh.)

A grey-haired American man broke the silence. 'I hope you don't mind me saying this,' he said. He was leaning forward with one hand planted on his knee, looking directly at the Belfast man. 'But I really appreciate your honesty. It isn't easy to say something like that.'

The group murmured its agreement.

Gillian began counting her breaths.

The Belfast man stretched his legs out and crossed his ankles and looked at the floor.

The woman next to him put a hand to his back.

Gillian's breathing was getting smoother. She shifted in her chair and forced herself to make eye contact around the circle, to reconnect with the group. She suggested a moment of quiet time before breaking for tea.

'So we'll just close our eyes . . .' she said slowly (it was hard to keep her voice steady), '. . . and let today sink in . . . and think about how we might take care . . . of today . . . of what's been shared . . .' She trailed off. It was so quiet she could hear others breathing. In the silence she thought of Jonathan. She didn't think it was a déjà vu she'd just experienced but some uncanny premonition. He was ill. Or nearby. Or had died.

Opening her eyes, she said quietly, 'Back here in twenty minutes?'

Three weeks before Jonathan had been due to return to London, the department head he'd been covering for in Dublin opted for early retirement. Jonathan was offered his job on a permanent basis. Without discussing it with Gillian, he turned the offer down, and though she was hurt, she was also relieved. As long as he was here, she couldn't stop seeing him, and seeing him was becoming increasingly painful.

When he moved back to London, she relaxed for what seemed like the first time in six months. It was an exhausted, drained relaxation, like a post-fever fatigue. Her world appeared before her with a new clarity; the fact that she still possessed it felt like an instance of undeserved luck. She looked at Damien and saw a poignant innocence and was shocked at how close she'd come to destroying that. Heather seemed more or less where she'd left her, and this felt like a narrow escape from some unspecified danger, like how she'd felt when Heather was small and slipped out of sight for a moment. With only her own family in it, Gillian's life seemed suddenly self-evident, its particulars overt and unashamed. It was as though she'd entered a bright clearing, and she thought she understood then why people talk about affairs being the saviours of marriage.

But the relief had been short-lived. Very soon, she began to miss him. They had decided to stay in contact through e-mail, the idea being that they could remain friendly, but not as friendly as friends who phoned each other. By explicit agreement, they refrained from expressions of desire or affection, and though she stuck to the agreement and kept her e-mails breezy and devoid of anything she actually was feeling, she started to despise his similar discipline.

After four weeks of this, Gillian was nearly cracking. She began to drive past his old apartment in Smithfield, stopping sometimes for a moment to look up at the kitchen window, which was always dark. Nobody had moved in yet, and she was glad of that. She liked to imagine its emptiness as a testament to what had happened there and a mark of respect for its passing. She didn't feel good about it – loitering in the wake of his existence – but she told herself it was better than phoning him, better than hopping a plane to London.

Still, she had the strange feeling that she was more absent from her marriage now than she had been when she was actually seeing him. She was either thinking of him or had the nagging feeling that there was something she'd forgotten, and only when he sprang to mind again did she relax, realizing that what she had forgotten, for a moment, was him.

Six weeks and a day after he'd gone, she phoned him, half surprised that he should be there, on the other end of the line (it was so easy, why had it taken her this long?). The sound of his voice destroyed her guard and she became immediately rash.

'I can be in London tomorrow,' she said. 'I can be in London and back here before six o'clock tomorrow night.'

There was a silence. She felt horribly exposed but also relieved at having finally said something true to him, for the first time since he'd gone.

'Jonathan?'

'Gillian, think about what you're saying.'

'I have,' she lied.

'If you do that . . . what will happen then?'

He was on the mobile. She could hear cars in the background. She pictured him standing in the dark, in the middle of rush-hour pedestrian traffic, in a suit, smoking, the tiny blue phone in his hand. She had never wanted to be anywhere like she wanted to be in London just then, in the back of a black taxi on her way to him, with the whole night ahead of them.

'What are you wearing?' she asked.

He gave a little laugh, then she heard him taking a pull on his cigarette.

'You're smoking too much,' she said.

'I always smoke too much,' he said. 'I'm wearing a suit. It's the black one.'

'I miss you,' she said.

'I miss you, too,' he said, without hesitation.

'I won't tell him why I'm going to London, don't worry about that. I just want to see you.'

'What happened?' he said softly. 'I thought we were doing okay.'

'I was just being brave,' she said, hoping to sound wry.

He sighed. He smoked. In the background, someone shouted.

'You have a life,' he said. 'I can't do this . . .'

'You already have.'

'What do you mean?'

She could sense him becoming suddenly alert. 'I mean I can't go back there.'

'You mean you've left?'

'No,' she said. She almost wished she could have said yes. She wondered if it would have impressed him. 'It's just so hard.'

'Who is it harder for?'

'Is this a contest?'

She heard an ambulance siren. They waited for it to pass. Then two car horns sounded in a brief aggressive dialogue, or maybe teaming up against a common enemy. She heard a delicate pull on a cigarette. She pictured him with one hand clamped to his forehead. 'I'm standing on the street corner,' he said. 'Can we talk tomorrow?'

He'd phoned the next day at lunch hour. As soon as she heard his voice, she knew.

'I couldn't sleep last night,' he said.

'Me neither.' She was parked in the alcove just beyond the Forty Foot. It was bright and cold and the sun was hitting the water in a way she wanted him to see. 'I'm in Sandycove,' she said. 'It's beautiful.'

There was silence. Then he said, 'Gillian, I can't start up again.'

She wasn't sure whether to hate him or thank him. 'I know,' she said.

'Because if we did, it wouldn't end. And I can't take that on, that responsibility. I don't trust my thinking right now. I'm a mess, you know. I think I left Dublin a bigger mess than I arrived.'

'Glad I could help,' Gillian said. When he didn't answer, she felt mean. 'You seemed okay when you left.'

'I thought last night,' he said, 'I thought maybe once, you know, we could see each other. But I'd only be kidding myself. If I saw you once, I'd see you again, and again, and again . . . and I can't . . .'

She waited, but he didn't say anything else.

Already her world had begun to rearrange itself, her mind gathering again around the old realities. Over the past several months, Gillian had allowed new images of herself to take shape – the day-to-day of living with Jonathan, having Heather with them, the three of them, a Sunday afternoon in London, then the whole night ahead, shopping and dinner and sleeping and waking, and the next day, and the next after that. But a strange raggedness attached itself to those fantasies, as though she had literally torn herself away from her life.

And now they were receding and different images filling her head: herself and Damien, older. Never having to tell Heather any of it; not having to worry if Heather and Jonathan would like each other. Never having to make a lot of unpleasant decisions, or see the layers of untruth being peeled back, the lies totted up, so much more obvious in hindsight. To think of the times she'd nearly told Damien, those rare moments of feeling inexplicably close to him in the midst of it all – so close it was impossible to believe he didn't know – and how terrifyingly easy it would have been just to say it, one simple sentence; the vast gulf between the before and after of the revelation impossible for her mind to encompass; the perversely exhilarating knowledge that she held their future in her hands.

She'd resisted the temptation every time, opting for the obvious benefit of secret-keeping. Namely, power. Because that was what lying was, she thought, it was keeping the power for yourself, being the only one who got to make informed decisions. And now she was off the hook. She would never have to tell, because she wasn't going anywhere. She felt a sliver of relief in amongst the larger, dead weight of loss, and she marvelled at whatever instinct was behind it: inertia or fear or maybe even loyalty.

'I have to not do this,' he said.

'I heard you,' she said.

'Sorry,' he said. 'I'm repeating it for myself.'

'So . . .'

'Yeah?'

'So maybe we shouldn't . . .'

'Speak?'

'I'm just thinking . . .'

'I know.'

'That it'd be better.'

'Yeah,' he said. Then, 'Not at all?'

She hesitated. 'I don't know.'

'No, you're right.'

'For a while, anyway.'

'I won't write?'

'I don't think so.'

They sat there not saying anything.

Then Gillian said, 'Let's not hang up.'

'I don't want to hang up.'

'Where are you?'

'I'm at home,' he said. 'I'm working from home today.'

There was a silence, during which she knew they were picturing each other in their respective physical locations.

'I can't see you,' she said. 'I don't know what home looks like. I'm sure I've got it wrong.'

'I can see you.'

'I know,' she said. 'I brought you here one day to show you.'

'And you worried the whole time about your aunt driving by.'

'I wish I could touch you,' she said.

There was a pause. Then he said, 'I wish you could too.'

She didn't speak for a moment. This used to happen. She'd ring him on the mobile just to talk, on a weekend, say, when he was on one of his excursions to West Cork or Connemara, and they'd end up accidentally aroused; for her just the sound of his breathing was enough, a certain quality of silence that she knew meant he was thinking of making love to her.

She breathed so he could hear her. Then she said, 'Where are your hands?'

'One is between your legs and one is on me.'

'You're stroking yourself?'

'I'm rubbing the head of it against you. I'm teasing you.'

She shifted a bit in the bucket seat. 'You know I'm in broad daylight here.'

'So be discreet,' he whispered. 'Are you wearing a skirt?'

'Yes.' She wasn't actually, but it seemed helpful to pretend.

'Slide your hand up your skirt and tell me when you're touching yourself.'

She rolled her eyes and smiled to herself, and took a coat from the back seat and laid it over her lap. She felt suddenly, stupidly happy. Just as everything had seemed at its irretrievable worst, here they were again, whispering to each other. She unzipped her trousers and lifted the elastic of her knickers and slid her hand down and pushed her finger back and forth across herself.

'How are you?'

'Slippery,' she said.

'Where's my tongue?' he asked.

'It's on my nipple, you're tonguing me through this lace bra.' Her eyelids were getting heavy, but she couldn't close them because she had to keep a lookout.

'Aah. Now I'm moving up, up your neck, I'm kissing your neck now and behind your ear. I'm slipping the straps of your bra down and holding both of your breasts in my hands.'

She was trying to picture his hands on her breasts but it was impossible when she had her eyes open. She closed her eyes and let her head loll to one side, thinking the position might both make her look asleep and render the mobile invisible to anyone else out enjoying the view of the Forty Foot.

'Are you there?' he said.

'Yeah.'

'Stroke me, will you? Just slowly, up and down.'

'I am.'

He groaned.

'Do you know what I'm doing?' she said.

'Tell me.'

'I'm licking you. All around the smooth top and along underneath. Can you feel my tongue? Now I'm putting you in my mouth.'

'Oh my God,' he said slowly. 'Are you rubbing yourself?'

'Un-hunh.'

'Pretend it's my tongue,' he said. 'My tongue's going back and forth on you. Unh, I'm putting my tongue inside of you.'

She breathed heavily, audibly, and moved her finger in and out of herself. 'I want you inside me,' she said.

'Now?'

'Un-hunh. Kiss my breasts.'

'I love your breasts.'

'Unh . . .'

'Fuck me,' he whispered.

'I am.'

'Come over here and fuck me,' he whispered.

'I will.'

'Sweetheart . . .'

'I'm here.'

'I can't stand not touching you . . .'

'Faster,' she said.

'Come live with me . . .'

She swallowed hard.

He was repeating her name, and she was saying, 'I'm here, I'm here . . .' and then, for a moment, neither of them could say anything.

That was the last time they spoke.

The following morning, she removed every trace of him from her computer. She barred herself from his old neighbourhood. She didn't pass his office at work unless she absolutely had to, didn't go to the canteen, avoided the little Italian place on Abbey Street and La Belle Époque on Capel Street and every other place they'd been to. When a sweet thought of him arose, she countered the image with some unattractive moment of his, training herself to dislike him – his voice on the phone, for instance, during that last conversation, the hint of evasiveness when he'd said *I can't start up again*, as though attempting to let her down easy. And then the sex. He'd started it; she should have said no.

Come live with me . . .

That was the line that kept coming back to her. She nearly hated him for it, for having said it there and then, from the safe place of fantasy, where you weren't held accountable for what you said, and after they'd just decided that coming to live with him was exactly what she wasn't going to do.

Although Gillian had been visiting the Diax chat room since going on the capsules, she had never posted on it until tonight:

Something happened today, something about someone I used to be in love with. I saw him – I mean not saw him, but he was in my head like he used to be. Like it was yesterday. I hadn't felt that way in a long time. He was gone from my life, completely, and suddenly I'm missing him. Does anyone know what I'm talking about? I don't know if this is Diax and I don't know what to think. – G, Ireland

She checked her e-mails. By the time she went back to the chat room fifteen minutes later, three responses had been posted.

I don't know (I don't think anyone does yet) whether the drug does what I think you're suggesting (a 'freshening' of old memories?). But a recent study at a university in Berlin (I think) suggests that Diaxadril may result in a more vivid imagination. How this affects your emotional state (eg being in love) is anybody's guess . . . D, Maine

The second was from Madrid:

I am on Diax for ten months and do not notice one change in my memory or functions. I begin to believe it is placebo and farmaceuticals hoax.

And the third was from Gordon in London:

What you say interests me, G. My fiancée was killed in a motor accident twelve years ago. I believe that Diax has recently given me back something of her. It's not exactly like it was yesterday when I think of her now, but the memories I have retained of her all this time are somehow that bit sharper now. The difficult part is that more things can trigger the memory of her, which is painful. It also makes me ashamed of the relief I sometimes felt when I realized she was fading in my mind (but otherwise I would not have been able to go on . . . and now I have a wife and two children I must be here for). It's a mixed blessing for me, and I wonder am I being selfish. But it also feels like a part of my life I have a right to . . . Keep in touch

Twenty

Heather liked the island. It made Emile's kitchen sound as if it was in the Caribbean, even though it was just a big square wooden thing you could chop stuff on. She was spinning herself slowly on one of the high stools next to the island and watching Emile's sister unload the dishwasher. Nathalie was always doing stuff around the house now, trying to make up for having been a complete fuck-up all that time. She had just said something about the moon, which Heather hadn't caught because she'd been wondering where Emile was. He was meant to be here.

They were talking about the moon because they had both watched this programme on TV the other night about when the Americans landed on the moon. Heather had seen the film clip a million times but she still loved it. Apparently people back then thought that now that men had walked on the moon, it would only be a matter of ten years or something till there were people living up there, in spaceships on legs or in colonies of skyscrapers.

'One day people *will* live on the moon,' Nathalie was now insisting.

'It would be depressing. Because isn't it dark all the time on the moon?'

Nathalie thought about this. 'I don't know. Isn't there a, you know, "dark side of the moon"? So wouldn't that mean there's a not-dark side?'

Nathalie wasn't very smart, Heather thought. Not that she

herself was absolutely sure of the situation on the moon with regard to daylight. She peered into the teardrop-shaped sip-hole of her Red Bull and said, 'But now they just send stuff up there, right? Like robots and satellites and space stations, and let them float around for ever.'

'It's criminal,' Nathalie said, extracting a number of forks from a shiny bouquet of cutlery, 'that we are now leaving our rubbish in space.'

Nathalie was always going on like that. Like about how she was against war and pollution and racial discrimination. Like, *how radical*. But Nathalie was nice.

'Hey,' she said, 'I saw your father on *Ireland Tonight*.'

'Oh,' Heather said, and stared harder into the sip-hole. Loads of people at school had told her they'd seen her father on *Ireland Tonight*. Some of them had said, 'Is he going to lose his job now?'

Heather hadn't thought her father had done so badly but maybe she was just too thick to see it or maybe you couldn't see it if the person was your father. When she'd asked her mother, her mother had said of course he wasn't going to lose his job – he had created an award-winning development that was making loads of money for EI. It was controversial, but that didn't mean it was *bad*.

'He did pretty well,' Nathalie said.

Heather looked up. 'Do you think so?' It was a nice change, hearing someone say that. On the other hand, Nathalie wasn't very smart.

'Yeah. He made sense, a lot of the stuff he said. I can't remember exactly what now, but I remember thinking, yeah, that makes sense.'

Heather was trying to remember something her father had said that made sense so she could remind Nathalie and thereby reassure them both that Nathalie's assessment was correct. But she couldn't remember anything he'd said, sensible or otherwise.

Nathalie had finished unloading the dishes and was now leaning against the island. 'Anyway,' she said, 'he's lovely.'

Heather wrinkled her nose. 'Who?' she asked, though she knew who.

'Your father!' Nathalie said, and playfully swatted Heather on the arm, which meant, Heather knew, that Nathalie was embarrassed.

'Oh.' She felt like Nathalie was waiting for her to say something, but she didn't know what to say, so she spun herself and the stool slowly around again, wondering if she should report such comments to her mother.

She looked at her watch. It was now twenty to five. Where was Emile? Had he totally forgotten that Heather was meant to be helping him pick out a new fish for his aquarium? She had seen him only once since the night with Cormac. She'd come over last Sunday and they'd watched TV while his parents and Nathalie and Nathalie's new sort-of boyfriend were out at the theatre. She hadn't told him anything about Cormac, but maybe he'd heard somehow and was angry with her. Maybe she had done the wrong thing entirely and blown it with Emile. This thought, which had begun to creep up on her, now filled her with horror. She tried to reason with herself. How would Emile have heard? He wasn't friends with anyone else from her school. And Emile had texted her only last night and said CU4phish@4, like everything was fine.

Anyway, Heather had decided she was going to say something, today. After the pet store, she would declare her feelings. The episode with Cormac had emboldened her, especially as Cormac had phoned her four or five times since. She'd kept him at bay without ever really telling him she never wanted to see him again, because the truth was that although Heather wasn't very interested in speaking to Cormac when he phoned, she very much liked having him phone; it was her first taste of the pleasure of being wanted by someone she didn't want.

She was tempted to talk to Nathalie about Emile. It was one of those situations that she suspected had a really easy solution, and people who were slightly older, even if they weren't that smart, could tell you what the solution was, if only you'd ask. The thing was, Nathalie was Emile's sister, so she might tell Emile. On the other hand, she was a girl, so she might not.

'So,' Heather said, 'what's your new boyfriend like?'

'Neil?' Nathalie scrunched up her shoulders and smiled. 'He's lovely. We met at the gym.' She rolled her eyes. 'Can you imagine? Me, at the gym. But he's not like Mr Workout or anything. He's, I don't know, sweet.'

Heather nodded. She wasn't particularly interested in Nathalie's new boyfriend. She was just trying to get round to the topic of Emile. While she was thinking of what to say next, Nathalie said, 'D'you have a boyfriend?' She was looking at Heather like she was trying to remember something.

Heather pulled in her lips till they disappeared.

'*Wha-hut*!' Nathalie laughed. 'Go on, tell us. Who is he?'

'Well,' Heather said, having released her lips, 'I really like someone. And I think he likes me. But we're just friends. I wouldn't call him my boyfriend.'

'Not yet, maybe. Give it a couple of weeks. Boys are insecure. They're terrified of looking stupid. That's the first thing you should know about them.'

Heather looked forlornly at the wall. *A couple of weeks?* She'd known Emile way longer than that. Her heart was beating faster. Why was she so nervous? It wasn't even Emile, it was only his sister. But she'd never said it out loud, not to anyone, and now she was about to –

'Emile,' she said.

Nathalie got a strange look on her face. 'Emile . . . ?'

Heather swallowed. What did the strange look mean and why was Nathalie giving it to her? She knew well what it meant. It meant that Emile was not, and probably never would be, her boyfriend. It might mean that Emile was someone else's boyfriend. Someone at his school, probably, a girl who'd been to the house, who Nathalie probably knew, who Emile might even be with right now, picking out a new fish. A girl he'd never told Heather about because he knew Heather loved him and he didn't want to hurt her feelings so he was waiting for her to figure it out, but Heather was too thick, she hadn't figured it out. How could she have thought – she, Heather, the one with the red splotches on her cheeks! – that Emile would love her instead of, well, whoever he did love?

'What *about* Emile?' Nathalie asked. She had removed the strange look from her face and replaced it with a fake cheerful one.

Heather shrugged. 'He has a girlfriend, right?' It came out very quietly, but aside from that it seemed like a good recovery, a clever switch in tactics, pretending like she already knew about the girl and wasn't that bothered. Like, *That's cool, I'll just start liking someone else now*. She even managed a smile.

Nathalie's eyes roved strangely around the room, like in a film when someone's being strangled. She twisted her mouth to one side. Her mobile rang. She looked from the mobile to Heather and back again. Then she picked up the phone and checked the caller display.

'I won't be a minute,' she said. 'It's someone from my group, but I'll tell her I'll ring her back.'

Heather sat there with nothing to do but stare into her Red Bull while Nathalie got rid of her friend on the other end of the phone. She was laughing a lot and saying things like, *Well done, you! Did you ever think – no, I know! I'm the same, but listen, I'll ring you back*, and throwing worried looks in Heather's direction.

When Nathalie hung up, she turned the phone off. The seriousness with which she seemed to be taking this discussion was only increasing Heather's sense of foreboding. She was shaking her head now and looking intently into Heather's eyes.

'Emile . . . doesn't have . . . a girlfriend,' she said.

Nathalie delivered this line with such solemnity, Heather half expected her to follow it with, *but he does have a fatal disease, hasn't he told you?*

Heather blinked and looked sideways. Nathalie kept staring at her, waiting for her to say something, to ask a question. But Heather didn't need to ask.

Twenty-One

The buzz Gillian felt these days was more suited to the motorway, but tonight she was taking the old road home from Meath. The R108 was a good discipline. As it was only local traffic – farmers in old bangers, horses in horseboxes, people just nipping down to the shops, and trailers with hay piled so high it trembled – you couldn't go fast on it. Gillian had often used the 108 as an exercise in patience, a meditation; it was one long speed bump she'd incorporated into her commute, though she'd been taking it less and less lately.

It was early April and still bright. The sky was periwinkle. (In late summer the light could go an unearthly gold-green or, if it was warm and thundery, a deep velvety grey.) She passed the turn-off for Gormanstown, heading down into the valley again, the green fields spreading before her, then the last stretch into Naul, the first crude scratchings of suburbs before the turn-off for Lusk; the Hollywood Lakes; Ballyboughal; the St Francis Brewery – her litany of landmarks – then the scrubby bit as you neared the T-junction for Swords.

She saw him just before she reached the junction. He was building a wall off the hard shoulder, but at that moment he was standing still, holding his left hand around his right wrist, he'd hurt his hand, and Gillian slowed – she could hardly take her eyes off him – then pulled over because she'd begun to feel a little bit faint or perhaps anxious, she couldn't tell which and maybe it was both. She put the car in neutral, pulled the handbrake and looked at him, smaller now, in her side mirror.

The mirror made him tiny in an unsettling sort of way, standing all alone like that, only an inch high.

It wasn't the man himself, his face or the way he stood, or even his injury that did it. It was the way he looked, floating in her mirror, disconcerting the way people are disconcerting when viewed upside-down. She closed her eyes to let whatever it was pass (a panic attack? her first hot flash?), and when she did she saw her mother and that other man in the kitchen, upside-down, in the house she used to live in before Grace and Martin's, before her parents disappeared.

The man in her mother's kitchen must have been some kind of a tradesman because he was wearing those trousers that you can hang tools on, and his trousers and his white T-shirt had what looked like grey paint on them as well as blood, just like his shoes did and like the towel her mother was holding around his hand. Her mother and the man were upside-down because Gillian was playing the upside-down game, which involved curling into a ball and positioning herself on her head on the big sofa in the sitting room and watching people through the kitchen door as they moved about upside-downly.

But what was going on just then was too interesting – you could miss things when you were upside-down – so she righted herself in order to get a proper view of what looked like the unfolding of a major emergency. Then the man and her mother both gave a little laugh.

Gillian saw herself heading towards the kitchen, skirting the rug the way she always did and pushing herself along the wooden floor like a cross-country skier, not lifting her feet, not making a sound.

Her mother and the bleeding man turned to look at her. The man said something – she couldn't hear what, but her mother and the man smiled at her, then looked quickly back at his hand. Her mother peered closer at the man's hand, shook her head and said something else, this time to the man, something like: *I can't see anything.*

Gillian looked down at her socks. They had little scalloped eaves around their folded-over tops. She could see the tops of the socks clearly, which meant she was wearing shorts or a dress. Her socks were white and rather dirty around the toes, the way they got when she'd been wearing them around the house all day without shoes. Her mother had disappeared somewhere and left the brave man standing there alone. Gillian looked up at his hand, which was bleeding all over his clothes, and said, *Can I see?* Or maybe she didn't. Maybe she just thought it. Or maybe she was just thinking now that that's what she would have said at the time.

Gillian opened her eyes.

The car was still idling by the side of the road. She clicked open the glove box and fished for paper and found three old tax discs. On the backs of them she wrote down, as quickly as she could, every detail she could recall. Then she put the discs carefully into her bag. When she looked up again and checked the mirror, the man was gone.

Twenty-Two

The last time Damien saw Kate O'Loughlin, she was chained to a lamppost. He hadn't seen her in the flesh, only in the papers, but he remembered her, as did everyone he knew, including his mother, who had asked him, when he'd told her about the semi-famous woman who would be at the meeting, 'But why had she to be naked?'

'I think it's a Scandinavian thing,' he'd said. 'Stripping for a cause.'

'Tcht,' she'd said. 'She was only looking for attention.'

She had rung him at the office that morning. Since his stint on *Ireland Tonight* his mother had been taking a keener interest in his work. She regarded with near-reverence anyone who appeared on television – she didn't realize how easy it was now to get on television – though she wasn't entirely sure that Damien's new celebrity was cause for pride.

The reason Kate O'Loughlin had shackled herself naked to a lamppost was because, as a PhD candidate, she had staged a protest on the one-year anniversary of the Emigrant Ship and Visitors' Centre in New Ross. Under cover of darkness, she had painted

THE FAMINE WASN'T FUN

across the ground of the car park. When the Minister for Tourism had arrived first thing in the morning for a low-key celebratory photo op, he'd encountered Kate, who had

Sellotaped replicas of the centre's replicas of passenger tickets all over her otherwise naked body before slipping into the chains. Over her head, stretched between poles, was a banner that read:

MY DEATH CERT IS YOUR SOUVENIR

She wasn't there long before they cut her chains and hauled her into New Ross Garda station – attempting during the chain-cutting to cover her with a blanket, an attempt Kate fiercely resisted. Her writhing, combined with the breeze and the friction of the blanket, caused some of the tickets to come unstuck, leaving patches of flesh exposed. Damien had heard all this second-hand, from someone in the Minister's office, though he was able to imagine it from the photos in the various papers, each taken at a slightly different stage in the struggle. He remembered Gareth saying, as they'd gazed at the *Irish Independent* on Gareth's desk, 'She'd be brilliant in marketing.'

Kate had long since given up taking off her clothes in public. As keen on tenure as anyone, she had settled into a life of contributing papers to little-read journals, overseeing graduate theses in Cork and sitting on panels such as this one. Now she was here to discuss 'The Making of Kill', an exhibition to be housed in the interpretive centre. There were two others at the table with Kate. To her left was Dean, from Heritage Inc, a London-based marketing group promoting heritage sites and interpretive centres in the UK and Ireland. Next to Dean was Moira, who used to work for a now-defunct preservation body and was currently with Exhibit Design, a company that advised on museum exhibitions. Damien had already held meetings with Dean and Moira, but Kate hadn't joined them until now. In fact Damien hadn't known until yesterday that it would be

Kate on the panel – the list had simply said 'academic consultant'. Now that she was here, they needed to start finalizing the content. It had to be done quickly. The exhibition was due to open in June, in time for the summer season, and it was already March.

Damien had opposed the idea when Gareth put it to him, but Gareth had overruled him.

'Everything is process now,' Gareth had said. 'Setting aside a room or running a video to explain how a thing was reconstructed or discovered or dug up is almost standard.'

'But what's the benefit to us?'

'The benefit is that by agreeing to the project, we show that we're happy for our methods to be transparent. That we have nothing to be hostile or secretive about –'

'But we *don't* have anything to be hostile or secretive about.'

'Exactly.'

It was damage limitation. It was PR. Sean's memoir was due out in May, and some postgrad at Notre Dame was using Kill in a documentary short called *Reality Tourism: The New Subservience*. They needed to start, as Jimmy had said, liaising with the enemy.

'Sorry,' Damien said, pulling out a chair. 'Traffic.'

'No problem.' Moira smiled at him. 'There's sandwiches there.'

He sat down at the oval-shaped table and looked at the sections of filled ciabattas on the tray in front of him. He hated ciabattas – sometimes they were so hard they did something to his jaw so that for days afterwards it would make a disconcerting clicking noise as he chewed – but there was no getting away from them these days. He lifted a section containing some slabs of grey-white cheese and several stringy pieces of rocket and applied himself.

His glance made the rounds of the table, sweeping repeatedly across Kate, as she was sitting directly opposite him. Once or twice, he caught her eye and thought he detected a glint of cynical self-satisfaction.

'Couldn't she have Sellotaped the tickets to one of those body leotards?' his mother had asked.

'I'm not sure the impact would've been the same,' he'd said, not entirely comfortable discussing a naked woman with his mother, whose disapproval of nudity, he suspected, had extended to the marital bed.

Kate dropped her eyes to her lap, and Damien dropped his to her breasts. He imagined nudging tickets with his nose and tonguing the flesh underneath – how stiff her nipples must have been that morning! She had the kind of breasts you'd think a woman like her would have (that was interesting, the way women's breasts seemed to match their personalities, but it was probably just one of those things, like a nose or a car: once you were used to someone having a certain kind, you couldn't imagine them having any other kind). Kate's breasts were large, not comically or artificially, but more offhandedly. She wore them as though she had agreed, at some throwaway moment in the distant past, to look after them.

Damien reminded himself to look away. He knew that just because Kate had chained her naked body to a lamppost he was not entitled to mentally undress her at a meeting. He moved the ciabatta around his mouth, attempting to reduce the rock-hard crust to ingestible mush. He chewed and chewed, his jaw was clicking already, and as he chewed, he thought of crawling on all fours under the table and burying his face in Kate's crotch, a hand on each hip, tucking into her as though she were a slice of watermelon.

'You ready to get started?' he heard Dean say. Dean was pouring tea for all of them.

Damien nodded, shifting in his seat, trying to reel in his mind, which had wandered off into the little storage room he'd passed in the corridor and was having Kate amidst the cardboard boxes and the out-of-order photocopier and the stacks of last year's Eircom directories. He rubbed his eyes. He wasn't having enough sex. His libido was becoming far too free-range. If only Gillian . . .

If only Gillian what?

He was meeting Elspeth tonight at six. She wanted to talk to him. She hadn't said about what, exactly; just asked had he noticed anything odd about Gillian. She'd also asked him not to mention to Gillian that they were meeting.

'What's wrong?' he'd said.

'Don't worry,' she'd said. 'Really.'

But of course he was worrying. There was a handful of reasons he could think of for such secrecy, each one of them alarming. He was trying not to dwell on it – after all, it might have nothing to do with him; it might be a problem between Elspeth and Gillian – but the anxiety was there, simmering away at the back of his mind.

Moira turned over a page of her notes. 'So we were talking before you got here, Damien, about the Famine.'

'The Famine?' he said. 'What about the Famine?'

'In relation to the village,' Dean said.

Kate sat up straighter. 'Famine cottages line the road leading up to the interpretive centre,' she said. 'They were moved to that location. Am I right?'

Kate was obsessed with the Famine. People like her made Damien feel insufficiently obsessed. He offered the most minimal sign of assent he could manage.

'So we start by saying that,' Kate said.

Damien turned to Moira. 'Why?'

'The brief,' Moira said, eyeing her notes, 'is to "explore what the construction of the village reveals about representations of history".'

'I know what the brief is,' Damien said.

Kate scrutinized him, sardonically, then turned her head, slowly, deliberately, towards Moira. Damien looked over at Dean. Dean was an ally; he thought the exhibition was unnecessary. But he believed, along with Gareth, that – if handled right – it would add a certain 'intellectual cachet' to the project.

Damien disagreed; intellectual cachet could be off-putting. He hadn't forgotten the day he'd been standing outside the National Gallery and heard a little boy asking his mother, *Can anybody go in there?* Damien froze, waiting for her response, which, when it came (for she'd taken a moment to assess the building and the people entering and leaving it), was, *No, you have to belong.*

He turned back to Moira. 'So what's the idea vis-à-vis the Famine?'

'What Kate is suggesting is a panel explaining how the cottages were moved, what EI's rationale was in doing so, and how the move may have affected the original site.'

'Affected the original site?'

'Every time you remove something from a landscape, you alter it.' Kate narrowed her eyes. 'You've taken people's homes away –'

'People's homes? Nobody's lived in those cottages for a hundred and fifty years.'

'They were an*ces*tral homes. They signified something to those who saw them every day, they signified continuity.'

'They weren't even cottages any more,' Damien said, his

voice rising. He'd forgotten all about fucking her atop the Eircom directories. 'They were just gable ends and a few stones. *Now* they're cottages, because we rebuilt them.'

'Because where they were,' Kate said, leaning forward, 'they weren't serving a purpose any more, right? Their removal is a perfect opportunity to open up the topics of displacement, diaspora, ruptures in the stability of the community. It's essentially a metaphor for emigration, which is one of your themes . . . isn't it? The "American wake"? People migrating to where their labour is needed, whether they have an inherent connection with that place or not. It's landscape as commodity –'

'Okay, okay.' It was Dean. He held up his hands. Turning to Damien, he said, 'It seems to me that this kind of thing would be of interest to people. As well as a way of acknowledging that EI preserved those cottages that would otherwise have completely disintegrated.'

Moira nodded. 'You could have one standing panel,' she said. 'A few black-and-white images?'

Damien said nothing. He was almost smiling. They were, he was beginning to realize, humouring Kate. A couple of concessions to placate her, a sop to her Famine fixation, and maybe she'd be happy. Gareth had said as much: *The point is to make these people feel they've had their say. Once we've got them on side, it's a bit harder for them to criticize.*

Damien looked around the table. 'Could be interesting,' he said.

He was leaning against the wall, having just come back from the gents. He was thinking about the fact that Kate loathed him – it was clear to him by now that she did – and about how he was beginning to loathe her. She was supposed to be providing information, not dictating the content or tone or method of presentation, which, two hours into the meeting, she was still attempting to do.

She hadn't acknowledged his entry nor the fact that he had not reseated himself at the table. Instead she was looking intently at Moira, who was saying, '. . . because we want to avoid too much black and white.'

There were a dozen or so photos lying on the table. 'Who are these people?' Damien asked, nodding at the one closest to him.

'These people,' Kate said, 'are part of the protest that took place outside of the EI offices in February.'

'Oh, that,' he said, without looking up at her.

The six people in Kate's photo were not 'part of' the protest, they *were* the protest. Each of the six wore a white T-shirt, and on the front and back of each shirt was printed a single characteristic, an allusion to both the Seven Dwarfs and to the latest EI Worldwide Visitor Survey of tourist expectations. There was WITTY, SNEAKY, CHATTY, TIPSY, LAZY and (SOOO) FRIENDLY. Damien and Jimmy had watched them from the fifth-floor window, trudging after one another in a small circle, and had agreed that it was pretty sad that the protesters couldn't rustle up a seventh.

Damien took the few steps towards the table and tapped a finger on the photos. He looked at Kate. 'So what have you in mind here?'

'The controversy at Kill reflects larger issues over heritage and public interest. These,' she nodded towards the photos, 'are from various battles over the past few years.'

'*Battles?*' Damien leaned forward. He scanned the pile for the car-park shot of Kate, but there was only an enlarged reproduction of an *Irish Times* piece headlined:

Jaysus. Damien was exhausted. He felt the fleeting temptation to walk out. His half-eaten ciabatta looked up at him forlornly, the strands of escaping rocket having gone limp. He still had Elspeth ahead of him.

'So what's your point about the black-and-white?' Dean asked.

'Black-and-white,' Kate said, 'is the visual medium of protest. Therefore the continuity with that tradition is foregrounded if you use black-and-white. It's more psychologically and sociologically accurate.'

Damien succeeded in saying nothing.

'It's a good point.' It was Moira.

'It *is*?' Damien said. He noticed that each of the three others had a sheet of paper in front of them – it must have been handed out while he was in the gents – titled 'Suggested text to accompany protest photos from The People v EI'.

'"The People versus EI"?'

'We don't have to go with that, of course,' Dean said. 'Those exact words.'

Damien stared at him, then shifted his gaze to Moira. He didn't look at Kate. It was obvious by now that Dean and Moira were not his allies – they were Kate's. And Kate was not the one being humoured here; he was.

By a quarter to six, Damien was in the car heading into town. By now he was pretty certain that Elspeth knew something about Gillian that he didn't and that the only reason she hadn't told him yesterday was because it was too huge, too awful, for the phone, and that when she'd asked him if he'd noticed anything odd lately she was only sounding him out, confirming her suspicions: that he was totally ignorant of the fact that his wife was in love with someone else.

His mistake, he'd begun to believe, had been in never telling Gillian that he knew about what she'd done. If he'd told her, he'd have got credit for forgiving her. As it was, she had no idea how hard it had been, how much it had taken out of him, to see her touching someone else like that – standing in that restaurant, straightening his collar, caressing his neck before dropping her hand and glancing quickly behind her, a deplorable furtiveness in her expression. If she knew, she'd feel ashamed, and he resented her freedom from shame almost as much as he did her infidelity.

He was inching up Pearse Street. There was always a tailback here at rush hour. Up ahead and to his left, a split-screen billboard announced:

WHY WAIT? SHE WON'T.

Damien blinked. Was it an ad for the cock clinic? Good Lord. They'd become almost bullying. He studied the images. There was a man on the left side, waiting. On the right was a woman, not waiting; in fact, going off with another man. All three of them were holding mobile phones. The ad wasn't for the cock clinic at all, Damien realized, it was for Nokia, and the two who were going off together (you just knew) had more ways of communicating through their mobiles than the poor bastard left behind did, or maybe their ways were faster because they had some high-speed option the poor bastard didn't have, as a result of which he'd been twenty seconds later ringing the woman, or texting or e-mailing or whatever.

Fucking hell, Damien thought. Not much margin for error these days. It depressed him that he was able, at a glance, to decipher the billboard's message. Wouldn't it be nice, he thought, to be from another planet for a day and not be able to understand any of this shit? He chewed on his knuckles and stared out at the bleakness of Pearse Street.

Elspeth was waiting for him at a little bar and restaurant on the north quays. It was Monday and the bar was quiet. She stood up when she saw him and gave him a small smile that he couldn't read. He leaned down and she kissed him once on each cheek. He had his hand on her hip and wanted to pull her close – he wanted to hug her, he needed to. But Elspeth didn't hug.

He sat down and banged his knee on the low table while attempting to pull his chair closer. The table was square and too big, he was miles from Elspeth and his chair was so deep that if he tried to rest his back against its back, his feet would lift off the ground.

'What the fuck?' he said.

'Did you hurt your knee?'

He twisted and put his briefcase in the large accidental storage area that existed behind his back. 'Why do we have to go fucking with things that can't be improved upon? Like the relationship between the height of a table and the height of a chair. Like the dimensions of a seat. Look at me.' He slid all the way back. 'It's like I'm Alice in fucking Wonderland.'

Elspeth cringed, gently.

The barman came over. Damien felt like lodging a complaint about the furniture. But the barman would say what everyone in the service industry (was it still called that?) said now if you complained –

Nobody else has complained . . .

– which encouraged a kind of self-censorship because who

wants to look like the lone malcontent? Damien felt like complaining about that. That idiotic riposte.

'Gin and tonic,' he said, and squeezed the bridge of his nose between his thumb and first finger.

Elspeth was already having a martini. She didn't say anything. She was waiting for him to relax.

When Damien's drink arrived, he took a long swallow, eyeing her over the rim of the glass.

'Better?' she said.

He shook his head. 'Sorry.' He told her about the meeting. 'Do you remember the woman who chained herself to a lamppost in the car park of the Famine ship a few years ago?'

Elspeth squinted. 'I don't know. Do I?'

'She was naked.'

'Oh, her!'

'She's on the panel that's deciding what goes into the exhibition.'

Elspeth looked surprised. 'Wasn't she a bit mad?'

'No,' Damien said. 'She just pretended to be for a while.'

'So was she naked at the meeting?'

'Only in my mind,' Damien said, and felt suddenly, fleetingly, randy. Not towards Elspeth. Despite her manner of indiscriminate flirtation, Elspeth's complete lack of sexual intent with regard to him was so obvious that he'd stopped thinking of her in that way a long time ago. Besides, she wasn't really his type. She was too bony. No, he was thinking of – what was her name? Natalia? Nathalie? something like that – Heather's friend, or her boyfriend's sister. Heather had told him just the other day that Nathalie, who was twenty-one or something, had seen him on TV and thought he was handsome.

Handsome, eh?

She says you're lovely.

He'd pretended mild amusement and resisted the temptation to press for Nathalie's exact words.

He knocked his top and bottom teeth against each other, three, four, five times.

Elspeth sipped her martini. Damien had never acquired a taste for martinis and felt incompletely grown up as a result. 'You're bad,' she said.

'If only I were,' he said, meaning to sound coy and sounding, instead, miserable. They both fell silent. 'So,' he said.

She put her drink down and folded her hands on her lap.

'Tell me.'

Elspeth gave a big, drawn-out shrug. 'I don't know,' she said.

'Well, you wanted to talk about *some*thing.'

She shook her head. 'Maybe it's nothing. I just find her . . . odd lately. Skittish. She'll hardly sit down and have a conversation with me any more. I keep thinking there's something she's not telling me. I don't know what it is. Maybe she's thinking of selling?' She glanced at Damien. 'I ask her what's going on and she just says, "Nothing," and I feel like I'm intruding. But it's getting hard to work together. She's so secretive.'

'She's always been secretive,' Damien said, leaning back, before he remembered how far away back was. 'She'll tell you that herself.'

'It's the only thing she'll tell me.'

He was wondering how he should say it because it looked as if Elspeth was going to leave it up to him.

She picked up the toothpick on which her olive was impaled, caught the olive behind her teeth and withdrew the toothpick, like she was unsheathing a sword. She disembowelled the olive and put the stone on a saucer. 'So you're not worried?'

'I didn't say I wasn't worried.'

'Then you are worried.'

Damien looked around the bar. The crowd had trebled. He'd already drained his drink. 'You ready for another?' He nodded at her glass.

'Are you driving?'

'One more.' He motioned to the barman, then turned in his chair, using the armrest as a backrest and wedging his uninjured knee against the opposite armrest. He felt like a pretzel. 'I'm worried,' he said, 'but not about her selling.'

Elspeth bit down on the toothpick. 'What do you mean?'

'I thought you were going to tell me she was seeing someone else.'

Elspeth's mouth opened. She put a hand to her heart and almost smiled. 'You thought *I* was going to tell you that?'

'Well . . .' The barman brought the drinks. Damien unpacked himself from the chair and stirred his gin and tonic with his finger, a habit he'd had for years which Heather had recently told him was unhygienic.

You can get salmonella that way.

She says you're lovely.

'Okay, wait.' Both of Elspeth's hands were up now, palms facing him. 'First of all, as far as I'm aware, there's nothing. I have nothing to tell you. But even if there was something, I mean, Damien . . . my God. You couldn't expect me . . . that's your stuff.'

He tapped a fingernail against his tooth, then stopped. 'So what you're saying is, there's nothing to tell but if there was something to tell you wouldn't tell it anyway.'

She rolled her eyes, but her annoyance wasn't genuine. 'I'm saying that to my knowledge, there's nothing to tell. But if you have suspicions, you should talk to her. They're probably totally unfounded. I think she's going through something. But,' she shook her head, 'I don't think it's that.'

He sipped his drink, then set it back on the table.

'She did seem depressed,' he said. 'After Grace died. But then, lately, I actually thought she was better. She seemed, I don't know. Perkier.'

'So you took that to mean she was seeing someone else?'

He crossed his arms over his chest. Was that a very fucked-up conclusion to have drawn? The way Elspeth put it, it sounded like it was. But Elspeth didn't know the whole story.

'I don't know,' he said, shaking his head. 'I don't know what to think.'

Elsepth put the toothpick on the saucer, next to the olive stone. She was puzzled. 'Have you asked her?'

Damien stared at the saucer. 'No.'

'Well . . .'

'Yeah.'

'Why kill yourself wondering?' she said.

He looked up and shook his head. He didn't know why.

Twenty-Three

She talked dirty to him, but not in the old way.

. . . so rather than trying to slow down and do less with the time we have left, we should fill every minute, do everything we can, go places, meet people, pack it all in. A new line of clinics: Having It All At Sixty. It's heresy!

Her excuse for re-establishing contact, after five years of silence, was the visitation, as she'd come to think of it, which had been so uncanny that she'd convinced herself it might well have been the moment of his death. And even if he hadn't died, the experience had made her realize that if he did she'd have no way of knowing. When they'd ceased communication, they'd made no allowance for such a morbid eventuality; the present had contained drama enough. But it seemed wrong to her now, offensively casual, that one of them might vanish from the world without the other knowing.

She hadn't expected there to be much on-line. He wasn't exactly a public figure. What did come up she initially thought must be a reference to another Jonathan Tran. It was all about noise. Whoever this Jonathan Tran was, he was extremely interested in noise. She went to a site where Jonathan Tran was listed among a group of members of a London-based research team. She clicked on it.

b. London. Studied town planning and information systems. Formerly employed as a manager at an information consultancy firm. Currently engaged in analysis of the changing nature of urban noise, comparing noise-growth patterns in the developed world with those in the developing world, and exploring whether strategies for combating rising noise levels in the former may be equally effective in the latter.

Beside this brief CV was a small photo. His hair was too neatly combed and his smile alien in its bland frankness. He looked corporate, mid-management, lacking in imagination. Looking at this visage of banal virtue, she felt betrayed, as though he were denying who he'd been with her. Or maybe it was the fact that he had changed at all, moved on, recovered; that he wasn't exactly as she'd left him. *You want me to fall apart*, she heard him saying. She didn't. She just wanted proof that it had left a mark on him.

She clicked on MISSION STATEMENT:

Our interest in urban noise includes both an academic and a psychological perspective. We trace the escalation of noise and explore the subtle and not-so-subtle effects on the human psyche of living in increasingly noisy environments. We are investigating whether forms of aural adaptation exact some as yet unidentified or unattributed psychological or physical cost.

Bizarre. She didn't remember him having been particularly interested in noise. In fact, she couldn't recall his ever having mentioned it. And now that she thought about it, his apartment had been surrounded by construction work and he had never once complained.

Along the top of the page that contained his bio was a series of tabs – VIEW (EST.) NOISE LEVEL RATES IN CAPITAL CITIES, BECOME A PARTICIPANT IN OUR STUDY, HISTORY OF

URBAN NOISE RESEARCH COUNCIL (UNRC). The last one said CONTACT ME.

They were guarded with each other at first. They talked about their work and whatever was in the news. But then he asked, with a tentativeness that managed somehow to come through, *Are you still married?*

She felt oddly offended by the question. As though he were suggesting the marriage had been on a certain inevitable course.

Yes, she wrote, with a curtness she hoped would come through. *I am*.

He was seeing someone. For over a year now. She lived in Kent and they spent most weekends together, at his place or at hers. They'd met through work; she was a town planner with an interest in eco-friendly development. Gillian felt frivolous in comparison, though Jonathan seemed genuinely impressed by what she'd done. He'd read an article about her, somewhere.

You did?

She thought of him sitting in his kitchen some morning, a page full of words about her in front of him, a photo, holding the story of her life in his hands. She imagined how she might have haunted him afterwards. She wondered had he kept it, tucked away in a drawer somewhere. He said that, after he'd read it, he'd been on the verge of making contact, but he hadn't wanted to disrupt her life.

You? she wrote. *Disrupt my life? Impossible.*

She didn't ask about the woman in Kent, and he didn't volunteer much. Gillian liked to believe that his reticence was a sign of the woman's insignificance, rather than a sign of her importance. If she didn't hear from him on a given weekend, she knew they were together, and she got angry with herself for feeling angry. She wanted to know if the woman knew about her. She wanted to know what Jonathan's intentions were with this woman. And with her. She wanted to say: Who are we kidding? This was more than a game, more than a warm or offhanded exchange between exes, and they needed to acknowledge this. But come Monday, he'd be back on-line, his tone as breezy as ever. Her unease would vanish and she'd tell herself she was being melodramatic. She had a whole life, after all. Wasn't that what he used to say? And then she learned to disappear herself some days, skipping the daily instalment and leaving his latest note hanging, read but unanswered, until she could no longer stand its look of abandonment.

He sent her a photo. (She'd teased him about the one on the website.) It wasn't quite a close-up, but it was close enough. He looked a little older, his face was thinner, the eyes a bit tired. His hair was slightly tousled and his smile diffident and good-natured. He was outdoors, under a leaden sky, in rain gear zipped up to his chin, as though he'd been out walking. Gillian figured the woman in Kent had taken it, and she wondered if his choice of this particular photo was an attempt to remind her of the existence of a life that excluded her.

She zoomed in on him, the image jumping each time she clicked, a nose, a cheek, an eye. He got grainier and grainier until he looked like a missing person.

The only text accompanying the photo was: *What do YOU look like now?*

She downloaded the image to My Pictures, typed *I look just the way you remember me . . .* and logged off.

He told her about noise. He'd become interested in it through a research project he'd worked on as a consultant. The Noise Research Council had him analysing findings about Third World noise levels. They were putting together a worldwide noise level index, like the one that exists for air quality.

I never thought noise could be so interesting . . . but it is, at least to me. The effects on us are more insidious than with other kinds of pollution. We work with psychologists and neurologists, and it's like detective work. But it's also (maybe) research that could produce actual changes in quality of life within the foreseeable future.

The break from London, and especially those trips to the West of Ireland, had heightened his awareness of all the racket in which he had spent his life immersed. Once he'd started hearing it, he couldn't seem to tune it out, and he began to think that aural desensitization wasn't such a positive form of adaptation.

She told him about Grace – how just when she'd got used to the idea of her slowly disappearing, she had quickly disappeared. But she didn't tell him how lonely the death had left her. Nor did she tell him how much she was thinking about him. And she never mentioned the medication.

He understood her frustration with the Farm. *The problem is that you've got too correct. Maybe you need to do something to contradict it. Drive fast, or no, too dangerous. Speedwalking? A release. Something 'naughty'. We can't be good all the time. Channel surf. Eat something full of additives. Make a lot of noise. Sometimes, secretly, I make a lot of noise.*

When she heard a hammer drill, she thought of him; when she heard car alarms and buses rumbling and when helicopters hovered. Noise made her smile now, like it was some sweet aspect of him, a keepsake or a personal effect she'd stumbled upon.

He was cropping up in places that had long since ceased to contain him. Her attention sought out things that referred to him, however obliquely. A teapot in a shop window the same colour as the cups in his old pre-stocked kitchen. Clementines. Camel Filters. A certain colour skin. Socks with little diamonds on them in the window of Brown Thomas. School House Lane that always reeked of steak from a restaurant's extractor fan. The smell of ginger.

He kept materializing in her mind, superimposing himself upon her field of vision, the way he used to right after she'd come from him. She saw him in the shower, his head bowed beneath the water, his palm against the tiles and his arm outstretched, solid as she rested her hand on it. She saw him from behind as he stood looking out the window of the apartment. And she saw the day he'd slept on the bed after bathing and she'd laid down beside him and watched him, poring over the terrain of his face as though it were a map of somewhere marvellous.

She felt unsettled, but at the same time invigorated. In fact, she liked the way she felt – curious, edgy, in possession of something she didn't know the nature of, or hadn't seen for so long she didn't recognize it. She was eager for the next thing to happen, though she had no idea what the next thing was.

And then she saw her father.

She was in the car when it happened, this time with Damien, coming home from dinner in town. It was dark and raining, and he was driving. The wipers were slipping silently back and forth across the glass in a way she had always found soothing. She wanted to burrow into the moment, hemmed in by blackness and rain, moving slowly out along the Howth road. She was aware, out of the corner of her eye, of Damien's head in silhouette, its outline against the glass, then, without noticing exactly when, she became aware of the noise of the engine, a soft drone enveloping them. She rested in it all for a moment, feeling oddly calm, and then suddenly there she was – just for an instant – in the back of her parents' car, hunkered down in the seat behind them, safe from the black wet night pressing in from outside. She could see the backs of their heads, so high, it seemed, above her. And then her father glanced over his shoulder and said, *All right back there, Pinky?*

She nearly gasped. He used to call her that. She might have forgotten had Grace not reminded her as she was growing up; she'd certainly never remembered hearing him call her that. But now she had heard him. She had his voice in her head, and the words, she knew, were going to stay with her, like one of those lines someone says that you remember for ever because it was wonderful or hurtful or just distressingly accurate, those lines that years later you can hear in your head as clearly as the first time you ever heard them.

She tried to focus her mind to flesh out the scene, but nothing more came. She looked at Damien, to see would his silhouette prompt her again.

'What?' he said, feeling her eyes on him.

She shook her head. 'Nothing,' and put her hand on the back of his neck and massaged it, to steady herself.

Twenty-Four

Two half-packed suitcases were open on the sofa and a large black bin bag sat gaping beside the desk. On top of the desk were boxes with disks in them. Dr Harding was checking over the labels. He'd already thrown several disks into the black bag, but he was hesitating with the one he held in his hand. It was labelled '*Merchant of Venice*, Rome, 2021'. He looked around the room, as though he was afraid he was being watched, then put that disk off to the side with a few others.

This was the final episode of *NY25* before the summer hiatus, and Emile had invited Heather over to watch it. It was the first time she had seen Emile since just before the day of their fish-shopping date, when he hadn't shown up and Heather had cried into the pieces of kitchen roll Nathalie kept tearing off, and everything about Emile fell into place and Heather wondered why she had pretended for so long not to know – or had she pretended? Maybe it just seemed like that now. It was hard to say what she had known, now that she definitely knew it.

Without moving her head, Heather looked over at him. He was closer to her now than he'd been in more than two months, and yet it was like he'd gone away somewhere remote and strange and impossible to reach. Somewhere like Greenland.

They hadn't really talked about it. Emile had said that he was sorry, though he hadn't said about what, and Heather hadn't asked, she'd just said, 'Yeah . . . okay.'

Then he'd said, 'I've missed you!' Really cheerful, like she'd just got back from her holidays or something.

Heather couldn't bring herself to say she'd missed him, too. She'd said, 'Unh-huh . . .'

Loads had happened since she and Emile had last watched *NY25* together. Emile said he had known straight away that the woman with the French manicure was Dr Harding's ex-wife.

'That's why he wouldn't go public with the recording,' Emile insisted. 'Otherwise, he wouldn't have cared so much. He'd have totally gone for the government *and* Mnemon.'

Heather hadn't guessed that the manicure was also the ex-wife. She'd had to wait for about three episodes until the scriptwriters spelled it out for her. But she didn't want to call attention to her general inability to read between the lines, so stopped herself just as she was about to say, *I completely missed that*.

Tonight was the night of the bombing. What had finally convinced Dr Harding to back the Colombo plan was the second recording his ex-wife had sent him. It was of an in-house meeting of Mnemon executives that showed them planning how, even after they did the deal with the government, they would protect certain of their clients – the elite, the wealthy, the money-laundering, the criminal – from the government's prying eyes.

Dr Harding was really nervous. He'd spent his life saving people's lives, and now he was part of something that might end up killing people. But Claire had assured him that the Refuseniks had taken every precaution.

It was almost 8 p.m. in New York. The 6 a.m. shift at the Colombo plant was winding up. Dr Harding and Claire were at Claire's apartment. They had a satellite feed from Colombo that offered a sweeping view of the plant, which was floodlit and surrounded by palm trees, but still looked eerie and deserted.

A buzzer sounded and suddenly people were streaming out of the building, thousands of them, it seemed. Dr Harding reached for Claire's hand where it was resting in her lap, but he didn't look at her. He didn't dare take his eyes off the satellite feed.

After tonight, everything could change. If the bomb was a success, Mnemon and the US government would freak. Nobody seemed worried about the Sri Lankan government freaking. Apparently, in certain parts of the world, they were used to buildings blowing up. Mnemon would probably find out about the Refuseniks, and then it would be a matter of whether they could pin the bombing on any particular individuals. If they did, all the Refuseniks, including Dr Harding, could wind up dead, or in prison, sitting on death row. But Heather didn't think either of those things would happen. The series was continuing in the autumn. Mymar, Claire and Dr Harding were all way too popular to kill off, and death row would be a total bore. Heather's guess was that Dr Harding would have to go underground, disguise himself as a member of the steaming underclass.

The building was empty now except for the robots. The security check had begun. The robots had been sweeping ever since Mnemon had been the target of threats a few years ago, before the Refuseniks had formed. Nobody ever found out who'd made the threats, and Mymar suspected they were invented by Mnemon to win public sympathy and justify a hike in implant prices.

The two guards who were undercover Refuseniks looked around and stepped in through a back door. Everything was dead still, and Dr Harding lifted Claire's hand and put it on top of his knee, so that he could squeeze it between his two hands. He looked more scared than Claire did. The seconds ticked by (though you were meant to think they were minutes), and you saw the guards opening the back door again just as the bank blew.

'Oh!' Emile said.

'Oh my God!'

'They are so fucked!' Emile was totally surprised. Heather was, too. She'd thought it would be a clean operation with a zero body count, if only because she was sure Claire and Dr Harding were going to get it together after the bomb, to celebrate and end the season on a romantic note, and now there was no way they could get it together, not after they'd just watched two Refuseniks getting blown to bits.

On Claire's satellite feed mayhem was already erupting. Police sirens and fire engines and people running every which way waving their hands in the air and shouting in a language that wasn't English.

Dr Harding and Claire looked hard at each other. 'They knew the risks, Bill,' Claire said.

'Did they? Or did you tell them what you told me? That there would be no casualties.'

Claire shook her head, just once and slowly. 'I never said that. I said we had minimized the chances. Don't do this, Bill,' she said. 'Don't pretend you didn't know there was a possibility. They had all the information we had. Something must've gone wrong with the timer.'

There was a guy being interviewed on the satellite feed. He was one of the workers at the memory bank, and clearly a member of the steaming underclass. Claire and Dr Harding turned to look.

'We . . . we like-ah . . . to have the-ah . . .' – he pointed to his head – 'the memory. We like. We don't agree terrorist activities.' He raised both hands and tapped his fingers to the sides of his head. 'All my ideas,' he said, then pointed to the burning bank, 'in there.'

'Jesus,' Dr Harding said.

'Ssh,' Claire said. 'Let's listen.'

'My fam-a-lee,' another man was saying. 'Birthday party. One year ago. Gone.' His hands made the gesture of an explosion. 'My mother, dead. I have films.' He pointed to the bank. 'No more. Gone. Who are these people make this? Why they destroy thoughts of us?'

Dr Harding sighed and hung his head.

'Bill,' Claire said, 'they're mourning the loss of something they haven't really lost. That man still remembers his mother –'

Dr Harding turned to her and put his fingers to her lips and rested his forehead against hers.

After a moment's silence during which Claire and Dr Harding sort of rubbed their faces slowly over one another, Claire whispered, 'There's no going back now.'

'I know.'

She ran her hand through Dr Harding's hair and brushed the back of her fingers down along his temple and his cheek and his jaw. 'I want you to switch off now,' Claire said.

Dr Harding had never had the removal surgery. He hadn't performed the removals on other people either, not after the Reactive Dementia case. He'd said he wasn't going to make guinea pigs of anyone. Emile thought Dr Harding was just scared, and Heather said, 'Yeah, he might be,' but she thought he was wise, too, and that he'd probably have the surgery next season.

Dr Harding looked down at Claire's hands, which he was holding in his own. 'I don't know what's going to happen,' he said. 'To any of us.'

Claire put her finger under his chin and lifted his head a bit and gazed at him with such tenderness it was like she was about to dissolve.

'I can't help it,' Dr Harding said, 'I want to have something . . . I want to be able to see you if I'm somewhere far away or if . . . if anything . . .'

'It's okay,' Claire said, 'you can say it. If anything happens to me.'

'I want to remember you just like this, just like you are now. This beautiful, this alive, this close.'

Claire brought his hands to her lips and kissed them. It was the first time either of their lips had actually touched anywhere on the other's body. Claire looked at him again in that tender and amazing way that was so convincing Heather wondered if they were in love in real life. A tiny wave of sadness broke inside her chest.

'Bill, this will only happen once in exactly this way. Let it.'

Dr Harding looked at her. He was giving in.

Claire said, 'You'll hold on to what you need from it.'

In the triangular space between their bodies, you could still see the satellite feed. It showed a blur of smoke and flames, but the background was now the colour of twilight. Dr Harding reached for his remote and glanced at Claire before switching his implant off.

When he looked up again, she held him in a gaze of such intensity it was like he was powerless to look away. She said, 'Do you have any idea how long I've loved you?'

Dr Harding's lips parted slightly. He was stunned. Clearly he had no idea how long Claire had loved him but, under the circumstances, he did the right thing. He put his lips to hers and he kissed her, properly, his lips parting a bit more now, then more, his mouth moving on Claire's, then slipping down to her neck, which was arched, her shoulders, back up to her jaw, then finding her lips again. As their bodies pressed closer and the triangular space between them shrank, the camera zoomed in slowly on the satellite feed, on the flames and the crowd and then the sky, zooming, zooming, until Emile's whole wall screen was the dusk-blue of a bombed-out tropical dawn.

Heather and Emile sat staring at the screen. She didn't dare look at him. Neither of them spoke. Emile swallowed so loud she heard it. She didn't know why it was that only when you were trying to swallow quietly did your swallow get really loud.

A woman's cool, mechanical voice said: *'NY25' will return in September with a brand-new season of episodes.*

'Do you know what we should do?' Emile said.

'Hunh?' She looked over at him.

'What we should do. We should write a TV series. Just for the hell of it.'

Heather thought about this. She wasn't that into the idea. In fact, she thought it was kind of stupid, a waste of time, which was odd. It was the first time she had ever thought any idea of Emile's was stupid, which did not mean, she realized in a flash of insight, that it was the first stupid idea Emile had ever had.

The world turned on its axis.

'Uh . . . a series about what?'

Emile had the cap of a bottle of Perrier in his hand and was flicking it up in the air. 'Like something like . . . virtual. But you don't know, I mean the viewer doesn't know, if it's virtual or not, and the characters don't either. And it's like a mystery, where you keep trying to figure it out.'

Heather was tired of virtual. 'Yeah,' she said absently, 'that'd be cool.'

She sighed up at the ceiling. At the roof, at the sky, at satellites, heaven or outer space. It wasn't an unhappy sigh; it was just huge. Like when she let out her breath after holding it for as long as she could. She closed her eyes and imagined she was in a boat, a slow one, like the ones they have in Venice, and she was moving out, gliding away, and it was cool, it was nice, she was happy or she was sad, she didn't know what to call it, but it didn't matter.

Twenty-Five

It was seven-twenty. She was meeting him at eight. For the past hour, she'd been lying on the bed in her hotel room, flicking through a *Time Out* guide to Edinburgh she'd borrowed from reception. She couldn't concentrate enough to read, but the glossy pictures, all of which she had now looked at several times, were distracting enough to keep her nerves at a manageable level.

I have to go listen to Edinburgh soon, Jonathan had written.

Edinburgh? Gillian had answered. *When? I've got meetings coming up there, but the dates are flexible.*

This afternoon, she'd seen an editor who wanted her to contribute to a health and leisure publication, had lunch with a Scottish therapist she'd met at a conference on attention deficit disorder in adults, then spoken to someone who was researching a book on Deceleration. The meetings had been mostly for the purpose of convincing Elspeth and Damien of the trip's legitimacy, as well as of preventing Jonathan from suspecting that he was the only reason she was here.

She had become a liar again. She turned the page and stared at a photo of the Scottish Ballet performing *Prince Rama and the Demons*.

Maybe Elspeth was right. Maybe Damien was, too. 'You're somewhere else,' Elspeth had said. 'You're not with us.' Damien would look at her intently and ask, 'Are you okay?'

She felt okay. She felt sharp, in fact. Decisive. She didn't cry any more. But she was out on her own, she knew that, and she knew from before that that was what lying did. It cordoned you off, first in your own mind, then in a way others could see.

The Diax occurred to her, too, of course. She'd been thinking about lowering her dosage, from 30mg to 15. But she was reluctant. She remembered the day she listened to Elspeth's choosing-a-toothbrush spiel and how quick and alert Elspeth had seemed compared to how she was feeling herself at the time, muffled and woolly. She didn't want to go back to that. Why should she?

There'd been talk in the chat room recently about dosages, and a few postings from people who'd gone off Diax. This morning, Dieter from Frankfurt had written:

I went off Diax after three months (could not stand the side effect) and when I stop it, I feel I had become suddenly stupid. I think I have now become normal again, but it make me wonder how the drug is working that my normal mind now feel like slow motion.

Gillian had been tempted to ask Dieter more about it, but she'd been reluctant to post since she'd described the scene with her mother and the man with the bloody hand, and two people had heckled her – *whoa, sounds like you're in the Twilight Zone* – and a third had written something quite disturbing.

If you remember things you did'nt before (like your mother doing crimanal things to you, like mine did and loads of other peoples mothers and fathers did), you should be careful. I did'nt go on this drug (no way), but I started to remember without it. Could be you will remember things that will effect you deeply. BE CAREFUL. Only word of advise because I have been there and only tons of therapy saved me.

Gillian had never posted about the thing in the car – *You all right back there, Pinky?* They'd have thought she was mad.

She scrolled down. BF from Michigan had responded to Dieter:

You are better off without it. do not waste your money on this product Diaxadril is only one farther example of drug compinies trying sell you something you don't need! There website should be called diaxadril.CON. There is no hard evadence that it does ANYTHING! The best way of decresing your chances of MCI/AD is to stay "cognatively active" and avoid arterosclerosis etc which can be done WITHOUT DRUGS!

In answer, Roy S from Birmingham wrote:

Why is it that conspiracy theorists can never spell?

Gillian hadn't come across Roy S before, but she liked his style.

Juliette, Paris, had come down on the side of Diax:

Taking this Diaxadril is no stupider than to take vitamins. No large risks are detected and benefits are reported on clinical trials. It is preventative, so means that maybe you never know if it is the thing that prevents the disease, or one helpful factor or just a placebo. Of course there is this chance that you don't need Diax, but I am high risk for AD and prefer to invest in its possibility of help.

To which Mark, Vernonia, Oregon, had answered:

Yes no stupider than vitamins, but Diax is a lot more expensive than vitamins (which have been shown just as unnecessary), unless you go to Mexico for your prescription (or maybe Moscow for you) and anyway, everyone knows that the French are number one druggies in western world and take ten pills every time they sneeze!

Idiot, Gillian thought. She'd felt like writing a note of support to Juliette. But she knew her posting would only provoke another imbecilic comment from Vernonia or some other outback of reason, which she would then feel compelled to refute. It was the frustrated desire to have the last word in a world in which there were no last words – no expert opinions to which everyone deferred, no definitive answers, no filtering of misinformation and, apparently, no spell check. Just as she'd been about to log off, she saw a posting from Gordon, the man from London who had lost his fiancée. Gordon's note was addressed to her.

G, he'd written, *where have you been? How are you? Have you seen anyone . . . of interest lately?*

Busy, she'd typed. *Fine*. And, *No, I haven't seen anybody lately*.

He was thinner, and he'd quit smoking. He had one of those little white nicotine things and he sucked on it from time to time – it was like a cross between a ceramic hash pipe and an o.b. tampon. When she was ordering, she'd noticed him changing the pellet in it. Gillian was not pro-smoking, but she did feel a certain nostalgia for his smoking, and it seemed a little sad, this change in him. She could remember him in the white vest and boxers, sitting in the kitchen, blowing blue-grey smoke straight up into the air as though nothing could touch him.

'I thought people gained weight when they quit,' she said.

He shrugged. 'Hill walking.'

Gillian arched her brows, trying to look impressed. *Hill walking*. He was smiling tentatively at her and she was thinking how effeminate his new hobby sounded. She shook her head to make the thought go away.

'What?' he said.

Gillian took a deep breath. 'Oh . . .' she said, with a slow shrug, 'this.'

Jonathan nodded. 'Yeah,' he said.

She couldn't get over how thin he looked. But he also looked looser and more relaxed; when she'd known him before he'd been like something wound very tightly. She wondered how she seemed to him, but it was too soon to ask. The waiter came with the wine, and Jonathan gestured for her to taste it. She realized she'd never been out to dinner with him before.

When she'd okayed the wine, they touched their glasses gently together. Then he set his down and said, 'So . . .'

She smiled. He shook his head. *Imagine. Us. Sitting here.*

There was a moment of silence, an acknowledgement that there was no obvious place to begin.

Finally, she said, 'So it's getting noisier in Edinburgh?'

'Seems that way,' he said. A good-natured vexation. 'Noise is like an arms race. It just keeps escalating. You can witness it any time you're in a pub. In trying to rise above existing noise you unwittingly create more of it that others in turn must rise above. And it isn't just noise, it's vulgarity.' He leaned back in his chair. 'The more crap that's coming at us, the more outrageous people and things have to be to attract our attention. Talk louder. Say something more shocking. Show more cleavage.'

Gillian considered the cleavage she was showing. It was minimal. She had dressed conservatively. 'So what's the solution?' she said.

'Solution? Do people really use that word any more?'

'You sound like Elspeth. "There's no such thing as problem or solution; there is only process."'

'Well,' he said, 'I don't know if I agree with that. But half the time I suspect that all we're doing is reminding people of the questions, trying to keep conclusions from becoming foregone.'

Gillian managed a thin smile. 'It's funny,' she said, 'how we ended up in sort of similar lines of work. I mean, in a way. We're both in the less-is-more business.'

'Yeah,' he said, 'it is funny.'

'You should come and give a talk at my place,' she said.

He looked surprised.

'I'm joking,' she said quickly.

'Oh. Well.'

'Well.'

'You never know,' he offered, trying to head off her embarrassment. There was a silence.

The waiter appeared with a plate of antipasto.

Jonathan took a last pull on his inhaler before slipping it into his breast pocket. 'You know,' he said, 'I was amazed when I read about the Farm. I was really glad for you, that you'd got out of that office – not that it was such a bad place . . .'

She smiled, more sardonically than she'd meant to. He didn't smile at all. The pause was his acknowledgement.

'. . . but just that you'd done something so' – his eyes went wide – 'risky.'

'It didn't feel risky,' Gillian said. 'It was like I was a different person then. I was so sure I was right.'

'And now?' He picked up his fork and speared a slice of carpaccio. She looked at his hand and saw it turning the key in the lock of his apartment on one of those lunch hours. 'Now you're not so sure?' he said.

For a moment she couldn't look at him. This was what they used to dream of – getting away to some city, any city, where they could be anonymous and take their time – and here they were, five years later, talking shop.

She took a breath and said, 'Now I think: who am I to be telling people how to live? There was a kind of a hubris about it, I think, but also an innocence. I was burned out at that office . . .' She stopped. She saw him approaching her desk, the look in his eyes on the days they were going to meet.

'. . . so it was kind of . . . in reaction to that, everything I did. But really, what do I know?'

'Well, you must be doing something right.'

She cut an artichoke heart in two and slipped half in her mouth. When she'd swallowed, she began her recitation. 'The average doctor visit now lasts eight minutes. There is an over-the-counter medication for women who "don't have time for a yeast infection". Developers of high-rises have discovered an upper limit to the number of storeys in a building; it's determined by the amount of time people are willing to wait for a lift. In Tokyo, all-you-can-eat buffets charge by the minute: the faster you eat, the cheaper it is. Etcetera, etcetera.'

He was listening, watching her.

'So I thought I could change the world, you know?'

'You did?' He laughed. Then said, 'Sorry,' noticing the look on her face. 'It's just, at some stage you have to say, "So what?" Not take the world so personally.'

She shook her head. 'I don't think I take the world personally.'

'What I mean is, let go of all that questioning and just do whatever you're doing. Not take yourself so seriously.'

'So I take the world personally and myself too seriously.'

He leaned back again in his chair and eyed her, as though remembering how defensive she could be. 'I didn't mean *you*. I meant all of us.'

His certainty made Gillian feel lonely. She looked down at her plate.

'But,' he said, 'if it doesn't feel right any more, trust your instincts and do something else.'

She heard a double meaning in everything he said.

The waiter smiled at her as he approached to clear their

plates. He seemed to understand that she was having difficulty.

Jonathan smiled, too. 'Just make sure you get a good price from whoever buys you out.'

When the waiter had disappeared again, she said, 'You know, I don't want to talk about work.'

Another silence.

'I'm sorry,' he said.

'It's okay.'

'It just seemed like a safe place to start.'

He asked about Heather. Gillian said, 'She hardly speaks to me these days.'

'It's the age,' he said. His kids were at university now. He and his first wife had started young.

'Let's hope.'

Jonathan told her about the house he'd bought and the new floors he'd put in and what the neighbourhood was like.

'You sound settled,' she said.

'Settled?' He looked at her and rolled his eyes. 'I think I've given up on that idea.'

'How do you mean?'

'I mean any time I've ever thought, *Okay, this is it, this is where I stay, this is who I stay with*, it's always sort of exploded in my face, sometimes in a way I can laugh at, sometimes not. Now, I don't know. It seems wiser just to watch, see what unfolds. You know what I mean?'

'I do,' she said, though she'd never managed it herself.

He asked her to tell him more about how it had been having Grace with them, and how she'd been getting on since Grace's death. She said she thought she was coming around. She told him a bit about the trip to France, making clear she'd gone with Damien without ever actually mentioning his name.

'I felt guilty going,' she said, 'so soon after. But then I thought, no. No, this is exactly what I should do. Grace was dead, okay. But I still loved the South of France. And I mean that's the point, isn't it? That's the gift the dead give. They remind us how much we love living.'

He was looking at her like he used to, way back in the beginning, when who she was was only just dawning on him and every day was a revelation.

Halfway through the main course, he said, 'Did you ever tell him?'

Gillian froze. Her face felt hot and prickly.

'No,' she said.

He nodded and kept chewing, and didn't lift his eyes from his plate.

'Should I have?' she asked.

She could see immediately that the question bothered him. It was how all their old arguments had started. He used to say he felt sorry for Damien, and Gillian had always heard it as an accusation.

Jonathan was having agnolotti, pasta in the shape of pillows, and as he punctured a pillow with his fork he said, 'I told her I was having dinner with you tonight.'

'You told who?' Gillian said, though she knew.

'Dorothy.'

Dorothy. The sound of her name came as a shock, as though he'd used profanity (up to now she'd been *the woman I'm seeing*). Gillian turned it over in her mind. *Dorothy*. Who was named Dorothy any more?

'So you told her about us?' she said. 'About when we knew each other . . . before.'

'I told her not long after I met her.'

'Hnh,' Gillian managed. Her face was growing warm with shame, as though some private thing of hers had been brought out in the light and mocked.

He lifted the napkin from his lap and wiped his mouth. 'How is it?' he said, nodding towards her plate. She was having a linguine dish that involved lots of fish, some of it in shells; it was like a mini-ecosystem.

'Good,' she said.

'I had to tell her about tonight,' he said.

Of course, she thought. He was reminding her that she was the one who'd done the lying, that it wasn't the sort of thing he did.

'I'm not suggesting you shouldn't have told her,' she said.

Jonathan stared at her plate.

'It's good that you're honest,' she added.

'It isn't just nobility,' he said. 'It's protection, too.'

'Protection from what?'

'From what? From you, from the past. Do you think I wasn't nervous to meet you?'

Gillian stared at her pasta, twirled some into a small cylinder and found a mussel. 'You seem to be handling it fine,' she said, not looking at him.

'Would you rather I weren't?'

'I'd rather you behave as you feel.'

Jonathan rubbed his neck as though it was suddenly stiff and said, 'We used to have this conversation . . .'

Of course they did. They had it and had it and had it. The conversation had been ongoing, and still it had no resolution.

'Can I ask you something?' she said.

'Of course.'

'Do you regret it?'

He shook his head immediately. 'I don't,' he said.

'Are you glad the way it turned out?'

His expression changed. 'Are you?'

She surprised him with what she remembered. What he was wearing the afternoon she met him on Henry Street. The shoes he had on that first day they'd arranged to meet in the canteen after work. The exact wording of an e-mail he had sent her one day after they'd been together. The name of a pub in West Cork he'd phoned her from.

'I can't believe you remember that,' he kept saying.

'Really? Does it seem odd?'

'It seems' – he shook his head – 'amazing.'

'Well, they say women have better memories for things like that.'

'Maybe,' he said. And then, offhandedly, 'I remember reading once that the secret of a good marriage is a short memory.'

She tried to smile, but she knew the line and didn't like it. She suspected it was a jibe at women. 'And are you planning to get married?' she said teasingly.

He opened his eyes wider, though he was looking at the tablecloth when he said it. 'In July.'

She was stunned. Though why should she be? 'Well, I guess . . . congratulations.'

Jonathan was shaking his head. 'I suppose I should've said it in an e-mail. It's just we didn't talk much about, you know, our . . .'

'No, no, it's fine.'

They sipped their coffee. Jonathan pulled on his inhaler, while Gillian arranged and rearranged three brown sugar cubes atop the tablecloth.

He said, 'Can I ask you something?'

'Of course.'

He picked up his teaspoon. He was holding it at arm's length, like a mirror, the way kids do to see themselves upside-down, then he pressed his thumb into the bowl of it. 'Why did you want to see me?'

Gillian stopped playing with the sugar cubes and sat back in her chair. She wasn't sure what to say, or what she wanted to say, so she stalled. 'Did it surprise you that I wanted to?'

He thought for a moment, then put the spoon down, ran his finger along its handle and said, 'Yeah. Actually.'

In the small bedroom in Smithfield, he was lying on his back, looking up at her. She was straddling him, her palms resting easily on his chest. They were just talking, about something, nothing much, judging by his expression, which was tender and a little bit amused . . . How she had loved that room, the loneliness of it, the anonymity, the worlds within its four walls and yet its elemental simplicity. When they made love there, she never wanted to leave. She'd lie beside him afterwards, feeling like she'd finally come home (it didn't make sense; the room wasn't even his home). He'd smoke a cigarette and she'd hear the quiet sizzle, amplified in the semi-dark, and in the background, the traffic, the occasional siren, and sometimes people shouting to each other or a passing car blasting hip-hop. It was always hip-hop. They'd lie for a long time sometimes, saying nothing, just lying there, acutely alive.

She'd wanted to see him again because she'd wanted to feel that way again, to know that she could, that such things were still possible in her life. She had wanted to see him again because she'd wanted to see herself.

She looked up and met his eyes across the table. He was watching her, but not, she noticed, like he used to. She wanted to say, *Remember that?* She could have drawn such a picture of the two of them in that room, he could have closed his eyes and she'd have whispered it to him, and for a moment their minds would have held the same image, and she thought if they could do that, it would be enough, or as close to enough as they could get.

But something told her not to try. Instead, by way of an answer, she said, 'I really loved you.'

He blinked a few times, quickly. It wasn't what he'd expected.

'Can I say that?' she asked.

He nodded. He put his hand to his mouth; he was biting his thumbnail and looking at her. Then he closed his eyes and she watched him. But not like she used to.

Twenty-Six

The book was called *Village People: Playing Myself in Kill*, and Kate had been carrying around a copy since she'd walked into the centre tonight. Sometimes she held it as though she'd been reading it on the way and couldn't, literally, put it down; other times she used it as a plate for the dainty puffs of pastry and tiny squares of focaccia that were making the rounds. A lot of people were talking about the book – in whispers – and Damien had seen Kate showing a few people passages from it. She'd become quite friendly with Sean and his American girlfriend, Amanda, who had co-authored the book; they'd thanked her in the acknowledgements for her 'tireless support'. But having it with her tonight, at the launch of 'The Making of Kill', was a dig at Damien, who'd borne the brunt of the book's criticism.

Fortunately, the criticism was relatively restrained. Partly out of fear of libel and partly, Damien suspected, because Sean and Amanda, or perhaps their publishers, didn't want to alienate readers by being too vitriolic, the book consisted largely of humorous anecdotes from inside Kill mixed with a sprinkling of observations about the tourist industry, all woven into the love story of Sean and Amanda. (Amanda had been brought to Kill by some well-meaning Irish cousins who, God love them, had seen nothing amiss and were initially confused by Amanda's reservations, though they had since seen the light and become active in a watchdog movement monitoring EI's long-term strategies.) This was the most cringe-inducing part of the book, Amanda describing her 'discovery' and 'rescue' of Sean, as though she had sprung him from some archaic mental ward.

When I first met Sean, the line between his own personality and the one he was being asked to project had become blurred. He was unable to step out of his role as 'poet-philosopher'. When I would ask him a question about himself, he tended to answer by quoting Shakespeare or Joyce. Later, he admitted to me that he had come to believe that his own personality was insufficiently interesting. I suggested Sean might like to talk with a therapist, a friend of mine in New York, and Sean agreed . . .

In his loathing of *Village People*, Damien was in the minority. Sean and Amanda were the current darlings of the academy, as well as of the people. The academy liked them because they sang their tune, in a way the people could understand. The people liked them because they were anti-Establishment. But what really sold Sean and Amanda to the public was the fact that they'd found love in their sixties. They were a romance for the new millennium – the age of the pensioner. They made the cover of the *RTE Guide*, alongside the headline:

When they're sixty-four . . .
for Sean and Amanda,
life is only just beginning!

They did the rounds of radio call-in programmes and appeared on an inexplicably popular television chat show. *Village People* was Waterstone's Irish Book of the Month. It was getting fairly good coverage in London, too. Only the *Sunday Times* damned it, accusing Sean and Amanda of having taken victim literature to a new low.

Damien looked at his watch. Gillian was late. She was

coming from meetings in Edinburgh, but her flight had got in at midday, which would have given her plenty of time to make it to Kill by now. She'd promised to be here. Damien put a hand to his forehead. He was feeling the onset of nausea.

Someone rang a little bell. The speeches were about to begin. Kate was first and made her way to the podium, smiling to her left and right as she went, as though she were the queen of somewhere. Her eyes were shining. She was wearing a flowing brightly coloured embroidered robe, something you had to be very large and possibly African to do justice to.

'It is by now a platitude to say of this country,' Kate began, 'that it moved from the pre-modern to the postmodern with no intervening period of modernity. Or, as some would have it, we didn't know what we had until somebody told us to sell tickets to it.'

A few of Kate's colleagues were there, and they laughed. Jimmy smiled wryly. Judith, who loathed Kate even more than Damien did, stared impassively at her. Judith was standing next to Matt. They'd come out as a couple. Damien was somewhat mystified. Judith seemed to be viewing the thing with Matt as more than just an ironic interlude. He looked at his watch again. He'd tried Gillian on the mobile earlier but couldn't get her.

Kate droned on about the elevation of Kill from an amusement park to a site of important cultural interrogation.

Blah blah blah.

Damien looked at Jimmy. Jimmy was looking at a little boy who was pressing his thumb against the roof of his mouth. He looked like he was attempted to prise his head off. Jimmy grinned goofily, raising his eyebrows as high as they could go. The boy smiled and twisted shyly into the folds of his mother's skirt.

Damien's mother had been meant to come tonight, but had had a bit of a fall on the step outside her front door and had bruised her hip badly. Damien knew this was how it started. The doctor told her she should try to shed some weight. It seemed like a cruel prescription. How many pleasures did his mother have?

'. . . and we hope that this is the beginning of a fruitful dialogue and working relationship between EI and those sectors of the community – wherever that community is – that have an interest in how they are represented. In other words,' Kate said earnestly, 'all of us.'

Perfunctory applause.

Damien did not share her hope. His hope was that he would never have to see her again.

While Kate was being replaced at the podium by Tommy Geraghty, the local TD, Damien slipped out to the car park to try Gillian again. But she was still out of range or had her phone off. He heard laughter from inside. Tommy was a bigger hit than Kate had been; these were his people, after all, people who were glad to see the back of the fifties and didn't give a shite whether Kill was pre- or postmodern or both.

'Real?' one of the old folks working in the village had said to Damien. 'What would I want real for? Sure wasn't I there once already?'

Damien dropped the mobile into his pocket and walked the length of the car park. He stood at the entrance, squinting in the direction of Castleplunket, straining to hear Gillian's Renault. But there was no sign. He turned around and scanned the rows of cars, thinking, but not really believing, that she might have arrived without his realizing it. When he didn't see anything, he headed back towards the centre. Two little girls were playing a game of hide-and-seek between the cars in which they both hid and both sought, popping up and down and squealing gleefully. He thought: if we split up, who will Heather go with?

A woman stood near the door, watching absently. One of the girls' mothers. She was wearing a ring, Damien noticed. She was married. If he wasn't married any more, is this what he'd check first? Weeding out the unavailable, an evolved labour-saving reflex. Or maybe not. Gillian wore a ring, and she hadn't been weeded out.

He paused at the paving. He and the woman agreed it was a lovely evening, though it was clear neither of them felt lovely. A wave of empathy passed through him, and he fought the absurd impulse to solicit reassurance.

He turned away and took the mobile out again and tried home. When he heard his own voice on the answering machine, he hung up. From inside, he could hear applause. Tommy was finishing. He was on next. He looked once more towards the road but it was dead quiet.

'Duty calls,' he said, sounding sheepish, and the woman gave him a pained smile. She didn't know who he was, he realized. She thought he was talking about going to the jacks.

Judith was already standing at the podium, waiting to introduce him. Damien could tell by the look of her that she'd been searching the room for him and was in something of a panic. He caught her eye as he was making his way to the front.

'Ah!' she cried. 'And here he is.'

He was going to do the Irish-cottages-in-Amsterdam thing. With slight alterations of emphasis, it was applicable to practically any EI occasion.

'The Father of Kill,' Judith gushed, by way of introduction.

Damien gave her a look. Judith had become goofily effusive since she'd begun taking her relationship with Matt seriously.

He slid behind the podium and smiled at his audience, waiting for them to settle.

'About ten years ago,' he began, 'I was in a hotel bar in Amsterdam. One of those bars where they have books on the shelves that nobody ever looks at, and you're not even sure if the books are real. Like most people, I never look at those books, but that night, one of the volumes caught my eye. It was Eamonn O'Reilly's photographs of Irish cottages. I took it down and spent more than two hours with it. I had seen this book on several occasions but for some reason, probably because I was away from home, it affected me as it never had before. These three-roomed cottages with their thatched roofs and brilliantly painted doors – regatta blue and periwinkle and post-office green . . .'

He let his eyes roam over the crowd. They were all listening. All except Kate, who was making a point of staring over her left shoulder at nothing.

'. . . there were planters with red geraniums flowering. An old teapot. Bicycles. And the light: indigo and lemon-lime and something like tangerine that I've never seen anywhere but in the West of Ireland. I was utterly transfixed. I was in tears . . .' – he paused – '. . . I admit. And I thought: I want to go there. I want to *live* there. It was as though I'd never seen my own country before . . .'

Damien spread his hands in a gesture of mystification. 'I grew up in Mayo,' he shrugged, 'in the bogs of Mayo. It's not as though I'd never seen a thatched cottage before.'

People chuckled.

A wine glass shattered. Damien twitched. Groans of mock disapproval were sent in the general direction of the culprit. He swallowed hard and waited for everyone to quiet down. He'd forgotten what he was saying. Their eyes were all on him again. He scratched his head and stared down at the podium. The nausea had been replaced by the bodily heat of self-consciousness. He was rattled. He put a hand on his heart and tried to look ironically rattled. 'Where was I?' he asked, lifting his gaze from the podium.

More chuckling, and someone said, 'The bog.'

'Mayo!'

'Amsterdam!'

'You had just started to cry,' Jimmy called out, and there was laughter.

'Right, right, right,' Damien said, nodding. 'Thank you, Jimmy.'

He could feel his hands shaking and he gripped the sides of the podium to steady himself. This kind of thing didn't happen to him, ever.

'So there I was,' he managed, 'in the bog . . . in Mayo . . . in Amsterdam . . .'

He was holding on tightly to the podium and still he could feel the tremors moving up his arms, as though he'd touched something electric and live. His throat seemed to be closing and his legs felt alarmingly weak.

What was the point he was coming to? The point, he knew, was that all the work he'd done since that night in Amsterdam had been guided by his encounter with those photographs, by the thing, whatever it was, that he'd seen in them, which was the essential something of his birthplace, the thing he wanted to share with people from all over the world . . .

That was the point. That was the point his cottages-in-Amsterdam speech always arrived at. But it suddenly seemed an incredibly complex sequence of events and emotions to relate.

He looked up, tentatively. He saw Kate, who was looking

at Judith, who was surveying the crowd. Jimmy had stopped playing funny faces with the little boy and was eyeing him now instead, worried, while the little boy was looking at everything and nothing, swivelling his head quickly left and right in an effort to amuse himself. Damien's anxiety now seemed to be gathering itself in his still-constricting throat. He felt a sting behind his eyes that was like a surge of pinpricks, warm pinpricks of light.

He let go of the podium and lifted his right hand and pressed his fingers to his eyes. He could hear the silence now, it was a special kind of silence, the kind that descends when the person who is standing at the front of the room, meant to be giving a speech, starts looking like he's going to cry.

Twenty-Seven

She was already late and still at least ten miles from Kill. They'd been delayed for more than an hour boarding in Edinburgh, then had sat in the plane for nearly another hour waiting to take off. Something about debris on the runway. Gillian had had a window seat and she'd sat, drained but calm, watching men in hooded yellow slickers, their stride brisk in the rain, their figures indistinguishable and oddly reassuring. It had been raining all morning and the world looked saturated, muffled and unbearably grim, the way it does to a child stuck indoors.

When they'd finally touched down in Dublin the rain was easing, and by the time Gillian reached Enfield the clouds had broken up and vanished. The sky had a fresh blue brilliance and the fields either side of the road glistened. The world looked rinsed, dazzling and intense, as though she was seeing it all through a too-clean window. It was the kind of afternoon, she had thought, that would have caused Grace to clasp her hands and say, 'Isn't it *mar*vellous! Isn't it *just* gorgeous!' Grace took nothing for granted and so was always primed for astonishment.

Gillian had been thinking about Grace on and off all day, missing her, wanting to know things about her that she'd never know now. What it had felt like to be her. Did anybody ever ask another person that? It was such a simple question, really, and yet it wasn't asked: what does it *feel* like? To wake up as yourself every morning, to look in the mirror and see what you see. What had it felt like for Grace as she moved through the dark and bright patches of her garden (were they her happiest hours?), or assembled cups and saucers on a tray – the set with the gold rims she'd owned for ever – or later even, when she'd lived with them, doing one of the 'helpful household tasks' suggested at the centre or simply sitting, staring, her thoughts rising up slow and separate through the murk. But by then Grace couldn't have told her.

The traffic started to slow just beyond Mullingar. She should have rung Damien to say she'd be late, but her battery hadn't enough charge and the lead was in her bag in the boot, and she didn't bother. The thing wouldn't start on time anyway. Nothing ever did. And, in fact, she was grateful for the chance to sit with herself a little longer. Last night was still resounding, in her nerves and her heart. She felt as though she'd shed a layer of herself.

It had all been over so fast. They had held each other outside the restaurant before saying goodbye; one minute he'd been pressing her tightly to him and the next he wasn't any more; she could see him receding down the street and then she couldn't see him; he'd turned a corner and was gone and she knew that she would never see him again.

She'd turned away herself then and headed back in the direction of her hotel. The air still had a trace of warmth and she'd walked slowly, listening to the sound of her footsteps and feeling the air on her face. She was thinking that you reached the point where there were only endings, where there were no real beginnings any more. It was a melodramatic notion, she knew, but that didn't mean it wasn't true.

She reached Tulsk and took the turn towards Castleplunket, from where it was just a few miles to Kill. When she pulled into the centre's car park, it was still bright; at eight o'clock a light that could have been mid-morning. There were a few people milling around outside, smoking and drinking glasses of wine. Gillian didn't recognize them. She spotted Damien's car. Two little girls stood on the paving. One of them whispered something in the other's ear, then they drew back and eyed each other, aghast with delight. Gillian got out of the car and headed towards the centre, nodding at the people she didn't know. She opened the glass door and slipped into the back of the crowd. When she looked up, she saw him, standing at the front behind the podium, just standing there, standing there and saying nothing, like he was waiting for the signal to begin again.